INSERT GROOM HERE

This Large Print Book carries the
Seal of Approval of N.A.V.H.

UNCONVENTIONAL BRIDES
ROMANCE SERIES

INSERT GROOM HERE

K.M. JACKSON

THORNDIKE PRESS
A part of Gale, Cengage Learning

Farmington Hills, Mich • San Francisco • New York • Waterville, Maine
Meriden, Conn • Mason, Ohio • Chicago

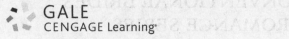

GALE
CENGAGE Learning·

LIBRARY OF CONGRESS CATALOGING-IN-PUBLICATION DATA

Names: Jackson, K. M., author.
Title: Insert groom here / by K. M. Jackson.
Description: Large print edition. | Waterville, Maine : Thorndike Press, 2017. |
    Series: Thorndike Press large print African-American | Series: Unconventional
    brides romance series
Identifiers: LCCN 2016052492| ISBN 9781410498045 (hardcover) | ISBN 1410498042
    (hardcover)
Subjects: LCSH: African Americans—Fiction. | Large type books. | GSAFD: Love
    stories.
Classification: LCC PS3610.A3526 I57 2017 | DDC 813/.6—dc23
LC record available at https://lccn.loc.gov/2016052492

Published in 2017 by arrangement with Dafina Books, an imprint of
Kensington Publishing Corp.

Printed in Mexico
1 2 3 4 5 6 7 21 20 19 18 17

For Will,
I'm so glad to have taken that
walk with you.

ACKNOWLEDGMENTS

To say seeing *Insert Groom Here* in print is a dream come true is an understatement to end all understatements. To thank God for making it happen, well, the tiny words don't do the feeling justice. But God has been in this project from the very beginning. You see, I have to give a huge thank-you to Bishop W. Darin Moore, who at the time was my pastor and during a sermon on marriage first said the words "Insert Groom Here" and got my mind whirring on a story. Yeah, I know I should have stayed focused on the sermon at hand, but this is where my brain went, and I took the ride! Thank you so much, Bishop Moore!

And another big thank-you for the support and love to my GC Bowling Angels, who have been in my corner, cheering me, all the way through this process. And I'd like to give an extra special thank-you to GC Angel Wesley Battle for being my

7

behind-the-scenes TV consultant on the project, answering all my questions on TV sets and production. And to his wife, my teammate Carmery, for her positive "That's doable!" reinforcement! With all these wonderful folks cheering me on, I feel truly blessed.

To my editor, Selena James, and the amazing Kensington family. You all are a joy. I can't thank you enough for making my dream come true. And to my wonderful agent, Rachel Brooks, and the rest of the L. Perkins Agency, thank you for being in my corner.

To Farrah, for always being a friend and a support. You are the very best! To the Destin Divas: you ladies make me want to be better at all of it! To Dren: you make the day better! Thank you. To Amy, thank you for your keen eye and for being the fabulous you!

And to all my friends, supporters, readers and cheerleaders over the years, your kindness can never be repaid. Thank you.

And now to my family . . . bring on the mush!

To my husband, Will, and my twins, Kayla and William, I hope to make you all as proud as you do me. I am the luckiest wife and mother there ever was. You are my treasure and have my whole heart.

To Ma, thank you for being there for me and dreaming this dream with me. I Love You. To James, Ashley, and Semaj, thank you for holding me down.

To Nana, I hope I'm still making you proud and that you are telling the stories in heaven. #WeNeedDiverseRomance always.

CHAPTER 1

"I can't marry you."

Eva Ward knew words were being murmured over her shoulder, but for the life of her she couldn't quite make them out. The red light above the camera transfixed her, and Kevin's voice sounded like it came from somewhere far away, as if from down a long corridor. To top things off, she was fighting a chill. The temperature in the blasted television studio had to be set at fifty degrees at the highest. Eva thought about the frigid air a moment and hoped the cold didn't show on her face — or, lord help her — anywhere else on her anatomy. That would be all she needed, for her nipples to make a surprise appearance on national morning television. Eva pushed back a frown as she brought her thoughts back to that blasted red light and Kevin. *Okay, focus time. What is he going on about?*

"I can't marry you," Kevin repeated, and

11

Eva blinked.

Wait. What?

"Wait. What?!" Jim Bauer, *The Morning Show*'s co-host, took Eva's confused thoughts and echoed them out loud, punctuated with his usual everyman laugh. But this was a bad time to laugh. In fact, it was the absolute worst time to laugh. "I don't think we heard you correctly, Kevin. It sounded for a moment like you were calling off the wedding."

Eva fought to keep her smile in place as Kevin turned from her to Jim. "That's right, Jim. I am."

She blinked again as the words really begin to sink in. *He is calling off what?* Anger bubbled up, heating Eva more quickly than could possibly be safe. She caught another glimpse of the red light and forced herself to push it back down. *Hold on there. This is not the time to go off the rails,* Eva told herself. She could do this. She'd practiced being on live TV, and she'd been put on the spot plenty of times. She was trained for these moments. Media relations was her job, for chrissake.

Eva pulled her attention away from the maddening red light that reminded her millions of people were watching this debacle over their morning coffee and toast. Instead,

12

she plastered on a well-trained smile and focused on what her fiancé, Kevin, and the talk show's co-hosts were now saying. But try as she might, she couldn't wrap her head around the words as they trickled toward her in dribs and drabs.

Something about being "confused," Kevin said. "Just not the right time," he went on. And wait, did she really hear the words "moving too fast"?

Hold up, this was madness! It was as if she was having some sort of odd bout of both inner and out-of-body experience, and she couldn't get the two to gel. But she had to, because Kevin was talking about her as if she wasn't there, sitting by his side on TV. National freaking TV! It was time to take control of the situation.

Eva blinked again, her lashes feeling thick and gloppy from the extra coats of mascara plus the individual false lashes the makeup woman had put on her that morning. She had thought they were a bit much at the time. Now she was afraid that with all the ridiculous blinking she was doing, she probably looked like Bambi gone drag. Eva forced her eyes wide, as if that would somehow make her appear saner, and stared at Kevin. Oh hell, Mr. Smooth was starting to sweat, despite the fact that if it was two degrees colder, you'd be able to see your breath as you welcomed Satan into the studio. His sleek, ultra-groomed, dark cocoa skin was starting to glisten, and Eva now noticed a hint of fear in his eyes.

Eva's heart raced, but despite this, she caught Kevin's eye and gave him a smile that she hoped said, "Come on, honey, don't lose your cool now," as she reached over and gave his hand a pat. She could do this. Just a little damage control, and she'd reel this right in.

Eva turned to her other side and looked at Diane Parker, one of *The Morning Show*'s other co-hosts, but Diane's blue eyes only seemed to mirror Eva's own internal confusion.

Just perfect. No help from blondie.

So Eva turned her gaze to Jim. Good ol' Jim. Surely Mr. All America would help save the day. But in that moment, a clear sound finally reached Eva's ears, punctuated by good ol' Jim's good ol' laugh. The loud, false pang rang against her eardrums. "Har, har! Good one, Kevin," Jim said, as Eva took in the obvious tension playing around the corners of his mouth, causing some of his pancake makeup to crease. "Of course you're joking."

"No, Jim, I'm not," Kevin said, his voice

clear, strong, and surprisingly absolute as he turned Eva's way. "I'm sorry, Eva. I can't go through with this."

Despite her best efforts at bracing, Eva winced as the words penetrated. The full impact hit her like a crosstown bus trying to make up for lost time.

This was not happening. It couldn't be happening. Not here. Not now. Not to her.

But Kevin continued, his voice getting higher with each word. The more his lips moved and the words washed over her, the more of a blur he became. His handsome features, smooth skin, close-cropped hair, fine button-down oxford shirt, new three-button jacket, pocket square — all becoming a washed-out mass of swirly rejection under the bright studio lights. For a moment, Eva felt like she might be sick, so she bent her head, her gaze hitting Kevin's highly polished leather shoes. The ones that she had picked up for him last week so he would be perfect for their big television appearance this morning. Eva felt her chest tighten as her throat squeezed shut.

"I really am sorry, babe. But I can't do it. It's all too much, and I've realized I'm not ready to get married."

It was like a physical blow. Like he had kicked her in the gut while wearing the shoes she paid for.

Eva's head snapped up then, away from the shoes and away from Kevin too. She saw the camera and the red light as it flashed before her like a beacon. She shut her eyes for a moment and thought once again about how many people watched this while they sipped their morning coffee and ate their sugar-toasted oats. What were they thinking as they stared at the seemingly normal-looking woman in her pink twinset and sharply pleated skirt? Damn it, she was wearing her grandmother's pearls. How does one go about getting dumped in heirloom pearls?

The nausea twisted at her again, and Eva had the distinct feeling that her normally caramel-hued skin was probably taking on a green cast to match the bile now churning in her belly. She wondered if the color would be picked up and broadcast in HD. Now there was ideal breakfast entertainment for you.

And then it hit her, and her worry doubled. Practically tripled. Shit. Her mother was watching this. Watching and most likely fuming. She could imagine the look on Valerie Ward's face right now. She was sure to be yelling into a phone right that moment to have her assistant and the rest of

16

the staff come in early to get started on damage control. The thought sent Eva over the edge. Probably even more than experiencing disappointment herself, she hated the idea of letting her mother down. She'd had enough of that in her life, and though she came off as a human fire-breather, Eva knew it was mostly a mask to cover past hurts.

Not ready to get married.

Kevin's words echoed through Eva's head, along with visions of her mother's impending tirade, and she felt the heat rise. First, it was a burning in the soles of her feet, then it licked up her legs, moving on to radiate through her stomach before finally making its way to her face.

She paused, her breathing virtually stopping a moment as the stomach churning turned to a full-on boil. Was this bastard really breaking up with her on national television merely months, hell, practically weeks, before her perfectly planned wedding?

Eva finally turned and looked at Kevin, fighting hard to keep her emotions in line. She laughed. A belly laugh that would make even ol' Jim proud. *It's a joke. It has to be.* Diane and Jim cautiously joined her in the chuckle and bolstered her spirits. *Whew.*

She couldn't believe she'd almost fallen for it. Of course, Kevin would never do that to her. He also had too much riding on this marriage. Too much riding on them. It must have been some silly producer thing. They were always doing something to try and jack up the ratings. And she played along and fell for it, for a moment. She should have known it was a stunt. What better fodder for the gossip mill and ratings than an on-air breakup and makeup from America's, at least for the moment, sweetheart couple? But Kevin knew how important this was. How much this wedding meant to her. To them and their future. Both personally and professionally. But he had been a fool to go for it in the first place and not let her in on the joke.

Eva strained out a smile. "Funny. But come on, sweetie. Joke's over," she said. "Now tell me you were just playing." She turned to the camera and raised a perfectly arched brow. "Tell America you were playing. We will be married and have our dream wedding right here on *The Morning Show* courtesy of Tied Knot Style and Bliss." Eva smiled wide. Her mother would appreciate the advertiser tie-in. One never missed out on the opportunity to thank a sponsor. It was a cardinal rule of marketing. Always keep the sponsors happy and coming back to write another check.

But instead of laughing with her and getting in on the joke, good ol' Jim clammed up and flipped through his blue cards, looking confused, and Diane, well, she was still a grinning zero as she nodded in a bobble-headed way that couldn't quite be declared for or against the joke theory. And wait, was that sweat on her brow now too? *Holy hell.*

Eva looked back at Kevin for reassurance, and he shrugged. *The bastard shrugged!*

"I really am sorry, Eva. You know I always cared for you."

Cared? Did he say *cared*? A rock thudded where her heart was supposed to be. Cared. As in, what you do for your late grandmother, as in how you felt about your childhood dog. Cared, "ed," as in past tense?

Kevin turned to the camera and laid on that old Kevin charm, looking ever so innocent and sincere. "I'm, um, sorry, America. I'd like to apologize to you too. And this is not Eva's fault. It's all me."

Jim piped in, "Well, I'm not really sure what to say here. We'll, well, take a commercial break and be right back?" He then held his ear and with an awkward look turned to Eva. "Oh, uh, I really am sorry; it seems we can't go to commercial. Not for

19

ninety more seconds." Jim gave Eva a look that said, "Tough break, kid."

Eva bit her lip and tried to steady her breathing, since her heart was beating so hard and fast she was sure the mics must be picking up every erratic thump. Crap! In ninety seconds, she was sure to be dead from humiliation.

Diane shifted her eyes away before speaking to the camera. Her voice took on a funereal tone. "We are truly sad to hear of this development. We were all looking forward to your wedding. But I guess now, given the circumstances, and as per the rules of the competition, we'll have to choose another couple." Diane smiled and changed her voice on a dime. "Luckily, we still have Sherri and Brad from Des Moines, who are our runner-up couple. Hey, as they say, it's for the best to find out before the marriage that the two of you don't suit. Don't you think?"

Just perfect. It's now that she turns into a freaking all-star chatterbox, spouting rules and crap.

"No."

The word came out before Eva could stop to think about what she was saying.

"Excuse me?" Diane asked, her wispy brows drawing together. "Maybe you didn't hear what Kevin said. He does not want to marry you."

Eva shot Diane a look that said *Thanks, but no thanks for the clarification,* then turned back to Kevin as he piped up again.

"Yes, Eva." Kevin put his hand across her forearm. "What are you talking about? I said I won't marry you. There won't be a wedding." He rubbed his hand gently across her forearm. Eva looked down at it, not knowing if it was supposed to be comforting or controlling. It didn't matter.

It wasn't either.

She looked up at him, eyes blazing, and jerked her arm away. Then, catching the red light out of the corner of her eye, Eva thought briefly of her mother, before giving Kevin a huge smile that would probably make the most venomous snake proud. "I don't give a damn what you said. I will have my wedding with or without you." It was like a fire had ignited and was rushing through her veins, threatening to burn out of control.

Kevin pulled back, shaking his head. "Eva, come on. Stop, you're not making sense." Then he lowered his voice to a stage whisper, as if the mics still couldn't pick him up. "Plus you're embarrassing yourself."

For the second time that morning, Eva

21

laughed inappropriately on national TV. *Goody, maybe hysterics are setting in.* She supposed it was natural, given the circumstances.

"Oh, really? Tell me, how can I embarrass myself any more than you already have? Freaking all of America is watching my national dumpation!" She waved her hands wildly in a gesture to the studio. Beyond them there were multiple cameras and overhead lights, and you could see the silhouettes of the burly cameramen nodding their heads in the distance. Behind Eva, Jim, Diane, and Kevin was a large window with people jockeying for their moment of fame, holding up signs saying hi to mom. Eva blew a guy in a cheese hat a kiss when he made an obscene gesture toward his crotch.

She turned back to Kevin and nodded. "See there! I'm already fielding promising offers."

A mumble of laughter traveled throughout the studio. Kevin looked down at the floor. Coward. She should have known he wasn't up to the challenge when she had to push him to retake the bar exam. No, he was ready, after one little setback, to squander it all and spend his life living between her couch and his rich stepfather's bungalow, making it party-hopping off his good looks and charm. Well, no more.

Eva jabbed a finger into his chest, and Kevin looked back up. This time satisfaction nipped at her as she saw a glimmer of anger in his eyes. "Six years! I have wasted six years dealing with your wishy-washy indecisiveness, and here we are about at the finish line, and you go and back out now. Stopping in the fourth quarter? Eighth inning? On the last lap? What kind of man are you? Well, I'll tell you. You're the type to use up all the best years a woman has, and then when it's time to commit, you bail." As she said the words, she felt a lump form in her throat and tears well in her eyes.

Oh hell no. There was no way she would let that happen. No way would she let Kevin know he'd gotten to her.

She swallowed and then continued, "Well, I've got news for you. There are plenty of men who I'm sure would be happy to take your place. Just ask Cheese Head." Eva looked back to the window, but Cheese Head was gone. She guessed the cheese was fine, but apparently pointing out your sausage was a bit much for morning TV. She turned back to Kevin and continued, "No matter, I will still have my wedding. You are replaceable. The question is, Who's got next? I will have my wedding! And I'll have it on the date as planned!" She pointed to the empty spot beside her. "All I have to do is just insert groom here!"

It was then that Eva detected a murmur going through the studio. Oh crap. Did she really say what she had just said out loud? She looked up and saw the red light flashing like a beacon out to New York, Chicago, Iowa, and beyond. And did she really just say it to not only Kevin, but to Jim, Diane, and the rest of America?

Eva closed her eyes. *Oh God. Please make this a bad dream. It has to be.* But when she opened them and focused on everyone around the studio, the same people who had smiled at her with admiration moments ago were all staring at her now like she was the Wicked Witch of the West or someone ready for a straitjacket. *Shit. This dream is way too real.*

Panicked, Eva jumped off the raised stool; pushing back sharply, she heard it crash to the ground behind her as she ran off the set.

"Well, um, that was spirited. We'll be right back, folks, and in our next half hour, bringing romance back into the kitchen!" The irony of Jim's words almost had Eva cringing as they echoed through the studio's speakers. His ridiculous "Har, har, har" laugh kept time with the clanking of Eva's retreating heels.

CHAPTER 2

"Shit, shit, shit!" Eva couldn't stop herself from kicking the worn leather couch in the studio's surprisingly not at all green green-room. And if she had thought about it for more than fifteen seconds, then, well, she probably could have stopped herself — that is, if she really had wanted to — but the physical release of her anger felt too dammed good.

It felt new. It felt real. It felt free.

So she turned and banged her fists against the wall without a care for her hands, then regretted it as hot pain shot up through her arm. "Freaking hell!"

Add that to her list of dumb moves of the morning. Funny, though not even, it never looked that painful on TV. "Ugh!" She let out a hard, un-lady-like grunt. The thought of TV instantly brought the scene she'd just escaped from back to her mind. Who the hell breaks up with someone on national

TV? But, worse, who flips out like she did?

Eva sucked in a breath. What was she thinking? She never lost her cool and went off like that. At least not so publicly. If there was one thing she knew, it was the value of keeping her true emotions hidden. But then Kevin's nonchalant shrug came back to the forefront of her mind, and once again without thinking, Eva went for the wall.

Like Kevin, the wall won.

"Damn. It!" Eva looked down at her red, quickly swelling knuckles and winced. *And damn you, Kevin. You piece of crap, spineless betrayer!* If he wanted to do the breakup in a public place, why couldn't he pick a Starbucks like a normal human being?

Eva felt a hot tear fall and swiped it away. She didn't even know why she was crying. In the moment, it certainly wasn't over love lost or any such nonsense. She didn't have time for that type of bull. Not that she didn't care for Kevin. Sure she did. If she didn't, she wouldn't have put so much time and energy into him and their relationship. But now that she thought about it, she guessed it was the betrayal and, worse, the embarrassment that hurt so much. She was sure she didn't deserve it. In their time together, she'd done nothing but raise Kevin's low-performing stock.

27

Sure, she knew she came off at times as a tad cold and had a reputation for being somewhat demanding, and yes, there were some who referred to her as straitlaced, perhaps stuffy for her age. The word *uptight* may have been bantered around. And probably she should have beat Kevin to the breakup punch when he had the nerve to call her a prude because she wouldn't go all in for some of his kinkier tie-me-up antics in bed. But what did he know? She could get plenty kinky and have just as much fun as any woman if given the right incentive, but lately he'd been barely any incentive at all. The funny, kind, attentive, okay maybe he was a little too into video games guy she'd first met had somehow morphed into this pompous, pocket-square-wearing asshole the world saw dumping her this morning. So the last thing she wanted to do was jump through some sort of fetish hoops when, both inside and outside the bedroom, he was a total bore. But still, the fact remained that she'd stayed and had invested years of time and energy in Kevin for just this moment. Bailing was not an option.

As her mother often said, "Bailing is never an option."

Eva sucked in a breath and stilled when the low hum hit her ears. Her cell phone was on VIBRATE in her purse on the glass coffee table, and it was currently pulsing so much the whole purse did a little shimmy. It was her mother. Without even looking, Eva knew it had to be. Valerie Ward was probably sitting with either her finger or her assistant's finger pressed hard on the RE-DIAL button at that moment. Suddenly Eva had the desire to kick the table, just to hear the glass smash. But of course, she didn't. She couldn't. She had to pull herself together. Get some control here. Her moment of going full-blown nutter was done and over.

Instead, Eva ignored the phone and rested her forehead on the wall, forcing herself to take slow, deep breaths. She'd deal with her mother soon enough. She had to come up with a plan. Or they'd come up with one together. Either way she had to get a handle on what had happened this morning and get started on her own damage control. She'd handled worse for her celebrity clients, and she was a nobody, so this should be easy to handle with a bit of rug sweeping. She just had to step back and look at things objectively.

A lump lodged in her throat. Still it made no sense. She and Kevin were perfect — despite the kinkiness non-compatibility factor — and she *had* invested the right amount of time and energy into the relationship. More than enough, actually. They were right on track with her plans. And at the age of twenty-eight, she was precisely on schedule. On schedule to be Mrs. Kevin Rucker Esq. before age twenty-nine. Add a couple of years of them being an "it" couple about town and then, bam, the first child by thirty-three and then baby number two by thirty-five. There would be no bar hopping, awkward setups by friends, or code-worded online profiles for her in her mid-thirties. She was getting her shit together. *Well, to hell with you, Kevin, for totally messing this up.*

Thoughts of the gorgeous monogrammed towels she had pre-ordered for their registry with their initials — ERK, in script — on Pima cotton came to her mind. Damn. She really wanted those towels. Had bought into the whole stupid fantasy of them.

"Well, screw you, Kevin, and your sorry-assed I love yous!" Eva yelled as she swiped once more at an errant tear and stomped her foot. Tendrils of her shoulder-length brown hair came undone from her chignon and fell into her eyes.

Then she heard it. A slight shuffling of feet that caused Eva to freeze, then turn around. And there he was. Right in the doorway, capturing her every sad and desperate move, stood a very tall man, and that was a lot for her to say, since she was five nine without her heels. His skin was a burnished tan, mostly natural, though some, she could tell, came from being outdoors in the sun, his worn T-shirt showing the tan line around his muscular biceps. She looked down, and said tee was tucked haphazardly into well-fitting faded jeans. When her eyes came back up to his face, the sexy scruff on his jaw showed he hadn't taken time to shave that morning, or maybe the past few mornings, before coming to work. *Work.* That was the worst part of it all. His work. Because slung over the top of this man's very broad shoulder was a TV camera, and in that moment it was trained directly on Eva in all her overly emotional meltdown glory.

"What the hell are you doing?" Eva inwardly cringed as she heard her own voice come out in an unflattering high shriek. "Haven't I been humiliated enough?"

Nothing.

Just silence from T-shirt camera dude for one long beat, and then another, as Eva stared at him open-mouthed, waiting for some sort of answer or apology, or at least

31

for him to put the blasted camera down, anything but this blank, emotionless stare.

And then he did it. He finally moved. The hunky camera guy's left brow went up, and at the same time so did his shoulders. They went up, and then they slumped right back down again. Eva took a step back, bumping into the coffee table behind her. Did he just shrug? Hunky freaking body-hugging tee, faded-jeans, perfect-stubble camera guy looked at her and shrugged. *What the total hell!* She was having a perfect, full-on meltdown, and he shrugged.

This was her second dismissive shrug of the day. Flashbacks of Kevin's casual shrug mere moments ago washed over her, along with even worse images of Kevin's eyes lingering too long on other women's legs in short skirts or paying special attention and laying on that old Kev charm with any woman with boobs over a C cup. When she'd catch him, he'd shrug then too, in a "Well, boys will be boys" kind of way. Well, she'd had enough of this bullshit. This was her last shrug of the day. She wasn't taking it anymore.

Sucking in a deep breath, Eva smoothed her hair as best as she could, then tugged down, straightening her disheveled skirt. She reached toward the table and slung her purse carefully over her shoulder before finally straightening her pearls.

Then, churning on pure hate, Eva walked toward him. She couldn't see his full face, since it was half hidden behind the camera that was taking in her supposedly private meltdown, but she did get a closer look now at the challenge in his one sparkling, heavily lidded, dark brown eye. She thought she may have seen that eye, that sexy frame once or twice wander in and out of the studio, but she wasn't sure. Letting her own eyes wander, Eva also caught a hint of a tattoo peeking out from beneath the cuff of his tee. When she looked back to his full lips, they twitched up at one corner.

"You find me amusing?" she asked, holding tight to the reigns of her control. "Cool. It's nice to see someone getting a chuckle out of this day." *Too bad it is at my expense,* she thought. Just like Kevin was probably laughing now. Just like all of *The Morning Show*'s viewers were probably laughing too.

Eva's blood boiled over at the hitch of that too-pretty lip and the smug look in his one dark eye. And then everything seemed to go dark. Her world turned to pinpoint tunnel vision as she continued to be propelled forward, only seeing that sparkling eye of his and that twitching lip. And as if on autopilot, Eva bit her own lip, gave it a light lick. At the last moment, she put her freshly manicured hand up to the front of the camera's lens and watched as Mr. Hunk quickly shifted his head from behind the camera and looked at her, hitting her with the full force of his masculine beauty. Bam! Smooth skin, dark slashes of brows, a strong square jaw, and those full, generously curved lips made her mouth instantly water. She saw him begin to open those lips in protest over her hand on his camera, but before he could get a word out, Eva moved in and covered his mouth with her own, capturing him in a hard, searing kiss.

His lips were at first firm and unyielding, but after a few seconds she felt a shift when they went soft and pliant as her pressure was returned. Then he surprised her by kissing her back. Instantly, Eva was swept up in a haze. It was a sensual fog of her own making, and in that moment, she felt herself swept up on a soft ocean breeze as her body seemed to awaken and come to life like never before. A slow wave of dangerous pleasure washed over her, and then — wham — the wave broke as if hitting a sharp rock when awareness struck, bringing Eva back to herself.

She pulled away, making a quick assessment of herself and the situation.

Quirking her own lip in a half smile, she looked into camera guy's dark-chocolate-colored eyes and saw his expression change from amused to confused, and as Eva looked deeper and briefly lower, she could see he was aroused. Her gaze shifted. He still held tight to the camera high on his broad shoulders, though.

That freaking camera, the cause of all her humiliation. Well, that and Kevin, of course. Kevin and his shrug. But Kevin was not there, so Eva focused on camera dude and gave him what she hoped was a saucy wink, then swiftly raised her right knee, slamming it hard and fast between his widespread legs.

For a moment she felt bad. Only for a moment.

That one went out to all the shruggers.

It was satisfying. And now she was amused by the sound of his weak yelp as he doubled over in pain and made his way to the floor. "Next time, you'll ask permission before you go around filming people like some type of new-age Peeping Tom."

And you'll think before you shrug, she silently added. She was not one to be screwed with or dismissed. Now, if only Kevin were around to get the next knee to the balls.

With that, Eva pivoted on the toe of her red-bottomed heels and walked down the hall, turning right at the end and out the studio door with her head held high and straight into the blinding light of dozens of flashing bulbs.

Oh crap, this morning just kept getting better and better.

CHAPTER 3

As Aidan Walker sank to the floor, all he could think was he hoped he didn't black out from the pain radiating throughout his groin, because he was really enjoying the view of her walking away.

Still, on the way down, nice view or not, through his pain-blurred eyes he found it hard to focus on the sway of his assailant's slim hips as she took her long, confidant strides down the studio's corridor. He shifted against his poorly timed, hardening erection as searing heat hit him anew, flaming through his body, licking at all the wrong spots. "Shit, shit, shit!" he muttered through closed eyes, then paused. Wasn't that what she'd said not three minutes ago as her on-air humiliation hit her? And to think he actually had felt a smidge of sympathy for her when that asshole had publicly jerked her over in the studio.

Aidan shook his head. This was what he

got for letting his guard down. He, more than anyone, knew never to let your guard down. Letting your guard down only led to trouble. At worst, it could get your ass shot off or, at near worst, your balls repositioned somewhere near your throat. All were lessons he should have learned from his last failed assignment overseas. He shifted again as the ache in his groin subsided and the now more intense pain of humiliation began to set in. Damn, he hadn't been caught off guard like that since his early days on assignment. But come on, how was he supposed to expect a low blow like that from the prim, straitlaced package that was Eva Ward? And he sure as hell wasn't expecting that kiss.

Subconsciously, he licked his lips, still tasting the lingering hint of sweetness from her tongue. His dick throbbed in response, and pain flared anew. *Holy fuck!*

She sure was some piece of work. Talk about fire and ice. And she had the nerve to taste like honey and whipped cream. Aidan narrowed his eyes, forcing himself to see things objectively. But there was no reading that woman. The kneeing and the kiss both came out of left field. She was an enigma, and it was damned frustrating since Aidan prided himself on being able to read people.

Hell, as a reporter, it was his job. In the time he'd been watching her, he'd thought he had her pegged, and now it seemed he was all wrong.

Not that he'd been watching her any further than his job of observing a subject required; he knew how important staying detached was. And not that she was even one of his subjects — she was no more than an intrigue that caught his eye on the way to fulfilling his obligations. Still, he could admit the jam to his balls, no matter how painful, sparked his interests even more. She didn't strike him as the type, all buttoned up as she was, with her sweater set and pearls. No way, or he never would have stood there like he did. All open and wide-legged and stupidly self-assured. Ridiculously sure that he knew her next move. Aidan couldn't help the chuckle escaping his lips. Man, his father would laugh his smug ass off if he could see him now. This was just the sort of situation that proved his point when he'd taken him off field investigations. Women were always the Walker downfall. Women, and leaping before one looked. He'd always said that Aidan was too impulsive, and this little episode was just another thing to add to his outtakes.

For a moment, Aidan thought of Kate

Harmon, his sometimes — well, now former — partner on assignment and in adventure, both in bed and out. Kate would probably shake her head at him too, seeing him on the floor as he was. And any laughter on her part would be well deserved. Any censure too. In the beginning, Kate had liked his impulsiveness. Like most of the women before her, it was a draw. But that sort of thing got old quick, especially when there was more than passion on the line.

Turns out, when things got dangerous, Kate wasn't as cut out for the adventurous life as she'd let on. Not that Aidan blamed her. Kate was ready to settle down, and after it got too dicey on that last assignment — well, it was Kate's last straw. Hey, he got it. It was perfectly normal for a young thirty-something to get bit by the marriage slash mommy bug when she was looking into the eyes of death and being held for ransom. Just then, telling a story might not have seemed all that important compared with getting back home and starting to live the quiet, carefree life portrayed on TV between the peak hours of eight and ten PM.

Aidan blamed himself for the mess he'd made of that last assignment and the danger he'd gotten his crew into. He'd screwed that up royally and should have had a better

40

handle on things. He should have been able to read their informant better. He was always a pretty good people reader, and there was no way that one should have slipped past his radar. No matter her watery, green eyes and sincere story of endangered children. He'd messed up. Didn't do the proper checks, and they'd paid the price. His lesson: Be sharper, work with a smaller team, and avoid entanglements. That way all the risks would be his own. He should have learned after all these years to never get too close to a story — or to a team anyway.

So all in all, Kate was smart getting out. She had decided the life wasn't for her, and subsequently neither was he. She'd pulled out of the relationship as soon as she was back stateside, taking an anchor job in the Midwest and an engagement ring from an old flame that came along with it. Aidan couldn't blame her at all for choosing the road more traveled. He could only congratulate her. Besides, they'd gotten what they both needed out of their time spent together; at least Kate was honest when the time came to say good-bye. There was no subterfuge from her, and for that he was grateful.

Suddenly Aidan's mind shifted back to

the matter and pain at hand, unlike Little Miss Double Punch with the kick to the groin after a kiss to harden him well and good. That was low, and he'd had his fair share of low blows. The kneeing and the kiss both came out of left field. She was an enigma, and it was damned frustrating. In the time he'd been watching her, he'd thought he had her pegged, and now it seemed he was all wrong.

Aiden knew he never should have been so quick to go off running after the lovely Miss Ward without thinking of the consequences. And damn Carter for playing right to his weakness, inviting him down when he did to watch the segment. If he'd given it more than a moment's thought, he might get suspicious, but no. She was blindsided. Still, Carter knew he was always one to run toward the story. It was his biggest failing as well as his greatest asset. Though it was what had also gotten him into hot water on his last assignment and what now had him back at home instead of out in the field, where he worked best, reporting on the stories that really mattered. But now he was here, where his father thought he was safest, playing corporate desk jockey and living up to the Walker name, getting the full lay of the studio land.

At least for the moment, it calmed his father, gave his on-edge nerves a rest, and kept him off Aidan's back. His father still got worked up thinking of Aidan's last dangerous assignment. Said it was time for him to play it safe stateside. Get a handle on the business and prepare to take over for him when he was gone. Aidan snorted at that thought. As if the old goat would ever go anywhere or give up the reigns to the likes of him. But still, he could play nice. At least for a while, until he could get on the road again. The stories he had to tell were too important to stay home chained to a desk full-time. And honestly, the way he saw it, even if he was sidelined for a bit, he could use that time to work his angle from the inside out. Shift the story from crap, like this overdone wedding spectacle, to something that really mattered.

Aidan shifted again and groaned. He couldn't believe it. He had made it out of some of the most terrifying places on earth, only to come home to New York and be easily taken down by an ice princess in pearls. There were some who would find this comical.

Some.

Over the past few weeks, while she had cunningly duked it out with the other couples for a shot at an on-air wedding, Eva Ward had expertly answered all the right questions and smiled at just the right times, all the while never letting a hair get out of place. No, he definitely wasn't expecting the kick from the tall slim woman with the well-manicured, well . . . everything. But maybe he should have been. She looked like she couldn't hurt a fly, let alone maim a man, but as he knew all too well, looks could be deceiving.

That morning, he was having fun, joking with some of the veteran camera guys while observing what was happening on the set. It was all a part of his father's plan: Work from the ground up, take in a little of all the key network shows in the major time slots, and then see where he could best fit in, and this part he didn't mind at all. At least doing this he wasn't chained to a desk or, worse, stuck in a boardroom. Also, the crew got to know him and would not just see him as the big guy's son. The one who would, deserving or not, probably inherit it all. And, as a bonus, he got to be in the background, watching the action — what action there was — and could keep an eye on Miss Ward as it were.

She wasn't hard to watch. Over the weeks, despite the syrupy crap this silly marriage puff piece was, Aidan had found himself either down on the set, hanging in the background, or glued to one of the many screens placed around the offices at just the right time to catch her segment and see every beautiful, perfectly thought out move she made. The woman was made for TV. But that morning he felt for her on some sort of deep emotional level. Maybe it was because for the first time he'd seen a crack in her perfectly polished façade.

And, yes, maybe he should have pulled back. Used some of that power that he didn't like to use and gone over everyone's head when he saw how things were going down and get Carter to get the director to cut and get her off the hook. Staunch the bleeding in the studio before it became a full-on bloodbath. But no. He had to go and be him, and instead he had let the story play out. Let her get stripped bare for the whole world to see. Then, to top it all off, when she'd run off the set, he'd done the unthinkable and grabbed a camera and gone off running after her. Aidan let out a sigh at his feeble attempt to come up with an excuse. No, this was all on him.

He was the one drawn to her. He was the one who had documented her meltdown. And he was the one who had grabbed the

45

camera and eagerly followed behind her when she ran from the studio. His — well, her — only saving grace was that they'd cut to commercial and then the cooking segment and didn't feed back into him while she was in the greenroom. Small mercies, but still he was grateful. Though he knew that exposés and gotcha journalism were what passed for news nowadays, he'd seen what it could do to a person's life and didn't want that for her.

Aidan let out a low curse. Hell, maybe he did deserve a payback for what he'd done. Not a kick to the balls, mind you, but that shrug he had given was a little over the top. Who wouldn't be pissed about being filmed while having a fit like the one she'd had?

He smiled then at the memory of her meltdown. Despite it all, she did look kind of cute, going wild like she did with her smooth black hair coming loose and that flush of color rising up, bringing a glow to her creamy tan cheeks, that spark of fire rearing up in those dark cinnamon eyes.

Aidan groaned as something too close to desire flamed inside him again. He couldn't help it. The image of her ranting and out of control was so polar opposite from the straitlaced Miss Perfect thing she'd dished out each time she'd sailed into the studio for the couples elimination rounds. He couldn't stop watching her even if he tried. And, truth be told, something nagging at him made him want to see more. Though he was ashamed to admit it, he liked seeing her come undone. Maybe it was because it was almost unnerving the way she didn't get her feathers ruffled like the rest of the contestants did. The way she handled every question like a pro. It was damned near bordering on robotic, and for some reason, it grated on his nerves. Which was ridiculous, because what should he care about a buttoned-up ice princess like her? But, hell, not even when it was the blindfolded bake-off — definitely not Carter's brightest idea — did she let a hair fall out of place. That was some kinda cool and at the same time some weird shit. The woman was unflappable.

At least she was until today. Today, after her jerko fiancé gave her that on-air sucker punch, she had good and well lost it. And for the first time, he saw a glimpse of her that made him want to look further. Go deeper. Made him want to reach out and touch her, see if that cold-as-ice exterior could thaw, and if there was actual flesh and blood underneath. Aidan grinned. *Oh yeah, she thawed, all right.* And if that kiss was any indication of how she did her thawing out, well, he was all for it.

"What are you doing down there, man? And why are you grinning like an idiot? I'm sure when your father told you to get acquainted with all aspects of the station, sweeping the floor with your face wasn't one of them."

At the interruption of his thoughts, Aidan lost his thin grip on humor and shifted his gaze to study the pointy tips of Carter Bain's high-shined loafers.

"She kicked me in the balls," he groaned out to *The Morning Show*'s segment producer and one of his oldest friends, purposefully omitting the part about the kiss. He didn't have more of a reason for keeping the kiss from Carter besides there being no reason for Carter to know about it. But Aidan knew in his gut that it went deeper, and if he told Carter, he'd be a dog with a bone, and Aidan wasn't in the mood for a tussle with his old friend.

He heard Carter suck in a breath as he barely bit back a chuckle. "Her? No, not her. I knew she was mad, but that mad?" He looked up as Carter shook his head. "Damn, if I knew she was such a loose cannon, I would have stopped you from going after her. Did you get it on camera?" Carter now chuckled out loud. "Of course you did. I can't wait to pull up the footage. Shit. We should have never cut to that stupid cooking segment. I knew she was a spitfire, but I didn't expect her to be that hot."

Aidan raised a brow. Carter was positively gleeful as he turned his body toward the now faraway Miss Ward, who turned the hall's corner. When she disappeared from view, he looked back down toward Aidan and gave him a sly grin.

Aidan shook his head. Different day, but still the same old Carter. Here Carter was, despite all hell having broken loose, his segment going to crap, and he still looked cool, smooth and polished, practically photo shoot ready, and giving a Cheshire cat grin that let Aidan know trouble was soon to follow.

Aidan had seen that look from Carter plenty of times over the years and had the battle scars to know what it meant. Carter was working some sort of angle. At times, Aidan couldn't believe this was the same guy he had hung with as a kid, spending every summer day and well into the nights catching waves off Third Point with him and Vin. The three of them trying hard to escape the various limitations and expectations life heaped on three young minority men grow-

49

ing up in the big city. So they'd take their escape where they could and when they could get away, pretending to live carefree lives as beach bums out on the Rockaways. The Three Amigos. And out of the three of them, it was only Vin who still had any semblance of the carefree beach-bum life, riding his bike and catching waves at will, and somehow in between making enough money off his beachside taco shack to turn it into a destination sensation and have folks clamoring for more. He'd turned himself into a renegade chef and business owner.

As for Carter, he had ended up getting his MBA and going full tilt corporate, quickly rising in the ranks of World Broadcasting Central, going from production assistant to segment producer in record time. He has been all too happy to use his friendship with Aidan and pull from Aidan's dad to get that first job. From anyone else the obvious nepotism would have annoyed Aidan, but from Carter, who was blatantly upfront with his bull, it didn't. Besides, it may have been nepotism that got him through the door, but Aidan couldn't deny that Carter's smarts and relentless work ethic had put him on top.

That Aidan could respect. Besides, Carter had always been a gamer. Had to be in order to survive, coming from the background he came from and floating in the circles he did, hobnobbing with those born with silver spoons when he'd barely had plastic.

Not that the corporate life was one Aidan would choose, and that was a sore spot for him and his father. And the fact that one of his best friends had stepped up to the business plate like "the son his father never had" should have really gotten under Aidan's skin, but somehow it didn't, and he thought that bugged his father all the more.

For all Aidan cared, Carter could take over the family business, at least the glad-handing and conference room bull, if his father would leave him alone to do the type of stories he felt were meaningful. Cut him loose and let him do the investigative work he loved and stop trying to pull him off the streets and into the confines of a boardroom.

His place was out in the real world. Telling the stories of the people. Not crunching numbers and trying to find the best way to pull in more ad revenue. Or worse, working on more projects like this on-air marriage sideshow. But Dad was the boss, and unfortunately for Aidan, he'd done the leap before looking thing one time too many.

This last time it was falling for the pouty lips and the sad eyes of a pretty government informant. What a dumbass move. He'd barely made it out without getting his ass blown off, and worse, so had his crew. In the end, threats were made, and money, lots of money, changed hands to assure their passage out of the country and back home. So because of that, he was back. Thankfully they all were, safe and sound, and Aidan was stuck doing penance for following his heart instead of his head.

Aidan focused back on Carter. "Hot or not, you know you would have sent me or someone else after her either way," he said, thinking of the groin kicker again. He paused before considering his next answer. "But what I got on tape I don't think is worth showing."

Carter frowned but then laughed. "Yeah, man. You're right. I would have. You know me too well. But I'd have warned you to watch your crotch. It's not like I'm completely heartless. And as far as what's worth showing, that little lady is fantastic. The camera loves her, and more importantly, the viewers love her. We need to show it all. I can have Seth pull up the footage and then make the call."

Aidan shot Carter a look. "Like I said. I

don't think we should show that footage."

Carter paused though he had already grabbed his cell, ready to call the director to pull up the feed, and stared down at Aidan, brows lifted. "Are you actually pulling rank on me here? I thought I was your boy."

Aidan raised a brow and let out a long breath as he ran his hands through his thick curly hair, taking time to rub at his scalp. It was getting long, his father would say, too long for the office. Looking at Carter, with his hair short and tapered, lined up perfectly, he was reminded he was way overdue for a trim. Little Miss Perfect probably thought she was being filmed by some sort of Neanderthal with a camera for an eye. "Go on with that pulling rank crap. You know I'm always your boy, but trust me on this. I don't have anything I think we should show."

Carter gave Aidan a long look before he shook his head and stuck the cell back in his inside pocket.

Aidan felt a brief moment of regret over not leveling with his friend, but still he was relieved when Carter tucked his phone away. He didn't know why he'd gone to bat for the woman who'd just unmanned him, but he did. Aidan stretched out his legs and mentally assessed his body. Good. At least the pain was subsiding. With any luck, he'd still be able to walk. Anything else, well, that was up to time and fate. He attempted to get up using the wall for leverage, taking it slow.

"Well, I think this was a dumb move," he said, ignoring Carter's outstretched hand, preferring to lean on the wall. "We should have stayed back. Viewer draw or not, she didn't deserve what that asshole of a boyfriend did to her — and on camera no less. I kind of feel like a jerk for following her."

"Yeah, but you did. And it's not like it's something new. Isn't it like you to always follow the story?"

"But how is she a story? This is nothing more than a fluff piece, and it's not like you knew she was going to have a meltdown."

Carter shuffled then, shifting his feet ever so slightly as he looked down, then back up again at Aidan. The movement was quick, and to an untrained eye, the tell would have been missed. But Aidan had known Carter for way too long to miss it. Carter was hiding something, and Aidan intended to find out what. Aidan straightened up further, ignoring his groin pain, and looked Carter in the eye. He lowered his voice to a low growl. "Like I said. It's not like you knew she'd have a meltdown, did you?"

Carter looked to the left.

"Shit, man, how could you?" Aidan spit out. "You pretty much turned that girl into a raving lunatic on national TV. That's low, even for you."

Carter put up his hands. "Jeez, were you always this dramatic when we were younger? It was just a little segment, and if you check the numbers, you'll see I pretty much just made her a star. Besides, I didn't think the guy would really go through with it. So I may have overheard him talking to some chick on his cell about a breakup and knew it was a possibility. And maybe I nudged him in the direction of doing it on the air due to contractual obligations, blah, blah blah. Like I said, I didn't really think he'd go through with it. I told him to think it over! Who would have thought he'd have the balls to actually do it?"

"Please," Aidan said, shifting his uncomfortable stance. "Lay off the balls talk." He stopped and thought a moment. "But really, C, if you thought the guy would do that, you should have stopped the show. Gone to commercial. Not encouraged that kind of bull."

Carter looked at Aidan as if he'd suddenly grown two heads. "Stop the show? Maybe it's you who has lost it. You know better than anyone that you never stop the show. The bigger the wreck, the bigger the viewership."

"Come on. You know you went too far. It wasn't right."

"What are you getting all bent out of shape for? Back in the day, you'd do whatever it took to chase down a story. What's going on? Did your last encounter make you squeamish?"

Aidan stilled, his mind quickly jumping to haunted places where he didn't want it to go. Pointedly, he shook them off, then bent over to pick up the camera, thankful he'd had the foresight to let it down easy and protect it when he hit the ground. "Yeah, and look where it's gotten me," he let out on a low breath. "Let's just say I've learned my lesson. Mark me down as reformed."

Carter's voice was lower now, as if he knew the dark journey Aidan's mind had gone on because he'd traveled there too. "Well, she signed up for the show, so that makes her fair game. You have nothing to feel guilty about."

Aidan easily slung the heavy camera onto his broad shoulder. He shook his head. "Fair game? What is she, an animal to be hunted? This is no game, and nothing about it is fair. Now you're sounding like my father. Be careful my friend, you're getting close to making a full transition into a first-class pompous ass. Turn away from the dark side. Stay with us in the light."

Carter laughed nervously and straightened his already straight tie. "Hey, don't go hitting below the belt. You're sounding like you're speaking out of Vin's mouth. I'm just working to give the people what they want, and that's good business."

Aidan scoffed. "Yeah, that's what those on the dark side all say to justify the unjustifiable."

Carter shook his head and looked down the hall toward where Eva stomped off.

"Enough about that. It is time to talk damage control, and that little lady and her not so little fit may have given us just what we need to take our ratings to the top and finally pass those blowhards over at CBN and *The Morning Perk*."

Aidan felt something in his chest tighten, and his stomach did a flip as he met Carter's piercing gaze with a challenging stare. Shit. For some reason, he felt the need to cover his balls all over again.

Chapter 4

The buzzing of her cell jolted Eva out of her sleep. Squinting, she looked at her bedside clock and frowned. *Oh God.* It was already well past nine, and the last thing she remembered was throwing a chopstick at the TV as a late-night host made a joke about her *Morning Show* meltdown. Maybe taking her best friend Cori's well-meaning advice of celebrating her newfound freedom with champagne and the comfort of a new man wasn't the best idea. Though she hadn't gone so far as to hunt out a one-night stand, she went full on with Cori's suggestion of the bubbly and uncharacteristically drank alone. Declining Cori's offer to come over and share in her misery and bubbles, Eva ensured her friend that she was fine, only exhausted over it all. And as for the man part of the advice, that was taken care of by delivered General Tsos from the Chinese restaurant down the block and her dusted-off nightstand playmate, Mr. Motivator. Or would have been if she'd gotten some use out of him in the past year and his batteries weren't dead. Seems the day was just full of disappointing male members.

Eva let out a sigh. Maybe she should have let Cori come over and possibly lend her a bit more backbone. They could have gone over to Kev's place and done a bit of tag team ass kicking. At least give him a good tell off. Thinking back, though her friend was loyal to a fault and followed the girl code of not outwardly bashing her choice of mate, she knew Kevin wasn't high on Cori's list of favorite people. And Eva knew that if she were seeing things through Cori's jade-colored lenses, she probably would have had her eyes opened sooner and seen Kevin for what he was up to before she had ever stepped foot on that studio's set and made a complete ass of herself. No matter. Done was done, and she had to deal with it. She told Cori she'd make a point to see her before she left for work. Another thought that brought Eva's spirits low was that her friend was about to be off sailing the globe, living the carefree life, at least for a while, working for a luxury cruise company. Eva smiled, though. Knowing Cori, there would be a new man in every port. There was no way Cori was getting tied down by — let her tell it — a ridiculous convention like marriage.

Thinking back, the joke the comedian made last night was kind of funny and would be downright hilarious to her if it wasn't at her expense. Besides, Cori was right. All this would blow over, and she'd be yesterday's news soon enough.

The phone buzzed again, and Eva moaned. She couldn't remember the last time she had slept so hard or so deep. It must have had something to do with washing down that last bit of chicken with half a bottle of Prosecco. Ignoring the phone, Eva stretched her body long, arched her back, and kicked her legs out, exploring the delicious coolness of the sheets on the right side of the bed. Inching toward the middle, she rolled onto her back and stretched wider still, making an X shape. Her long limbs just about hit all four corners of the mattress at once. She smiled. Oddly, it felt kind of good to wake up alone for a change. Kevin was a notorious space and cover hog, not to mention he made a lot of noise when he got up for his six AM sessions with his trainer. She hated to admit it, *but this,* she thought, reaching over and caressing the empty space where the indent from Kevin's body used to be, *this maybe she could get used to.*

The buzzing started again, and Eva turned once more, her face hit with a hard shaft of sunlight, causing her to squint. She pushed her leg arc out wide and let out a long sigh before quickly pulling her leg back in again, tight to her body, the coolness now giving her a surprising chill, reminding her that having the bed all to herself came at a price.

Reaching over to the side of the bed, Eva picked up the phone to look at the caller ID, now more than half hoping it was Kevin calling to apologize, saying he'd come back to his senses and was ready to make amends. It wasn't. A knot immediately clenched up in her belly as she saw her mother's office number. Of course it was her. She'd want to see how she was this morning, but also she'd want answers. Answers to questions that Eva knew she did not have. Not to mention, what could she say to placate her mother after her horrendous public meltdown? They were a PR firm, for goodness sake. Image was everything with them. And not even when her mother had been through her worst with her father and his death did she let it show through to the rest of the world. No, she took her lumps and shed her

61

tears in private and, in the process, taught Eva how to be strong in the face of what seemed an unimaginable heartbreak and embarrassment. And here she was, her only daughter, her legacy, and with a five-minute TV segment and a muttered line from a guy who probably wasn't worth the effort she'd put in, she'd gone off and lost it. Though she didn't want to face it, part of Eva knew that whatever questions or perhaps disappointment her mother directed her way was warranted.

She'd ask if she and Kev had been having troubles. No, nothing beyond the usual. Or so she thought. She'd want to know how come Eva didn't see this coming. She'd also want to know what her plans were to fix this and get her reputation — and, more importantly, the firm's reputation — back on track. All perfectly fine queries, to which, at the moment, Eva had no answers. It wasn't like Kevin was blowing up her phone or knocking down her door or even using his key to come in and apologize, ask for her back, or at least give her a valid reason for why he broke up with her on national TV. No, it seemed he was just . . . done. No calls, texts, or last-minute chase-downs with words of love or begging her forgiveness. Eva guessed he had said all he had to say on the air yesterday. And all his talk of love, well, that was the past. Mere words said when emotions needed to be manipulated.

The phone buzzed again, and this time Eva looked down and saw from the caller ID that it was her mother's assistant, Lance. She shook her head. So Mom was switching tactics. She knew Eva wouldn't ignore Lance forever since her mom would have him calling every five minutes on the minute until she picked up. She might as well get this over with and put the poor guy out of his misery. Eva swiped him over.

"Yes, Lance."

"Nope. I'm perfectly fine. Just running a bit late."

"Tell her majesty I'll be in shortly."

"No, I don't need you to send a car, but thank you."

Rolling over, she closed her eyes and treated herself to sixty more seconds of peace and quiet before the inevitable avalanche to come.

What am I doing here? Aidan's gut told him this was wrong, but still he was here. Fighting against the tight collar that gripped his neck, he finally gave in and ripped off the offending tie, shoving it into his suit pocket. The cute redheaded receptionist didn't even try to hide her smirk as she peered at him and Carter over the top of her sleek maple workstation. Aidan gave her a smile and took a moment to let his mind do its usual wanderings when taken in by a pretty woman, but his smile quickly changed to a frown when all that came up was the image of smooth caramel skin and creamy white pearls.

He ran his hands through his now shorter hair, cropped just this morning for today's meeting. *What the hell?* What was he doing thinking about her? Again. It was bad enough that he'd barely gotten a moment's rest last night, playing and then replaying their awful first meeting and that surprisingly seductive kiss that she'd hit him with. Still, it was maddening. Updos and twinsets were definitely not his type. Besides, he knew what sort of trouble she and her pearls were. Shit, he was just now getting proper feeling back to his nether regions and planned to keep them out of her knee range at all costs. So once again that brought up the question: What was he doing here?

"Really, man? You can't keep it together and look good for an hour?" Carter said from his side, bringing Aidan's thoughts back to the matter at hand. Aidan let his eyes sweep to his friend, who looked completely comfortable in his sharply tailored suit, tie notched just right as he sat casually perched on the reception area's most uncomfortable white leather couch.

"I'm fine. And it's not like I need a tie to take this meeting or look good." Carter's subtle nod let him know he had him there. But still he was uncomfortable, and it had nothing to do with his attire. "Honestly, it's not like you need me here. You can handle the pitch yourself. It's bad enough you wrangled me into this idea of yours."

"Wrangled?" Carter said, his brows drawing together. "Aren't you the convenient revisionist? When I told you the segment idea and suggested Rick Lancer for the lead producer, you practically jumped at the chance to take over and handle it yourself. So now you've got it. It's all yours, boss."

Aidan frowned at the mention of Rick, the self-proclaimed "reality king's" name. "I don't like being played, Carter, and you know as well as I do that calling out Rick was a play to pull me in. After what I said about not wanting to use her footage and being exploited by the show, you knew there was no way I'd let a snake like Rick within a hundred feet of the job. The man would chew her up, then spit her out, leaving her with no meat left on the bone."

"Yeah, but it would all make for great TV, and that's what we're after right now. Ratings. It's what the network needs."

Aidan let out a frustrated breath as Carter shook his head and continued. "I don't know what's gotten into you. It's as if you've gone soft. We're in the TV business here, not the hand-holding business, and you're home now, not on the battlefield. That female firecracker in pearls does not need saving." Aidan shot Carter a look with his last comment, and Carter tempered his next words. "Besides, I now have to fill three hours a morning with *news.* And barring, God forbid, a war on our shores, there is not enough real news to go around." Carter put his fingers up and did air quotes. "And there is only so much breaking news one can do on the latest celebrity meltdown. We've got to get creative."

Aidan shifted. "Fine, I hear you, but celebs are one thing. It's a different story when we screw over real people."

Carter gave him a hard look. "You know as well as do I that she stopped being a real person as soon as she signed that waiver." He smiled. "Besides. She's in PR. She knows the ropes. We're not dealing with a wounded bird here. If anyone should be wounded, it's you. She gave it to you good."

Aidan crossed his legs and groaned. "Don't remind me. That she sure did."

But despite his words, he was still torn. More than anything, he wanted to walk away — to steer as far afield from this project as he could, continue his getting-to-know-you company tour — but something wouldn't let him do it. When Carter told him his idea to keep up the pressure and to train a spotlight on the literally ball-busting Eva Ward, at first he had laughed. Stupidly, he had even chimed in with thoughts on the concept, a fast-paced dating show, something to make her follow through on her final words about still getting married anyway as she'd stormed out of the studio. But he should have known that Carter would pounce right on it, quickly calling in a production team to work up ideas and then wanting to name Rick Lancer as lead on-site producer.

But as soon as Aidan heard Rick's name, something in him wouldn't let it lie. Rick was a notorious life-ruiner. A real piece of work. A part-time body builder and full-time ass. Rick made no secret about his womanizing ways, and for some reason just the thought of him in close quarters with the hot-lipped ice princess instantly sent Aidan's blood boiling. Like her or not, she'd been through enough and didn't deserve the likes of Rick invading her space. So before he knew it, Aidan was stepping up to take the lead on a project that was out of his new normal of war zones and guns, and would have him playing backseat matchmaker to a woman in whom he'd literally met his match. Just by being here and entertaining the idea, he probably deserved every bit of busting he got from Carter on this one. Since it was business and Carter was getting what he wanted out of him, his old friend was keeping it to a minimum, but Aidan was sure it was coming. Carter knew him too well, and there was no way he'd let a good riffing opportunity lie.

Aidan was sure he'd been played. Hell, if he was honest, he was probably getting played by Carter yesterday when he just so happened to have him on the set when it all went down. It had all worked out a little too well, and Carter gave in way too easily and agreed in less time than it took for him to zone in on the perfect tie at Brooks Brothers. Oh well, screw it. What was done was done. At least now if she agreed and the project went through, he could be sure the ice princess came out of this ordeal without too many dings or chips. And he'd be sure to protect himself from getting run over in the process.

Snapping back to the moment, Aidan saw a tall, broad-bodied dude with dark skin and even darker eyes, who looked like he could be bouncing at any of the city's toughest clubs, come out to the reception area and give the saucy redhead a wide smile. He then turned toward Carter and Aidan, and the smile instantly vanished. "If you gentleman would follow me, Ms. Ward will see you now."

Carter shot up and gave the guy a broad smile. "After you, my good man!"

The big guy leveled him with a stony gaze. *Yep, definitely bouncer material.*

Aidan got up slowly; frowning, he resisted wiping his sweaty palms on his suit pants. He never sweated unless he was about to get into a tight spot, and right now, going up against Valerie Ward, Eva's mother, he had a feeling he was about to do just that.

Eva stepped into the elevator of the Parker Building on Madison Avenue, where the Ward Group's branding and PR consulting offices were housed. She immediately noticed the dawn of recognition in the eyes of one of the riders, a petite strawberry-blonde, who at first looked wide-eyed, and then that awful cloud of sympathy washed over her features, causing Eva's stomach to churn at the same time as her anger bubbled up. *Dammit!* She'd been getting *that* look all morning, and she was frankly over it. First her doorman, then the barista at her favorite coffee shop, not to mention the look from all the other patrons. Hell, they were just finally getting her coffee order right. Would she really have to now switch to the other Starbucks all the way up the street a whole block and a half away? And then there was the cabdriver.

Eva twisted her coffee cup as she pointedly tried to break eye contact with the blonde and looked toward the closing doors, catching her reflection in the shiny chrome. *It will be fine,* she told herself. Outwardly she was the same as she had been the day before. She chose her slim gray pants and white silk blouse carefully. She put her hair up in a smooth chignon, and her face looked flawless, with just the right balance of understated makeup. On any other day, she would blend in perfectly with the bustling New York morning crowd. Shifting her satchel in the crook of her arm, then looking up into the polished chrome's reflection, she caught the hint of defeat in her weary brown eyes. Just not on this day.

Eva looked back down and pretended to

concentrate on the coffee cup's familiar siren logo, then ran her hand along the edge, tracing the cover's rim. The sight of her now bare left ring finger caused her to pause, as she swallowed down on the simmering anger that was threatening to rise. The ring of her dreams currently sat idle in a silver dish on her dresser. Cold and alone, a diamond sparkling with no one to sparkle for. It somehow seemed an affront against her beliefs and the god of good jewelry that it should be there twinkling all alone and not on her finger being admired, as it should.

She thought once again of how Kevin had not called since the show. Coward. Maybe she should have changed the locks on her apartment before coming in to work. Thinking it over now, leaving the ring where she did was probably not the best idea. She wouldn't put it past Kevin's wimpy behind to try and sneak into her place to gather his few belongings when he knew she was at work. He was never big on confrontations, which is what made the TV breakup so surprising, and then again maybe not so much. She was sure he wasn't expecting her to go off like she did. It was probably his version of a restaurant breakup. A way to keep it public and minimize the scene. Eva let out a snort. A lot of good that did. Right now it would have been kinder if he'd sent her a text or at least gone old school *Sex and the City* and broken up with her with a Post-it or something equally impersonal.

Eva stared at her finger and made a mental note to call her doorman and put Kevin on the no-entry list. She'd be dammed if he got that ring back after what he'd done. And besides, she paid for half the damn ring anyway. Not that anyone but she and Kevin knew that. How embarrassing would it be if that news got out? And she was thought of as a sad case now. If folks knew that, she'd be positively tragic. Kevin took her to pick out her ring, and when she did, he steered her toward less-expensive, flawed diamonds. As if starting off their life together with a flawed symbol of commitment was acceptable. What a fool she was, listening to his crap about the ring not mattering, all the while happily picking out the best of everything when it came to himself.

There was a soft tap on her shoulder, and unfortunately the sigh escaped her lips before Eva could stop it. Damn. The strawberry blonde. She knew it was a mistake to let her emotions show, but Eva had been stopped four times already that morning. Just how many people really did watch that

stupid morning show? Weren't they supposed to be number two in the ratings? She
shook her head. First it was Carlos the
doorman, giving his kind regrets over Kevin.
Then it was the old woman with the two
poodles who stopped her not two seconds
later to tell her that she had an eligible
grandson. Next, it was the girl at Starbucks,
who gave her loud condolences over the
espresso machine, while the rest of the coffee shop nodded and looked at her like she
was terminally ill. All she wanted was a coffee, light with an extra shot, extra sweet,
hold the comments. Was that too much to
ask? The topper was the cab driver — she
didn't have the heart to jump on public
transportation today — who pronounced
what Kevin did as foul-assed and low-down
in his thick Caribbean accent. Eva just gave
a polite nod. She wouldn't voice it, but she
had to agree on that one. When Eva asked
the driver if he had watched the show, he
said no, but he got to see the highlights
when his daughter showed him the YouTube
clip.

Perfection. She was going viral.

There was another tap on her shoulder,
and Eva braced herself as she turned around
and gave an innocent smile to the
strawberry-blond woman looking at her like

the second coming of Jennifer Aniston or something.

"It *is* you! I knew it," the woman said, her voice echoing off the steel-paneled walls. "It was awful what he did to you. I'm sure it was going to be a beautiful wedding. I voted for you two, you know."

"Um, thanks?" What else was she supposed to say? The other three people in the elevator all stared at her now. She turned back and watched the floor numbers light up. Twelve, thirteen, fourteen.

"It was just terrible," the woman continued loudly over her shoulder. "Did you really have no clue? I mean, really, not a clue that he would dump you like that on national TV?"

Eva bit her bottom lip to keep from screaming. She could feel the eyes of the other passengers boring into the back of her head. Her face began to flame. Fifteen, sixteen. The woman tapped her again. "I said, did you *really* have no clue?"

Eva turned around. Fighting to keep a tight rein on her simmering temper and feeling tears threaten, she thought of her image and how she needed to focus on rebuilding it before she spoke. "No, um, I didn't."

The blonde shook her head. "Wow. Who

74

would have guessed? And here I was thinking all these reality shows were scripted. It kinda renews my faith."

Ding. Nineteen. *Thank God.* Eva let out a breath and smiled broadly at the woman. "Well, I'm glad my downfall helped." The woman's face fell in confusion as Eva stepped off the elevator. "To restore your faith in television, that is."

"Um, thanks!" the woman yelled at her back as the doors closed and Eva stepped into the waiting area of the Ward Group, only to be greeted by the open arms and lush bosom of Kimberly, the receptionist, as she ran around her desk and pulled her into an uncomfortable hug.

"There, there now. You're going to be fine," Kim said, petting her like one might a fallen toddler with a scraped knee.

"Oh, I know I will be fine," Eva said. "You, on the other hand, may lose that hand if you don't stop petting me like that."

CHAPTER 5

Kim pulled back abruptly, her hands holding tight to Eva's upper arms as she looked up into her eyes. "Aww, what a brave girl you are."

Eva fought not to roll her eyes and instead inserted her coffee and purse firmly between herself and Kim. She'd had it with the pity. It got old, and fast. "Thanks, Kim. I'm fine really. No need to worry about me. It's onward and upward," she said, extracting herself from the woman's surprisingly strong grasp.

Kim gave her a shaky smile, and for a moment, Eva was afraid she might actually burst into tears. "That's the way. You hang in there. What a trooper you are," Kim sniffed out. "But, hey, you told him, and good. And I'm sure you're right, you will find someone else. You won't end up a sad statistic. Filling out endless online dating profiles, constantly getting swiped left, then moving back in with your mom because your roommate moved out and you can't find anyone else to cover their half of the rent, all the while your boyfriend of eight years still won't commit because he says he doesn't want to be held down." On the word *down,* Kim let out a little choked cry, and she reached over the desk, going for a tissue, and blew her nose loudly.

So this is the day that just keeps on giving. Eva felt all her muscles go tight and seem to bunch up at once into her shoulders and neck area. Feeling the tables turn, she gave Kim an awkward pat on the arm, not quite comfortable getting too close to the overly emotional receptionist. "Are you all right? Hey, it's not so bad. As they say, plenty of fish and all."

Kim blinked, then gave Eva a surprised look as if she didn't quite get Eva's try at sympathy. She chuckled and waved her hand before letting out a delicate snort. "Oh no, I'm fine. It's you that got dumped on TV. Frankly, I'd be mortified. The way I see it, I'm sitting pretty good right now."

Eva threw her a sharp look and a cocked brow. "Well, okay then, thanks for the reminder. Glad I'm still the winner in the 'sucks to be me' contest of life. Now can we move on? Here's the rule. It's over and

77

done. I don't want to hear about Kevin, the show, or how sorry anyone is. I'm fine. I'm back, and I'm ready to move on. So how about you get on the phone and get to passing that message through the wires. Okay?"

Kim blinked harder this time before fumbling back to her desk area. "Um, sure, so I guess you don't want these messages left for you yesterday. They're mostly about . . . you know what."

When Eva maintained a stony silence, Kim swallowed, then nodded. "So maybe I should throw them away or pass them on to your assistant?"

Eva put her coffee cup on the receptionist station and took the pile of messages. It wasn't Kim's fault she was in this mess, so it was no use taking it out on her. "Don't worry about it. I'll take them. So many, huh?"

"Yeah, I'm sorry. Most of the calls did go to Jess, and I would have put these through to your voice mail, but I knew you probably didn't want to deal with listening to most of them, so I just routed them this way and took them myself."

Eva gave Kim a weak smile. Annoying or not, she was trying to help. There were so many messages, all contacts that had her direct line, and Kim had gone above and beyond in taking the messages for her. "Thanks, you didn't have to. You could have routed it all to Jess."

"Oh, believe me, she's had her hands plenty full. Her line has been ringing non-stop. Your clients have not stopped calling. It's been all hands on deck around here. Oh, and about that," Kim continued, lowering her voice enough to make her whispered tone more pronounced. "Valerie is waiting for you in her office. She said you should see her as soon as you got in."

Eva nodded. This was anticipated. Of course her mother had summoned her. She was surprised she'd patiently waited until she'd gotten into the office. She'd half expected her to use her emergency key and come barging in on her while she was still in bed last night or this morning. It wouldn't be the first time she made herself more than at home in Eva's space. But since she hadn't, maybe things weren't as bad as Eva imagined them to be.

Eva felt her heart pick up to trotter speed. Who was she fooling? Of course they were.

Her mother was probably out of her mind by now. She'd been after Eva to find the perfect man and get married for as long as she could remember. It was, Eva, thought, an odd and morbid aftereffect of Eva's

79

father passing away from an apparent heart attack brought on by the extreme physical exertion of a marathon sex session with his personal assistant after competing in a marathon road race with the New York Runners Society. Apparently, there were only so many marathons a middle-aged man could take.

Eva was only twelve when the veil of her perfect world was torn down. But worse, she thought at times, that losing her father was the dramatic shift in Eva's formerly carefree mother. It was as if all her mother's joy was suddenly gone with this one — okay, so it probably was not one, given how dad seemed to have a string of assistants — awful betrayal, only to be replaced by the drive to become the perfect socialite and businesswoman.

Valerie Ward was obsessed with maintaining an air of outward excellence. She took over Eva's father's spot at the head of the Ward Group and turned it, and herself, into the face of exceptional perfection. And to that, her daughter, Eva, became just another extension, a part of the machine, and this misstep with Kevin was unacceptable. There was a plan. College, a year for travel, and then three years in the business while she was groomed. Then marriage to a perfectly moldable man that would finish off the perfect portrait, completing their family image. But with his on-air breakup, Kevin had not only ruined the plan, he had completely obliterated the plan. Much as Eva's father had done to their family when he was carted out of that hotel room, as rumor had it, stiff as a board in all aspects of his anatomy and with his gym socks still on. Just humiliating.

Eva closed her eyes, then opened them again. The similarity of her and her mother's public humiliations was not lost on her. She was sure her mother was probably right now waiting for her, though, poised and polished, with a new list of eligible candidates vetted to her standard and ready to wed. Onward and . . . well, just onward. Failure was not an option when it came to the Ward women. *Never accept defeat, and never let them see you sweat.*

It was with that motto in mind that Eva gathered her things and headed down the marble hall to start her day and face the music that was her mother, Valerie Ward.

The office's exterior glass wall was set to dim, but Eva could see from the silhouettes that someone else was inside with her mother. She frowned, seeing that her mom's burly assistant, Lance, was not perched outside in his usual gatekeeper position and couldn't let her know who was inside. She hadn't been aware of them having any early-morning client meetings scheduled.

Smoothing the front of her blouse, Eva knocked quickly three times on the glass door.

"Come in, Eva."

At the command, Eva felt the instant beginnings of a frown. Of course someone would have called to tell Valerie she was on the way down — possibly Kim, or maybe even her own assistant. In the end, they all worked for Valerie, but going in there on the defensive was not the way to defuse the situation, and she knew it. Eva made a point to ease her features so that, she hoped, her expression was unreadable, especially when it was possible that clients were inside with her mother.

She saw her mother first, standing tall and commanding behind her desk in a vintage black and white abstract print wrap dress, her hair was pulled back tightly into her signature long, low ponytail. As always, she looked like she could either be about to do some sort of boardroom takeover or jet off for St. Barths at any moment. When it came to her globe-trotting mother and their exclusive list of clients, it was hard to say which might be the case. And it all worked for Val's cool persona.

"Good morning," Eva said with an outer confidence and smile she hoped hid her inner turmoil. "You wanted to see me, Mother?"

"Come in, Eva. I'd say you've kept us all waiting long enough. As I'm sure you know, we have quite a few things to iron out."

It was on the drop of the collective "us" that the two men seated opposite her mother's desk turned around, and Eva's perfectly poised but expertly expressionless smile sank. Still, it didn't escape her notice that only one of the men stood. The other, Carter Bain, *The Morning Show*'s producer, stayed in his seat. *As if he'd get up for anyone. Smug bastard.* Eva let out a long breath through her nose. Why was she even surprised? Carter seemed the type that expected people to rise for him, not the other way around. The fact that the man he was with, the one standing, was there at all — and standing, no less — was what really took her by surprise. Especially since when she last saw the tall, dark-haired man, he was laid out on the floor, holding what she was sure were his aching balls and probably cursing her everyway but Sunday, though she hadn't hung around for confirmation of that final part.

Eva's eyes narrowed in on her past take-down. She hoped he wasn't there to start more trouble. She saw a glimmer of a spark in his dark eyes and decided that he was there and with Carter, so of course he was. Briefly, she wondered if he was there to file some sort of charges. Talk damages. Bodily harm or some other such crap. That would be just what she needed on top of everything else, but with the spiral her life was currently on, she wouldn't have been surprised. Eva shook her head. She never should have agreed to do that damned show in the first place. Her eyes swept from his dark glimmer down to Carter Bain's unreadable gaze before she glanced back at her mother.

"What's he doing here?" It didn't matter which "he" her mother assumed at this point, since she didn't care to see either of the men ever again.

"Eva, take a seat," Valerie commanded. "Mr. Bain has been kind enough to come and see us today with an ingenious new show plan I think would be wonderful. Especially after all that, well, unpleasantness yesterday."

Eva sucked in a lung full of much needed air. Perfect, and so perfectly Ward Group. Her future ripped out from under her, neatly summarized down to just one word — *unpleasantness.*

She gave them each a quick once-over before landing back on her mother. "Wonderful for who? Them, or our company? Because I seriously doubt anything he comes up with will be wonderful for me."

"Miss Ward, won't you please at least hear us out?" Mr. Tall, Dark, and Suddenly Chivalrous Cameraman moved to the side. He offered up his chair to her, and Eva felt her brows come further together and the hairs on the back of her neck stand on edge. He was a far cry from the way he had looked the day before, when he held the camera, capturing her private meltdown for the whole world to see. He was a lot more polished, and his hair was still a little long, but neater, though she hated to admit caring — or even looking, for that matter. Most of that delicious scruff was gone, low and tapered, but blessedly, just enough was left to be slightly dangerous. Gone were the jeans and the wrinkled white tee. In their place was a well-cut designer suit, expensive Italian loafers, and a white button-down, open at the neck and showing off his deeply tanned throat. Yes, he was very different today out of his work clothes.

"No, I think I'll stand, thank you. I'm sure

this meeting will be short, Mr. —"

"Walker. Aidan Walker." His deep rich voice was smooth and commanding as he stated his name in that annoying, three-word Bond, James Bond kind of way. Still, it washed over Eva like a wave of silk, making every nerve in her body stand at attention as he held out his hand. But Eva stared at it for a beat before she looked back up into his eyes with newfound recognition.

She felt her brows go up as embarrassment brought heat to her cheeks. "Of course you are."

Shit. Aidan Walker. How could she not have recognized him immediately? Especially since media relations and PR were her job. Practically her life. It didn't matter that she was caught up in a wave of emotion yesterday. There was no excuse for being that far off her game that she didn't recognize a man with his reputation. Eva felt slightly sick but fought to cover it. Talk about a pile-on. Did she really embarrass herself to all holy hell, and then kiss and maim Aidan Walker? She stared at Walker, and something in his gaze sparked again, zinging her and lighting a fuse.

That was it.

It was officially official that she had the

worst taste in men. In business and in pleasure.

So it was bad boy Walker who was behind her public humiliation. Well, him and that asshole Kevin. But Carter was probably just Walker's lackey. Everyone knew it was Walker's father who was the head of WBC, and that made Aidan heir to the throne. And with his past history of taking risks and going too far, he should have known better than anyone what a weapon the camera could be. He was always in and out of the news, getting into some scrape or another. He was a notorious celebrity hound. Known for doing anything to get the story in his early days, he'd gotten quite the reputation for getting into scrape after scrape with celebs. And no matter that he was supposedly reformed and now into hard news, his latest misstep had almost gotten him and his crew into some very hot water on the wrong side of the Turkish border.

Eva swallowed before speaking. "No, thank you, Mr. Walker, I'll stand. Besides, I find this is my best angle. So what is it today? Is the camera hidden in your lapel or" — she looked around — "have you already tricked out my mother's office with micro cameras? You've been known to employ less than aboveboard tactics to get what you want."

As she made that comment, Eva not only saw a glimmer in his eye, but she thought she caught a spark. Fine. Maybe like her kick, it was hitting a little below the belt, but he was on her turf now, and like them she could play dirty too.

Walker leveled her with a challenging stare, then took a step back. Pulling his hand away, he walked over to the corner seating area and easily lifted one of the heavy chrome chairs and brought it over, taking a seat himself before looking back up at her. "No hidden cameras and nothing in my lapel. You also shouldn't believe everything you read about me, Miss Ward. I'm honest when it comes to the way I handle a story. My methods may be unconventional, but I do what it takes."

She noticed Carter Bain shoot him a look at his tone, but Walker ignored him and continued. "So, today it's just us, and we want to talk about what happened yesterday and how to fix it. Carter here thinks we have a good way for both you and the station to come out winners when all is said and done."

Eva continued to stand, staring at the three of them, probably for longer than need be, because the air got thick and — she hated to admit it — weird with an uncomfortable charge she wasn't in the mood to acknowledge.

Carter Bain gazed at her expectantly, as if he had a pocket full of magic beans to sell that would make, if not all of her dreams, than at least all of his own come true. Her mother took a seat, but not before giving her a look that let her know how disappointed she was in her and the whole sorry affair and that she needed to get in line and on board with trying to fix it. Hell, she was sorry too. She hated to disappoint her mom, no matter if to the rest of the world she was as Teflon as they came. Eva knew different. Disappointing her mother meant disappointing herself. That said, Eva still wanted out. Standing where she was, jilted and with all eyes on her, she wanted to run back to her apartment, shut the blinds, turn off the phone, and stay away from the TV until the next great celebrity disaster hit and she was nothing but a forgotten funny blip on the social media radar.

Eva looked back at Walker, and all she could see was him with his camera and the last image she had presented yesterday. Raving like some silly, little wounded child who'd gotten her favorite toy taken away. After dad and his dying debacle, her mother never raved. At least not publicly she didn't. No matter the talk in her face or behind her back, she was grace and elegance through and through.

Thankfully, Eva thought, her most unflattering footage had not aired, and for the life of her, she didn't know why not. She recorded the show, and when she arrived home, she thought she'd see both parts of her tirade on TV, but the footage ended after her awful proclamation to Kevin about getting married with or without him and her storming out of the studio. The next segment, after the break, was a poorly timed "bringing the romance back into the kitchen" cooking segment. Nothing on her and the rant in the not so greenroom. Still, what had aired was bad enough. She hated what it did to her reputation, how she now was looked at as one to be pitied. She'd had enough of that as a kid and then later after her father's affair. Ward women didn't do sad or pity.

Aidan Walker cleared his throat, bringing her attention to him once more, and surprisingly, the look he gave her wasn't one of disappointment, and it wasn't full of promises like Bain would probably offer; it came as even more of a surprise that it wasn't even apologetic, as it should have been, for filming her. No, it was the same look he had presented the day before, right at that moment when she'd decided she wanted to kiss him and, all at the same time, to kick him. Smug, self-assured, even a little detached, and way too cocky for his own good.

His hooded gaze went from her eyes to her lips, sending a fissure of some sort of strange airwave sparking across the expanse of space separating them. His full lips twisted ever so slightly as he looked farther down, sweeping from her collarbone to her breasts to her hips, all the way to her toes, then back up to her eyes again. Eva forced herself not to flinch. Just take him on, head on.

But then he did it. Again. Walker had the nerve to shrug.

It was as if the red ON AIR light suddenly flashed, bright and glaring, as if he was a matador waving the red flag. Eva sucked in a breath full of life-giving air and smoothly took the seat opposite him, looking him in the eye. "Really, Mr. Walker? You have got to be kidding me with that dammed shrug again."

Walker smiled, zinging her once again as his face seemed to change from dark and slightly menacing to all-out, knock you down with a sexual feather gorgeous. Eva sucked in a breath as she steeled her back, grateful she had taken the seat. She shook her head and turned to Carter. "Look, I don't know what type of game you two are playing, but you've got five minutes to fill me in before I call security and have you escorted out of our offices."

Carter put up a hand. "No need to go there, Miss Ward. Aidan is right. The offer we have for you would be mutually beneficial."

Eva narrowed her gaze. "Somehow I doubt that."

"Just hear them out," her mother said from her leather throne on the other side of the desk before she remembered they were in mixed company. "Please. Unfortunately, your quick declarations have gotten you, not to mention the firm, into a sticky situation. Now it's time to do what damage control you can."

Flames licked at Eva's face. It was bad enough that she was in the mess she was in, but to be publicly dressed down by her mother in front of these two? It was just about too much. Biting back a response, she fought not to look Walker's way and catch any more unearned bravado in his expression. Instead she kept her gaze trained on Carter Bain. "What is it you had in mind, Mr. Bain?"

Bain smiled, and on anyone else, she supposed it would be cute. But after her previous dealings, Eva was not biting. Her lips stayed firm as she crossed her legs and leaned back in her chair, frankly happy for the support. Carter's smile faded as he opened up a case and swiped at his tablet. "As of yesterday, the game's been changed. Now, normally, we'd go to the runner-up couple and give them the planned dream wedding. Easy and done. But it would seem that you are a big draw. According to our social media analyzers, you took the ratings off the charts yesterday, and for hours after the show you were a trending topic on twitter with the hashtag #GetEvaMarried, followed closely by my favorite, #InsertGoomHere.

Eva groaned at the thought of it. What a disaster. She was an unwanted YouTube sensation. And to emphasize the fact, he swiped the screen again and showed her a GIF of her yelling at Kevin, pushing back the chair, which fell behind her to the floor. The video repeated on a loop with the words I WILL GET MARRIED in big block letters underneath. She looked completely bonkers.

Carter continued, "Now, you know, press

93

like this we can't buy."

"Of course you can." Eva's mother chimed in, always the businesswoman. "But it's damned expensive." Valerie gave Eva a wink as if at least in this she'd done something right. Hey, press was press.

Carter cleared his throat and nodded. "Well, yes we can, it's just we'd rather not. And that said, you are the story. Everyone still wants to see you have your happily-ever-after. It will mean huge ratings for us and redemption for you."

Eva shook her head, then looked up at Carter. "Listen, once was enough. What if I'm done with the whole dating and marriage thing?"

Her mother sucked in a breath, and Eva raised a hand her way. "At least for now, Mother. Once publicly burned is enough for me. I made a mistake saying what I did. It was done in a fit of anger."

"We do know about your hot temper, Miss Ward," Walker piped in with a low chuckle.

Eva stilled. "Is that supposed to be funny? I'm actually quite levelheaded. You can ask anyone. I only show anger when I've been unjustly provoked."

"Duly noted. I'll be sure to let everyone know to keep provocation at a minimum."

Eva felt her pressure rise. "What are you

really here for? You said this was Mr. Bain's idea, so why are you even involved? Don't you have a real celebrity to chase or some war to exploit?"

Eva saw a muscle in his jaw tick as he leaned forward in his chair.

"Miss Ward, I think we're getting off topic," Carter Bain chimed in. "Please, let's stay focused on the issues at hand." He tapped his screen again. "See, here we're talking about a whole new direction for your image."

Eva bit at the inside of her cheek in order to hold off on commenting as she watched Carter swipe his screen again and saw an image of herself come to life. There she was, photoshopped and looking perky as all get out in an overly satined and tulled white, princess-style wedding dress with a cutout blank figure in the spot where the groom should be. The hashtag was above in bold letters: #InsertGroomHere. Carter grinned. "Isn't it fantastic?"

What the living hell? Eva blinked and wondered if she'd ever be able to close her mouth again as Carter continued to chatter on. "We're talking top-notch, full blitz and glitz all the way. The search will be on to finding you your perfect groom!"

He'd lost his mind. Eva looked at the trio

95

as they all looked back at her expectantly. Had they all lost their minds? Or maybe it was her who had gone over the bend. Eva shook her head. With the way things were going that was more than likely the fact. Trying her best to sound rational though, Eva directed her words and thoughts towards Carter Bain. "Mr. Bain there is no way this can work. Kevin and I were supposed to have our wedding next month. No one will believe I can find true love in a month."

Carter nodded soberly. "You're absolutely right." Then he grinned. "But they will get behind two months. Just think of it, eight men, eight weeks to the perfect end-of-summer wedding, leading into fall sweeps. We will get our ratings, and you will be a star."

"More importantly, you'll come out triumphant, darling, which is what you should be," Valerie chimed in. "Not like some victim with no recourse that this on-air breakup just happened to. It will end on your terms, not Kevin's, and the Ward name will be back fully intact."

That was it, she was officially in cray town. Giving herself a mental shake, Eva snapped out of her social-media trance and looked at her mother. In her gaze she could see she

96

was reliving all the embarrassment of her father's not-so-secret indiscretions. To her, there was no other option. Perfection and excellence were the only revenge for all past hurts. Never let them see you sweat, and definitely never let them see you cry. Eva would regret nothing more than the day they decided that going on that stupid show would be a good idea. She should have known better, and now her mother would never let her live it down. Not if she didn't fix it. Sure, in the beginning, her mom had been all for the increased exposure for the firm, but now that it was all screwed up, well, there was no way she could leave it that way. She couldn't have the Ward name tainted by yet another scandal. Eva felt her heart sink as her fate was sealed by her mother's expectant gaze.

But Eva turned from her mother and looked at Walker. Damn him. His look had changed. The indifference had gone, and now his gaze was full of pity. It was as if he saw the silent communication that had passed between her and her mother and read too much. Pity, just like the looks she had gotten all morning. Pity, just like the looks she got when people found out how her father had died in the arms of a woman who was not his wife. The same pity that brought on yesterday's "Oh, woe is poor me, I got dumped and then a shrug" wall-banging. Well, she wasn't having it. Eva could tell by Walker's look that he didn't think she could do it. He thought she'd bail and go running off to Saks or Bergdorf's on a shopping binge, or at least go off and hide away in her apartment or something. Well, she was not that girl. She would never be that girl. She was the woman who would face this head-on, with or without cameras in her face. And, at the moment, it seemed they would be there either way. All eyes were on her, whether she liked it or not, so she might as well make them ones she could control. She needed to turn this story around so she came out the victor and not the victim.

She was over this pity party. Time to call last dance and be out.

"No good-byes are easy, but I'm really hating this one," Eva said to Cori, the woman who had been her friend ever since they were paired as "the two roommates least likely to have anything in common ever" in college. For the life of her, Eva couldn't figure out how their friendship had lasted as long as it had, but somehow they just clicked. Cori was the light to her dark, the wind to her wing, and on most occasions the wing to her woman, though in reality that was vice versa since it was Cori who was the bigger pickup artist of the two of them. Without Cori, Eva could honestly say her college years would have been spent primarily studying and going to class, but thankfully she had had Cori to mix things up for her and give her a taste of some of life off campus.

They were in Cori's apartment, Eva having just finished helping — actually more like watching — Cori pack more swimsuits than seemed humanly possible for her latest stint abroad while they drank bubbly and shared cupcakes between plotting some never-to-be-carried-out revenge on Kevin.

"You know, this is a trip I really don't want to take. Especially not right now while you're going through this horror. But are you sure you don't want to at least go over to his place and egg his door or something?"

Eva let out a breath. "Cori, we are not in junior high."

Cori pulled a face. "I'm just going easy. I can get devious, but since I have to leave tomorrow, I don't want to leave you holding the bag."

Cori was a head marketing manager for a popular private cruise line, and she was about to jet off to the Mediterranean for the summer. The pay was not the best, but it was still not a bad gig if you could get it.

"No, I'm going to go aboveboard with this one. I have too much damage control to do."

Cori rolled her eyes. "Yes, I get that, but do you really think this show is the way to go?"

Eva bit her lip. "Of course I don't, but I don't see any other way."

Cori let out a long breath. "That's it. I'm calling off my trip. You need me this summer. There is no way you should go through this alone. I can work at Starbucks or — shudder — temp for your mother or something."

Eva gasped. "You'll do no such thing." She got up to hug her friend. "As if you really would anyway. Though the offer is appreciated. You really are loyal to a fault, but we both know what you think of both those jobs, having had them in the past. I don't need you making that kind of sacrifice. I'll be fine. I'm a big girl. I can handle myself." Cori raised a brow just when Eva gave a loud hiccup from the champagne.

"All right, big girl. How about you stay here tonight and I'll get you Ubered home in the morning."

CHAPTER 6

Eva sat with her back steely straight and tapped her nails on the highly polished veneer of the conference room table. Though she told herself that this time in the conference room was no different from the last meeting she had attended here, she knew it wasn't. Not by a long shot.

Glancing to her left once again, she noticed the empty chair and blinked as the threat of tears had the nerve to prick at her eyes.

Stop it! Don't you dare fall.

She'd already had this talk with herself on the way over. Told herself she'd be just fine on her own and was better off anyway. Still, self-talk was one thing, and action was altogether different. The last time she had been here, she at least had Kevin by her side. Not that he was the most staid or the most assuring, but at least he was there — another body on her side of the table, giving her support and having her back, so to speak. This time it was only her, and the empty chair punctuated that fact.

She woke that morning for some reason feeling less anger and more loss over the absence of Kevin than the morning before. She knew mentally it was wrong. But there it was. Annoyingly, everything reminded her of how thoroughly he'd woven his way into her life and how comfortable they'd been, despite the obvious flaws she should have seen sooner. Today the bed just felt cold and lonely, the absence of his emergency toothbrush and toiletries a reminder of the intimacy she'd miss out on. And hell, even though she hated to admit it, Kimberly at the front desk had rattled her. It wasn't easy finding a man in this city, and she didn't want to be another statistic. And more than anything, she didn't want to follow in her mother's footsteps and become the clichéd, angered, done-wronged woman who threw herself into her work, never again to find happiness with another partner.

Suddenly annoyed with her wimpish musings, Eva afforded herself one last tap, then stopped drumming her fingers and looked up. She swept her gaze across to the dynamic show of strength along the other side of the table. WBC was definitely well represented.

Carter Bain sat at the head of the table; to his left was his assistant, Karen Waters, a no-nonsense-looking woman with a dark bob that had a respectable amount of pouf for someone in what had to be only her mid-thirties. Next to Karen sat a casually dressed young woman with wild curly hair, introduced as the assistant GP and named Louisa Tera. Milly Parker and Jeffrey Nettles, a formidable couple of relationship experts, occupied the seats next to Louisa. Both of them smiled at Eva with slightly scary, overly enthusiastic grins, as if she was about to be pulled in for some sort of experimental shock therapy.

Yes, it was indeed lonely on her side of the table.

Milly smiled even wider than Eva thought possible, her petal-pink lipstick spreading uncomfortably broadly across her face as she began to speak. "Now, Eva," she said with a sniping, sharp punctuation on the *a* at the end, "how's about we get going on the search for your Mr. Right."

"Or at least Mr. Right Now," Jeffrey chimed in with a nudge to his partner's side as if the corny joke needed extra punctuation.

They both chuckled as the rest of the table stayed uncomfortably silent. Eva felt her lips go tight, so she forced herself to smooth her expression to her resting neutral face. This was not their fault, she silently told herself. This was hers. Her and her big mouth. It was her temper that had gotten her into this mess in the first place, and it would take all her cool to get herself out of it. They were just doing their job and capitalizing on her faux pas. She could understand that. Hell, she made her living off of that.

Carter cleared his throat. "What Jeffery is getting at is that we all know it's unlikely you'll find your soul mate in such a short time."

Eva turned to him and raised a brow. "Gee, you think?"

He continued, not taking the bait or skipping a beat. "But what we're at least trying to do here is find you someone that you'll feel comfortable with as you walk down the aisle, taking that big step into the at least immediate future."

"So you want me to lie," Eva said smoothly, somehow feeling better if he would just say the words and they could put everything out on the table, so to speak.

Carter coughed. "No, we —"

"That's exactly what they want you to do, but of course it won't be stated. Well . . . not on the record, at least."

Eva briefly closed her eyes and let out a breath before she looked up at the person attached to the voice of the candid interruption.

Aidan Walker.

For a moment, when she didn't see him at the meeting, Eva had convinced herself that he wasn't coming — that after their pitch meeting at the Ward offices, she was good and well done with him and that it was for the best and what she wanted. She refused to ask, of course, so she just ran with the thought that maybe, by some lucky twist of fate, he had had his fill of her and her public romantic woes. But of course not. Why would luck or fate or what have you do anything in her favor?

All heads were turned, and all attention was now paid to the fact that Aidan Walker — producer, reporter, cameraman, or whatever the hell he was besides a general pain in her ass — was stepping into the room.

After the meeting with her mother, Eva had given Aidan Walker one of her critical internet once-overs, looking him up to see how far she'd sunk herself with that embarrassing meltdown and knee to the privates.

All she knew of Aidan Walker was what she'd heard from gossip shows and Page Six. His more hard-hitting stuff lately hadn't been a thing that kept the press talking. After her brief investigation, she had to admit she was more than a little confused by the man who would eagerly invade her privacy and film her at one of the lowest points in her life and shrug it off like it was nothing.

As she looked him up, trying to get a better angle on who he was and what he was doing in New York, all she ended up with were more questions. For the life of her, she couldn't quite reconcile him in her mind. He seemed to be a man of duality. He'd received multiple awards for investigative journalism on stories running the gamut from illegal high-stakes celebrity fight clubs to, as of late, little-known reported rings of missing children and stories on the sex-trafficking trade. But then there was the image of him as the playboy wild child, son of the chief operating officer and principal shareholder of WBC, the one photographed on the arm of a different model or socialite every night he was in town.

She wondered: who was the real Aidan Walker? And what was he doing caring about her little puff piece on a morning talk show? More likely than not, his being there was punishment for his latest screwup. Though it didn't get much press, it was rumored to have cost the network a pretty penny.

Eva now watched as Aidan smoothly walked in, this time looking more like the man she thought was just another cameraman on the set the other day. Today he was back in jeans, only these were darker, not as faded, and he topped them with a button-down oxford shirt with the sleeves rolled to his elbows, his tanned, muscular forearms on display. In his hand was a paper cup of coffee, black, which he placed next to hers as he ignored the seat at the other end of the table, instead casually taking the empty seat that had haunted her moments ago.

"No, it's not," Carter countered, but Eva couldn't focus. As Aidan slid into the seat, a prickly warmth spread uncomfortably from her middle to her chest, rendering her mind unable to wrap around thoughts as it was supposed to. "We're not doing *The Bachelor* here," Carter continued, "We are genuinely trying to make a connection."

Aidan leaned back in the chair and gave Eva a quick shake of the head and an easy smile that really should come with a warning of some kind. She grimaced by way of reply as he turned back to Carter. "Sure you are. You keep telling yourself that, C, and you'll be at the top in no time. What is it, plausible deniability?"

He turned back Eva's way and gave her a wink.

The hell you say, sir! The wink brought Eva back to life, and she rebounded with an even deeper glare before turning back toward Carter. "Can we move on? And does he need to be here for this?" She flicked her hand Aidan's way.

Carter looked down and coughed, for the first time slumping a bit. "Well, actually he does. Mr. Walker is overseeing this project. He'll be my eyes and ears. On this, he has total control."

Eva pulled up straighter.

Total control. The words locked over her like a vice. "Not over me," she said, instinctively rising out of her chair.

From her side a chuckle sounded. A carefree rumble, mocking her inner turmoil. The laugh froze her in place as it grated down her spine.

"I don't doubt that for a second, Miss Ward. But if you could hold it for just a moment, sit down and think rationally, I think you'll see this will work out best for all of us."

108

Lowering her eyes, Eva let out a breath through her nose. Dammit, she was right. This was a punishment, though it wasn't his, it was hers. But why? Was he really so upset over her kneeing that this was his way of getting back at her? The thought brought up the possibility of him sabotaging the project and making her life a living hell. But then Eva remembered the kiss, and how when it started it was all her but had quickly changed to something based on mutual satisfaction and — lord help her — stimulation. For some reason, that thought filled her with more anxiety than the idea of him still being angry over the knee.

She glanced around the table at all the expectant faces. They were just waiting for her to bolt. She looked at Walker and caught the hint of challenge in his eye, but she also saw something more. Dammit, Walker was right. No matter that he rubbed her the wrong way all around. She needed to get past this. Get these next eight weeks over and done with and move on with the rest of her life. She couldn't let this debacle of hers hold up her life any more than need be, and this seemed to be the most painful but quickest way out.

Eva thought that careful deliberation last night with Ben, Jerry, and a bottle of pinot had it all squared away in her mind. She had it all mapped out. All she had to do was find a guy who would be as up for the PR as she was, suitable enough to be molded, and ready and willing to do anything to save face and keep her cover, at least for the short term. Once she found him, she'd be sure to get him on her side, go through with the wedding, have a quickie divorce within a suitable but not terribly long time period, and all would be perfect. So what if she had to spend a few weeks being shadowed by an overly pompous Aidan Walker? Getting over her initial embarrassing moment with him was a small price to pay for getting the press off her case and her life back on track. And who knew, once she had regained her dignity, she might yet meet her Mr. Right in due time.

Turning back to Aidan, she pasted on a smile. "You're right. I've got to do what I've got to do to get my reputation back, and hey, if this little puff piece is what daddy gave you to keep you busy and out of his hair," she shrugged her shoulders, "then so be it." She saw his dark eyes spark up ever so slightly as his jaw tightened, letting her know she'd indeed hit a nerve. Good. It was about time he knew what it was like. Her own nerves were frayed beyond belief.

With that, she turned back to Milly, irrationally content with that small hint of anger at the mention of his father. This time her smile was genuine. "As you were saying?"

Milly swallowed, her eyes shifting between Eva and Aidan as she cleared her throat. "Yes, as I was saying, we have screened for the very best candidates and have a wonderful variety of men set up for you — from a fitness expert to the CEO of an internet start-up company. If we can dim the lights, we'll begin."

At that pronouncement, Karen leaned forward and picked up a remote to bring down the shades and dim the lights, blocking out the picturesque skyscraper view through windows along the far wall. Instantly, Eva became even more hyperaware of Aidan's presence at her side.

No matter. She would ignore him, as one would a very large, very good-looking, sexy bug. Shit. She was in for it.

How does one go about trying to ignore the world's sexiest spider for eight weeks?

The ridiculousness of it almost made her laugh out loud, and as Eva reached into her bag to pull out her planner and start taking notes, Aidan shifted. It wasn't by much, just the tiniest bit, the smallest widening of his tentacles — well, legs, if she was being technical — as he leaned back to get a look at the image projected onto the screen. Too bad that that small shift was all it took to send Eva's hormones into a full-on tilt-a-whirl. As his leg briefly brushed hers, the shockwave sensation zipped from her leg to her sexual center, flaring up into her breast and bringing a heat to her face. She reached out to take a sip of her coffee. The warmth from the rich brew brought her no relief as the memory of his lips, as they went from hard and resistant to soft and compliant under hers, jumped to the forefront of her mind.

"Bret Meyers," Jeffrey said as Eva fought to concentrate on the words coming from the other side of the table. *Focus, Eva, focus.*

"Is the head of his own Fortune 500 company and the father of a three-year-old."

"No," Eva said curtly, finally catching the words and stopping Jeffrey before he could go further.

"No?"

"No kids, I'm sorry."

"Now, come on, Eva. Do you really want to come off as one of those hard-assed career women who can't stand kids? Besides, everyone loves a cute kid, and that means ratings," Carter piped up.

Eva opened her mouth to speak but was stopped by the sound of Aidan's voice. "Now wait." It was low and deep, but still commanding enough to fill the room. "Do you really think it's best if we drag kids into this sham, only to have it be a short-lived affair? How would that look for the station?"

Eva closed her mouth and looked at him wide-eyed. It was just what she was about to say, and frankly, she was surprised he had said it. But then he went and ruined it by giving her a cheeky little grin that told her he knew he'd surprised her. To top it off, the grin was altogether way too sexy, with his full lips and scruffy beard and perfect teeth and sparkling eyes. Eva twisted in her seat, and he grinned wider.

The jerk!

She narrowed her eyes. He had to be playing some sort of angle. The man who would follow her into the greenroom to tape her humiliation would not care a whit about dragging a kid through the mud right along with the rest of them for ratings.

Eva looked back up at the picture of Bret. Light, tan skin; expressive brown eyes; a nice smile; neat, close-cropped hair. She flipped over the head shot Milly slid her way. He was the CEO and founder of Uptech Media, a mobile media advertising platform voted one of the best start-ups this past year. Hmm, maybe she was being shortsighted kicking their first suggestion to the curb. Why should the kid thing be a deal breaker? At thirty-one, he was a little older than she was, but if she was going to go for men in their late twenties to mid-thirties, she was bound to meet a few that had been down the kid road and back again. Best not to eliminate prospects before sniffing them out fully. Besides, Carter did have a point. The image of her raging on Kevin came back to mind as did the GIFs and memes that followed. There were plenty that had her looking like a harpy. Coming off as sweet and child-loving wouldn't be the worst thing for her image right now. She had a long way to go to rebuild her level-headed brand and to get her mother off her back and their clients on surer ground. Putting the photograph down and ignoring Aidan at her side, she looked back to Carter. "You're right. I have my reputation to rebuild here, and his stats seem good. He's in."

Eva slid Aidan a glance, but his expression was now cool and unreadable. Good. One point in her column. Jeffrey clicked to the next photo, and a bright-eyed, to the point of almost manic man with close-cropped blond hair filled her field of view. "Trey Stone. Adventurer, champion at the X Games, and partner in CroxTrec Inc."

"You have got to be kidding me," Eva said. "Do I seem like I'd go for someone interested in any of those things?"

"No," Louisa, who up until this point had been silent, chimed in from where she had been pecking away on her phone for most of the meeting. She let out a bit of a maniacal chuckle and looked Eva's way. "That's why he would be perfect for the show."

From her side, Aidan let out a snort, and she could practically feel his eyes assessing her outfit choice of the day: slim white skirt, white linen blouse, dove-gray pumps, and dove satchel to match. She rolled her eyes at Louisa and then shot Aidan a look. "If you'll recall from my past appearances, Mr. Walker, I can handle myself fine in almost any situation. I'm pretty quick on my feet."

He sobered at that. "Oh, don't worry, your reflexes won't be forgotten, Miss Ward, and I'll be sure they are highlighted to their fullest over the course of this process."

What the hell does he mean by that? Highlighted to their fullest? "Listen, I'm not going into this to be exploited and made a fool of once again." She pushed back from the table, ready to leave the room, but he stilled her with a soft touch on her forearm. She glared, and he quickly pulled back.

"Sorry. I didn't mean to touch you." His voice was still low, but the apology rolled off his tongue quickly enough. "Please don't run off." His eyes held her in place. "Let's just get through this. Trust us, we are not going to make a fool of you. I personally am not going to let that happen. You were dealt a raw deal last time. Can you trust us to make it right?" His eyes continued to hold hers in a sincere gaze that, for some reason, she started to believe. "Can you trust *me* to make it right? If you don't, then you can leave now. We won't bother you any further."

"Now wait a mom—" Carter started to protest, but Aidan silenced his words with a sharp look. Carter let out a sigh. "Fine. If you're not comfortable with the direction of things, you can go. At any time."

"And," Aidan continued, "if it's me you really don't trust, say the word, and I'll pull myself off the project and leave you in the hands of Carter and his capable crew. The choice is yours, Miss Ward."

She looked from one man to the other. Carter embodied all slickness, and she knew he had screwed her over last time, and given the chance, he'd do it again. Her gaze went

116

back to Aidan. He'd done her dirty by filming her meltdown, but for some reason she
felt he knew it, and she also felt that somewhere, deep down, he was sincere about
making up for it. Besides, that footage had
never aired, and she had a feeling he might
have been the one behind it not going public.

She pushed her chair back forward,
smoothed her hair, and addressed Jeffrey
again, making sure her voice was calm and
steady. "Put the hulkster on the list, and
let's move onto the next one. The quicker
we're through this process, the quicker we'll
be done."

CHAPTER 7

Plain and simple, it was a full-blown invasion.

As she peered through her apartment door's peephole, Eva's groggy mind was still filled with lovely carnal images of faceless men with scruffy beards and toned muscles when it was brutally jolted to reality with the distorted, but still way-too-cocky smirk of Aidan Walker. Instinctively, she pulled back from her apartment door and looked down at her sleep tee and shorts, assessing the state of her morning dishevelment. Just perfect. Would this man always catch her off guard?

"Just a minute. I'm not ready for you all yet," she yelled through the door.

"There is no 'you all,'" he countered through the door. "It's only me. The rest of the crew will be up shortly. I came ahead. And I have coffee."

The magic of the C-word pulled Eva up short.

She angled back toward the door, her lips twisting as her suspicions went on full alert. How did he know how she liked her coffee, and why did he care? Eva leaned in close to the door. "You aren't armed with a camera now, are you? I swear, if I open this door and you shove a camera in my face, you will live to regret it." She leaned forward a bit more and looked back through the peephole again, only to be confronted by another cocky smirk and the baring of perfect white teeth.

"No. Scouts' honor. Just the coffee. Now, don't you think it's a little early to be shouting through a door? Want to open up and let me in, or do you want to wait until all of your neighbors are awake?"

Eva let out a sigh. Why did he always use logic on her and make it seem like she was being the irrational one? Besides, she should have thought of her neighbors. Though they had filming permission, and at this hour, especially on a Saturday, no one was up except the early-exercise fanatics, and she didn't have many of them on her floor besides the jogger in 12D. No need to get everyone mad at her on top of pitying her.

Reluctantly, Eva went for the dead bolt

119

and gave it a turn, opening the door. "As if they'd ever let the likes of you be a scout," she snorted. "Isn't there some sort of code of honor? I'm serious, if you've got some sort of hidden pen camera somewhere, I'll make our last encounter seem like foreplay."

Aidan stepped into the small foyer area, then looked down at her and slowly spread his arms wide, taking up all the space, his large span brushing both sides of the narrow entryway. "You want to frisk me, princess?"

Eva stared, wide-eyed at first, shocked at how appealing his challenge, though made in jest, sounded at the moment. She gave him a quick appraisal, eyes swooping from top to bottom in the span of one point five seconds. His jeans were well-worn so that they hugged his muscular thighs in all the right places. His tee, a gray jersey Henley that skimmed his toned chest and accentuated the fact that the man treated his body right, had two buttons open at the top, showing a hint of dark hair that matched the scruff on his chin he wore so well. His full lips, upturned at one corner, reminded her of the reckless and so out-of-character moment that she had had with him in the not-so-green greenroom.

What was she thinking kissing the man?

The knee, sure, that was awful and, yes, she shouldn't have done it, but the kiss? That was beyond out of bounds. Not that she would take it back. Looking at him now, she could still feel every moment — from when he went from shocked to pliant and from there to deliciously dominating — and if she were halfway honest with herself, that's when things got really interesting. Too bad it was also when she had come to her senses and backed off.

Eva felt the hairs on the back of her neck go up, and she blinked. She was getting into dangerous mind territory. Better to stop this before it went any further.

She swept her gaze up from his most gaze-able lips and back up to his dark chocolate eyes. Eva was taken aback by the underlying smolder there. She reached up and snatched the coffee from his outstretched hand. "Can you put your arms down? You look ridiculous."

"Sure, princess. I was giving you time to finish your, uh, assessment."

"Oh, trust me, my assessment is done. And you can drop the princ—,"

Her words were cut off midstream as his free arm slipped around her waist, and before she could get her protest out, his lips — those same lips that she had stared at for

121

just a little too long moments ago — were now on hers again. But this time there was no shock, at least not on his part. And in spite of herself, she leaned in toward him and gave just as she got. Her body folded toward his, head tilting, lips molding easily, maybe a little too naturally, conforming to his plump fullness. Instantly, shockingly, surprisingly she was aroused, her whole body now as warm as the cup of coffee she was having trouble balancing in her hand. She let out a soft moan as his tongue gently swept over the crease of her lips, and they parted in silent response.

But just that quickly he pulled back, holding her by an elbow with one hand as he softly retrieved the takeout coffee cup with the other. "Hey there, watch it. You don't want to spill this on your nice rug, do you?"

Her lashes fluttered, or maybe she blinked. Fluttering seemed such a silly thing to do and something she'd have neither the time nor the patience for. Either way, she opened her eyes and looked up, the world slowly coming back into focus. Walker smiled smugly down at her. Once again he'd caught her off balance and at her worst.

The bastard. She swallowed.

"What the hell was that all about?" she asked, hoping her voice held the appropriate appalled tone.

He grinned wide. "That was me evening the score. And after our meeting with the crew and then in my office, I got to thinking, you need to get your mind in the game. I figure we're good now. You kissed me, I kissed you. No biggie. Though I'm going to give you a pass on the balls kick because, one, it would lead to rightful assault charges, and two, I don't hurt women. It's not my thing. Also, three, I probably deserved something close to that for filming you without your knowledge. That will never happen again. So with this kiss, I figure now we're square. You can stop giving me wondering looks about where we stand after our first encounter. We stand where we stand. You snuck me one, now I've gotten you back. We're both on the up-and-up, and now we can get to work. Cool?"

He let her hand go and pressed the coffee cup firmly into it. It took all she had to stay steady, but Eva refused to give him the satisfaction of swaying.

"Perfect." He stood to his full height and looked down at her, his gaze more assessing than anything else. "Now that that's out of the way, I suggest you drink up and throw on some casual, Saturday, single-girl-about-town clothes, because in about fifteen minutes it's going to get pretty crowded in here."

All Eva could do was watch as he sailed right on by her, as if he hadn't just knocked her nonexistent socks off. In a few quick strides from the foyer, he was clear across her living room, and a few steps after that he made short work of her open-concept kitchen of her small apartment. One turn to the right and he would be at her bedroom door. Eva put her coffee cup on the kitchen island and ran to step in front of him.

"That space is off limits."

He raised a brow. "I hate to tell you, princess, but you signed an agreement that says otherwise."

She felt her face begin to heat. She knew what she had signed, but still, she didn't want all of America seeing her private space, as she knew her unmentionables didn't quite make it to the clothes hamper most days. *Or was it the fact that he would know?* Embarrassingly, it was the latter that caused her the most unease.

She crossed her arms and pulled herself up to her full height, raising her chin. "I know what I signed, and my private spaces are off limits . . . without mutual agreement, of course, and right now I'm not mutually agreeing." Her words sounded hollow even to her own ears, but she hoped she could fudge it. "I won't be embarrassed. You know as well as I do that the network can't afford any bad publicity out of this deal. The bedroom is out, at least until I straighten it up."

He looked down at her for a long moment, his eyes completely unreadable. Eva stared back. Unblinking. Trying her best to give as good as she got, when really she couldn't believe how he could be so cool after the kiss they just shared. The man was some sort of machine. Either that or she had no effect on him at all. She frowned. It was probably the latter, which really was for the best, no matter the blow to her ego.

The buzzer rang, causing her to jump at the sharp sound breaking the silence.

"Looks like your time is up," Walker said with a raised brow. "I'll give in for now. You go and get dressed. Clear out whatever it is . . ." Aidan paused. "Wait, it is an 'it' and not a 'who,' yes? I don't want to assume."

Eva crossed her arms. "Don't be an ass, Mr. Walker."

"Fine. Sorry, just making sure. And please, call me Aidan."

"Well then, don't be an ass, Aidan."

He grinned. "That's better, princess. And a word of advice. This will be a long eight

125

weeks if you take everything so seriously. If I were you, I'd lighten up a bit and thaw the icy rod you've got for a spine. With it as frozen as it is, it's liable to break at the lightest tap."

Eva fumed as thoughts of Kevin and accusations of him calling her frigid came to mind. "I'll have you know, I'm no princess, and I'm far from frigid."

Once again, he laughed. This time he looked down at her lips in such a way that her nipples hardened way too much for her to be comfortable in her T-shirt. Still, she wouldn't give him the satisfaction of fidgeting. His eyes met hers again. "No, princess. I'm starting to believe I can take your word on that." The buzzer rang again, leaving Eva no time to contemplate the meaning of his last comment.

"Okay, pri—,"

She raised a brow.

"I'm sorry, Miss Ward." He gave her a quick once-over. "As lovely as you are in your morning attire, how about you go get dressed." He took a step back and grabbed the cup of coffee, handing it back to her. "Sip some of this while you're at it. I'll handle the crew for now."

Eva took a sip of the perfect cup of coffee and gave him a wide-eyed look. He grinned.

"You're not the only one who does research."

CHAPTER 8

Aidan stood in the far corner of Eva's bedroom and gave himself a mental ass kicking as he replayed the kiss over and over in his mind. He didn't know what had gotten into him, but he knew for damn well he needed it or *her* to get out.

Shit. He was a total idiot going off and kissing her like he did and then coming up with that lame excuse about making them even. He was sure she didn't believe it for one moment. But like him, he was also sure she was telling herself the same lie or some such thing in order to get through the day, to keep things professional and on the up-and-up.

He shook his head. Dammit. He had almost ruined this job even before it got started, leaning down and kissing her like he did. And the worst part of it was he didn't regret it half as much as he should have. For all his talk about life and work lessons and being smart, he was acting like he'd learned nothing from his years of experience. One glimpse of a surprisingly cute-in-the-morning ice princess and he was tripping over his dick to get his hands on her again.

Aidan frowned — over his poor judgment, and when he thought about it, even more over the fact that it could possibly be more than just hormones when it came to her. With Eva it was the whole package. Yes, she was adorable in her wrinkled tee and shorts and her hair all tousled. But it was something else. Once again it was that hidden spark that pulled him in. That fire in her eyes that had him taking a job that was clearly not his taste or something he could say he believed in. That spark that had him showing up to woo her with coffee in the early-dawn hours as if she were an informant he had to win over with cash and promises. It was ridiculous and he knew it. And the most terrible part was that he knew it was a waste of his time since when this was done she'd have her groom and he'd be onto his next assignment.

So what was it all for?

Aidan shook his head in silent answer to himself. Enough of this. He needed to get his head in the game and focus on the task at hand. He looked down and tried to objectively study the image projected on the monitor before him, fighting to keep his expression emotionless.

The camera loved her. One thing both he and Carter could agree on was that she really was intriguing when she had her dander up. And right now, her dander was definitely up. Try as he might, it was difficult not to smile as he watched her squirm over the horror of having two cameramen, a sound engineer, a boom operator, the show's stylist, and herself all crammed into her walk-in closet. It was like a magic clown car, only better. And that didn't count the rest of the set people rigging up her small living room for after-date diary confessions. He was starting to think maybe they should have rented an apartment to double as her home. This was all around too tight.

But, surprisingly, Eva took it in stride. She teetered only a bit when Steve, the second cameraman, tripped over a pair of her strappy Jimmy Choos, crushing the dainty crystal heels under his steel-toed work boots. She didn't blow the expected gasket, but instead only let off a little silent steam, acutely aware now that there were cameras and mics trained on her every move and word. And at that moment, they captured the full awkward exchange in her closet between her and the station's quirky stylist, Mitzi Ackerman.

"I mean, come on, Eva, dear. Surely, you want to show your adventurous side to your dates now, don't you? Let a bit of that wild animal out now that you're on the market again?" Mitzi said, with an exaggerated shoulder shimmy for the cameras.

Eva looked at Mitzi, and her eyes shifted from Mitzi's bright, frizzed, tangerine hair to her cheetah top and her leatherette leggings, all the way down to her polka-dotted platform heels. To her credit, though she was clearly out of her depth, she kept up appearances. "I like to keep things pretty low-key," she said. "Let's just say I keep my adventures to myself."

There was an awkward pause, and her eyes went wide as she realized how what she'd just said might be construed and Aidan could see the embarrassment bloom under her golden hued skin.

Mitzi gave a chuckle and then a nudge and a wink. "I'll be the judge of that. Now let's go through this closet."

It was forty minutes later, and poor Mitzi was at a loss. She looked to the cameras and gave a weak grin. Aidan stood back. He suspected it was not often that Mitzi was

131

lost for words. "Really, I don't know how a person can have thirty matching twinsets in her wardrobe. It's inconceivable. And silk. That much silk. Your dry-cleaning bill must be astronomical." She pulled out her phone and seemed to hit SPEED DIAL. As she put the phone to her ear, she reached out and lightly touched Eva's pearls. "Charming. Pearls on a Saturday. You are original." Luckily, Eva's raised brow was caught on camera. And the simmering anger seemed to leap through the lens and grab him.

Mitzi's voice rang throughout the bedroom. "Hello, Carlo. Yes, darling, this is an emergency. Size six, bring it all. We're talking type A, to the max." She swiped at her phone and let out a dramatic sigh. "Not to worry," she announced to the room as a whole. "I have some things coming from the office. We'll get you going with hair and makeup, and you'll be fine."

Eva's eyes went wide. "Hair and makeup? Just how much hair and makeup? I thought this was supposed to be *me* going on dates, not some facsimile of me. I'm not going to be getting done up like a *Bachelorette* contestant and traipsing out of a car in an updo and an old prom dress."

She stormed out of the closet as Aidan moved forward. But Louisa, the segment's assistant director, got to her first, and Aidan stepped back. It was for the best. He had screwed up enough for one morning. It was better to let Lou take the lead here. So he hung back and observed Louisa's no-nonsense style.

One of the few women on the shoot, Lou wore multi-pocketed cargo pants, which no doubt held one of anything and everything that might be needed, and a simple black tank top. "Of course we're not going to do you up like that, Eva. But we also want to distance you a bit from the Eva you were when it was the couple's competition with you and Kevin. This time it's all about *you*. *Your* solo act. Now, I know it sucks and it's a total intrusion on your being, but can you bend a little and trust us to do our job?"

Aidan held his breath. He wanted so much to speak up but didn't dare. No need to spook her and send her running off. Besides, Lou had the right of it. Any words from him now wouldn't be wanted or received well.

He had pushed his luck far enough with that kiss, and he was damned lucky they were all even standing in her apartment after that stupid stunt. Sure, he played it off and acted like it was no big deal, just payback for what she had done, but in reality it was huge, way bigger than what was safe, he needed to pull back and seriously consider if staying on here was a good idea.

But what was the alternative? Step back and let Rick Lancer come in and take over? No way. With Rick, silly-looking dresses would be the least of her problems. Morning-show viewing be damned, Rick would have her visiting an underground sex den and dabbling in bondage by way of a first-date ice breaker. Not to mention how he'd probably come on to her. But shit, he was the one who'd kissed her. So how was he any better? With that thought, Aidan's brain threatened to overload. What was she doing to him? No matter, there was no way he was turning this over to Rick Lancer. That was not going to happen.

Besides, though he was sure to not pursue it any further, he could admit she rattled him. She rattled him *and* he enjoyed rattling her. That kiss she had planted on him after her meltdown was hard to shake, just as it was hard to shake how ridiculously alluring she was when knocked a little off her game. It was a turn-on. And it had been way too long since he had been that turned on by any woman. For so long he'd been out with what could only be considered cookie-cutter, model-esque, outdoorsy-adventure types. But this seemingly straitlaced city girl had him on his toes.

He liked seeing her a little off guard, slightly disheveled and not her usual perfect self. He loved it when her hair was down and not in that tight twist thing she preferred. And he could admit she was super-hot when she was in a bit of a temper and had a blush of color flaring on her cheeks.

"We'll start with cutting your hair," Mitzi declared.

"No," Aidan said.

"No," Eva echoed, but stopped short and looked at Aidan wide-eyed.

The three women stared at him, and Aidan realized he'd spoken out loud and probably a little more forcefully than he should have.

He coughed, then turned to Mitzi. "You'll do the makeover, but nothing too drastic. Social media is telling us that the public likes Eva as she is, so don't waver too far from her current image. Make the changes minimal and subliminal." He turned and stared at Eva, giving her what he hoped was a critical eye. It was hard to keep his composure and not crack a smile, because the look she gave him back was full of challenge and sass, and it took all his strength not to give some of that challenge right back. That, or lean back in and kiss those

135

sweet, pouty lips again.

Damn. What was it about this woman? Why did she distract him so? Aidan let out a breath and began to speak over his shoulder, directing his words at Mitzi and Louisa, knowing all the while that it would send Eva into a further state. No matter, she was the talent, and it was high time both of them learned it.

"A few highlights, maybe some curls now and again." His gaze went south to her tailored trousers, and he shook his head. "Some decent jeans, please, and some heels. Guys love that on dates, plus flirty skirts." Traveling north again, his eyes settled on the shell-pink twinset that skimmed her waist and hugged her full breasts perfectly. *What a lucky sweater.* "And for God's sake, lose the twinsets." He saw her swallow and knew she was tamping down her anger. The pearls at the hollow of her throat shifted ever so slightly, and he had the urge to lean in and lick, see what that beautiful throat tasted like. He let out a breath and continued. "She can keep the pearls, though. It will be her signature."

Catching the flame in her deep honey eyes, he practically had to step back so as not to get burned. So why was it part of him wanted to step in closer to her?

136

"Are you done?" Eva's sharp tone snapped him back to awareness.

He looked her over quickly, though it was more of a chance to get his response in line. "I think I am, thank you, Miss Ward."

The look she gave him was as frosty as a snow cone and as beautiful as anything he'd ever seen. But it was enough. She was dangerous, and his reactions to her had to stop. He was there for a job, and nothing more. Eva Ward was his subject, and in a little more than a handful of weeks he'd see her married on the air, and then his obligation to his father would be fulfilled. After that, hopefully the old man would be once again off his back and he'd be free, back out on the road and able to live his life and work as he chose.

CHAPTER 9

Eva had been plucked, pulled, dyed, and fried, and at that moment she was about at the end of her rope. She thought she'd never be free of the pack of wildings set loose on her life, but at last she was. She finally had her apartment to herself once again.

Or at least what was left of it.

She stomped out of her living room, which now held little resemblance to the calm sanctuary she had known earlier that very morning. Had this really only been one day? She was exhausted enough for it to feel like three. Looking around, she wondered how she was supposed to relax now that her normal beige space had been "spruced up," as the props people called it — so much so, with their ridiculous pops of color, that she hardly recognized it as her home. As if she'd ever have juvenile pink and yellow polka-dotted throw pillows anywhere in her life.

Eva shook her head.

She didn't get the whole idea of the apartment spruce-up slash makeover, but Louisa explained that though they would do some confessionals in the studio, they wanted shots of her after-date reactions at home, as well as a few getting-date-ready shots to pull readers into her story, have them really bond with her — as if any of the television voyeurs really wanted to know the real her. Come on, she knew the game, and even if they did, the real her wasn't the her they were currently selling. No matter, she thought, Operation Invade Eva's Life and Sell It for All It Was Worth was well underway. No way that train was pulling back into the station now.

Stepping into her bedroom only bought more angst when Eva caught a glimpse of a dizzying array of bright colors and fabrics strewn about on her bed. After the morning twinset summit, Mitzi had called in the big guns and obtained one of everything in every color imaginable. She could barely find her bed, and at that moment, all she wanted to do was put her new wavy extensions up, wash the three layers of natural-look, camera-ready makeup off her face, and crawl into said bed.

Her cell phone rang. A muffled sound from somewhere deep in the pile of garments had her diving into the colorful fabric abyss.

After a frantic search, she found the phone, swiped, and put it to her ear.

"You're my new screen saver!" Her best friend, Cori, bellowed out way too exuberantly.

Eva let out a groan. "Really, you too? You're supposed to have my back," she said. Her tone was annoyed, but still she was happy to hear Cori's voice.

She wished it was in person instead of via cell, as Cori was thousands of miles away, probably floating somewhere in the Mediterranean. Eva twisted at a hair extension, then dropped it, worried about pulling the blasted thing out and ruining the hours of hard work. Better yet, she wished she was on the ship with Cori — the sun beaming, blue water as far as the eye could see, and far away from the madness of New York that had become her life.

"You know I always have your back, no matter what," Cori said, sounding uncharacteristically somber. "It's killing me I'm not there with you to give that asshole the asskicking he rightly deserves. The more I think of it, the madder I get. Who the hell does he think he is, dumping you like that, and all before ten in the morning? Talk about no class. We really should have exacted some sort of tangible revenge before I left. Just say the word, though, and I can see what damage I can do from here. My reach is long, you know. No way should that dude get off scot-free."

"Cori, come on. You know revenge is not my style."

Eva heard a distinct scoff. "Yeah, but it's mine, and nobody screws over my best friend and gets away with it. Hey, speaking of screwing, did you take my advice and get yourself under or over a new guy yet? You know, work out some of that pent-up frustration and anger you're righteously bound to be having?"

"Cori, it's only been two days."

"Hey, that's forty-eight hours. Sounds to me like forty-seven more than you need."

The laugh she so desperately needed bubbled up in Eva's chest. "You are incorrigible! And no. Now how is it I'm your screen saver? You're practically in the middle of nowhere."

"The internet is a wonderful thing."

"Oh please. That depends on who you're talking to."

"Well, I'm talking to you, and at least the clips show that you didn't take his shit with a nod and a smile. You gave as good as you got. I'm really proud of you."

Eva let out a sigh. "Don't talk so fast. You wouldn't be if you knew the trouble I'm in now with this ridiculous follow-up show. I must have been temporarily insane."

Eva reached out and perused one of the dresses Mitzi swore was "ohmygodjust-eveything" on her. She looked at the body-hugging red evening dress and shook her head, fighting hard to push down on her ever-growing anxiety. "I'm telling you, Cori, they're planning to parade me around like a whore on a fire sale. You should see how they want me to get trussed up. There is so much red and Lycra I'm afraid I may start fires if I walk too fast. And we won't get into how low-cut so many of these outfits are. I'll look ridiculous."

There was a long pause, and Eva pulled back to look at her phone before returning it to her ear. Maybe they'd lost the connection. Cori's international cell service was excellent, but it could be spotty with her out in the middle of the sea. "Hello!" Eva yelled into the phone. "Are you still there?"

"Sorry, yep, I'm here."

"Well, then why are you being so quiet? I gave you the perfect segue to jump in and tell me I'm right."

It was Cori's turn to laugh. "That only

works if I agree. The outfits sound perfect. You know, I've been dying to get some vibrant color into your wardrobe forever. You do tend to gravitate to the neutral and the bland."

Eva felt her lips twist. Of course Cori would like the idea of some sort of low-cut body hugging, red dress. The woman never met a piece of Lycra she didn't want to shack up with.

"You know I don't do red, and as I've explained to you before, taupe *is* a color."

"Well, you also didn't do reality TV or have full-blown tell-off sessions on national TV, but now that's all changed, so what's a bit of color going to do at this point? I'm so proud to see my little caterpillar coming out of her cocoon, and taupe may be a color, but so is vomit."

"That's not even remotely cute, Cori."

Eva could practically see her friend's smile through the phone. She knew her protests were not fazing her a bit. "Maybe not to you, but I think it is. And hey, if you're going to go for it, you might as well go for broke. You know me. No halfzies on anything. I say go for the red. I know you'll look fantastic."

She hated to admit that her friend could be right. She reached out and ran her hand

143

across the hem of the dress and let out a sigh. If she was going for it, she might as well go all the way.

"Come on, don't be so melodramatic," Cori said. "Time to buck up, kiddo. You're going to rock this. Now, enough about the dress. What do you know about the men you're supposed to be dating? I want to hear all. Just think about it. So many delicious possibilities, and you get them all. That asshole Kevin did you a favor. By the way, have you heard from him?"

A knot twisted in Eva's stomach. "Not really, only a text saying he'll stop by to get his things soon."

"I hope you told him where he can shove his things!"

Eva shook her head as if Cori could see through the phone. "No, I can't afford to go off. Not after what I did on TV. It's too dangerous. Right now it's all about fixing my image. My mom is all up my behind about my image and the damage I did to the company by going off like I did. So because of that I just texted Kev and said his stuff would be in a box with the doorman."

"Humph. You're a better woman than me. He's so lucky I'm not in town, but I'll be back, and then it's on. And your mother needs to relax. She knows all press is good press."

Eva smiled. "You're right. And the free press is the only bright spot in all of this, according to my mother. She'd be glad to hear that your summers interning at the company weren't wasted. And you know that relaxing and my mother have never met. You're a great friend. But no. I don't need you in trouble for me. No covert, late-night drive-bys to Kev's place with you playing Thelma and me doing Louise, or would it be the other way around?"

"You know I'm Louise, but lately who knows? You do have quite the temper on you. Now, on to better things. Dish on the hot new prospects. All I have out here are moneyed retirees or nuevo-rich jerkos, and extra-oily cabana boys are becoming a bore."

"Yeah, you've got it real tough out in the open water. But really, I don't have much to tell. Walker seems determined to keep me in the dark as much as he possibly can. He says it will make my reactions more authentic. But if I know him, he's only do-ing it to get my goat. I swear, the man lives to infuriate me. It's like he's asking for another knee to the balls, or worse."

"What? Wait. I know it's been like five

145

minutes since we spoke. And honey, all jokes aside, I'm so sorry I'm out of town during your time of need and not there for you with Kevin and his bull. We'll have a right bonfire in his honor when I'm back in New York. But what is this about Walker and ball kicking? Shouldn't it be Kevin getting his balls smashed? Besides, I thought it was that Carter guy who was running the show."

Eva flopped back down on her bed with a thump as she fell back. "Carter is, or at least I thought he was, until Aidan Walker decided to slip onto the scene and take over everything." Eva told herself to get a hold of her nerves. Cori knew her too well and was too perceptive. And she purposely hadn't mentioned Aidan Walker when she was at Cori's the other night for that reason.

"So it seems to me you've traded one suit for another." Cori paused, and Eva could practically hear her wheels turning over the phone. "Wait a minute, are you talking about *the* Aidan Walker? Isn't he the hotshot reporter who got himself into trouble and also happens to be the heir to his father's entertainment holdings? Hold the phone! What do his balls have to do with anything? You and Aidan Walker's balls. Who would have thunk it? I had a feeling you were holding back on me the other night, but I thought it was just you being you. Now I come to find out you were holding out on Aidan Walker dish. I'd be full-on mad if you weren't a meme on my phone right now."

Eva let out another groan and shook her head. "The meme comment is low. But maybe I deserve it for holding out. First, who his father is doesn't change the fact that he's a jerk, and second, how would you know all that about him? Oh and C, I don't think you really want to know the balls part. It's not all that pretty."

Cori responded with a snort of laughter. "Have you lost your mind? What balls are? But we're talking about a rich-ass, with a capital R, good-looking dude, so of course I'd know at least general stats. You're dealing with me, and I'm no amateur. My business is dealing with folks with enough money to spend it on ridiculousness like weeks on yachts. And as for two, don't even think you're getting out of a hot, rich guy's balls convo. You know I live for this type of stuff. Now spill it."

With that, Eva gave up the fight and talked to Cori about her lowest of the low. She felt surprisingly lifted when, as she described Aidan's squeak before he hit the floor, Cori let out a bark of laughter and not the gasp of revulsion she would be sure to get from anyone else.

Aidan paced his bedroom and fought to keep his voice calm as he listened to his father rant over the speakerphone. He was running late and had planned to be out the door and on his way to Eva's by now to supervise her getting ready for her first official "date."

Not that she needed supervision, but still, he didn't have time to take this call with his father today or to indulge him by listening to his usual rantings. They had a packed schedule, and as it was a Sunday, there were people getting paid overtime for their services, a fact that he mentioned to his father in an effort to shorten the conversation, but still the man continued on. Aidan threw his towel aside and casually walked over to his dresser, pulling out a pair of boxer briefs and tugging them on. At this point, he was only half-listening. The rant was going on long past enough. He put on his jeans and was pulling his tee over his head when his father's voice stopped him.

"Dammit, Aidan, you know this is not what I meant. I'm pulling you off this project. There are better uses of your time than some ridiculous wedding piece. I called you in from the field to get involved in all aspects of the business. Now there's a shareholders meeting on Tuesday, and I expect you to be there."

Aidan bit back on telling his father what he could do with his shareholders meeting, but held to his control. It would do no good blowing up and getting into a fight; besides, he was almost as confused as just about anyone as to why he was voluntarily working on Eva's story, so how could he really fault his father for being bent out of shape? "Dad, I told you I'd handle it. You asked me to get involved with programming while I was here, and that's exactly what I'm doing. If you want me involved, you have to accept it my way, or I'm out. You have plenty of lackeys that can sit in a boardroom chair and smile, and I have plenty of other stories out in the field that I could be covering."

"I don't have to accept any such thing," His father said, his indignation clearly rising. "I could cut you off completely. How would you cover these stories you so badly want to cover without my backing you?"

Aidan stilled and told his tongue to stay in his mouth. Unfortunately, his tongue wasn't in the mood to listen to his brain. "Fine."

"Good." He felt his father's smug smile through the phone, and it burned him up. He'd used this ploy for years. He knew Aidan loved his life on the road, and he also knew that he loved the autonomy he was afforded by his position in the company, not to mention his family's wealth. But that freedom came at a high cost.

Eva's face appeared to him in his mind's eye. She was all done up in her pretty pink twinset, her pearls glistening, a sweet but carnal invitation to her beautiful neck. When she played at being little miss perfect ice princess, Eva was just the type his father would love to see him settled down with. A woman with the perfect image. So like his mother. Smooth, polished, never a hair out of place. Never a feather ruffled. So nothing like every woman his father cheated on his mother with.

Aidan spoke up. "Okay, fine. Cut me off if you must. Fire me if you have to. But I'm seeing this project through. I can do that and handle the board. I'll live up to my obligations, but it's going to be on my terms. You asked me to get involved and I am, but you can't hold me down. This is what I'm doing. I'm never going to be a behind-the-desk CEO like you. You have to take me as I am or not take me at all."

There was a long pause, and Aidan shook his head as he reached for his shoes as he fought to ignore his mounting anxiety. It didn't matter. This wasn't even really a gamble. His father would see things clearly. Aidan had proved himself time and again. And not that he wanted to leave WBC, but if he was a free agent, son of Everett Walker or not, he'd be snapped up by a rival network in an instant. His father knew that, and his competitive spirit wouldn't let that happen.

"You're too damned cocky for your own good, boy," his father finally said by way of acquiescence.

Aidan let out a breath. It annoyed him that he wasn't relieved about staying on with his father as much as he was about staying to see things through with Eva.

"So I've been told. Listen, I've got to go. Some of us don't golf on Sunday. Give my love to Mom." As he said the words, Aidan knew his father would probably not pass on the message; he and his mother barely talked. Sure, they were the image of domestic bliss for the media, but anyone who really knew them knew that their image was carefully manufactured for the press. His mother resided dually at their home on Long Island and their apartment on the Upper East Side, and his father spent the bulk of his time at a residence in Midtown, supposedly to be closer to the office. Aidan made a mental note to call his mother later. If he relied on his father, the message would get to his mom during their next charity gala.

With that, Aidan hung up and grabbed his keys before heading out the door, hopeful he could catch Eva while she was still sleepy and in need of her morning coffee.

"You're late."

Eva opened the door with a well-practiced smile that got markedly broader when she noticed Aidan's disappointed frown. With a flourish, she stepped aside to welcome him into the apartment while biting back a giggle. "What's the matter, Mr. Walker, think you'd once again catch me unawares?"

He looked down at her. She knew he was taking in her appearance. Her new extensions were loosely pulled back, then forward, into a flirty side ponytail, her face was a bit more made-up than usual, with brightly highlighted eyes, and there was a shot of pink gloss on her lips. The biggest change was in her casual attire — a light floral skirt and a sleeveless blouse. The transformation, though minimal, was still significant. But instead of looking pleased, Walker frowned. "Is the crew here already?"

"Nope," she said, casually taking the coffee cup from his hand. "Thanks. Didn't the schedule say the call time was eight? It's only seven-thirty. Even though you're late, you're still early." She paused as she put the coffee cup on the counter, then turned back and looked him in the eye. "Again."

He stepped into the living room. "Yeah, well, I like to get a jump on things. Early bird and all."

She raised a brow. "So what am I, the worm?"

His eyes narrowed on hers, then raked up and down her body way too slowly for her to be comfortable. "Hardly, Miss Ward."

She smiled. "Please, call me Eva, and I'll call you Aidan. No need to be formal this early in the morning. And really, you didn't have to bring me coffee. I have a perfectly good coffeemaker here, and I've already had a cup."

He nodded and took three quick steps around her as he went into her kitchen. "Great. I could use another cup."

Eva stared, her mouth gaping open. In less than thirty seconds he was in her kitchen, opening cabinets and pulling down a cup. She watched as he popped a pod into her

153

coffeemaker. Well, wasn't he one to go and make himself at home? He drummed his fingers for a moment as the coffee finished brewing, then took a sip and graced her with that damned sexy smile.

"Glad to see you're making yourself at home," she said, not hiding her sarcasm, and his lips spread wider, showing his gorgeous white teeth in a way that made her stomach do a little flip.

"Don't mind if I do. Hey, when we're working, things get pretty close. Of course, we try to be as inconspicuous as possible, but the crew does turn into a bit of a family. We like to keep it casual. You going to be all right with that, princess?"

Again with the princess. Eva knew that he knew it raked on her, but she wouldn't bite. Not today. Today was first-date day, and she had to keep her cool. Had to keep her game face on. This was the beginning of the start of her new image rebuild, and she was ready for it.

She'd felt remarkably better after she got off the phone with Cori last night. Talking with her friend put things in perspective, and she even felt that this crazy plan had a shot at working and could get her back on track to the start of a new life. She'd carry out her plans as originally stated — go on the few required dates, find her so-called prince charming, have the on-air wedding, and hopefully be a forgotten blip in the television radar by mid-fall. So what if the original rollout with Kev was a thing of the past. It would all work out.

It was a foolproof plan, and if it was executed properly, both she and her groom could come out on top. It was a win-win all around. She only had to keep her cool, and there was no way she would let another man get her to step out of character. Kevin had done it once; she would not be tripped up again.

Eva smiled. "I thought we were on a first-name basis, with me being Eva and you being Aidan, but if Eva doesn't work for you, and you keep up the 'princess' bull," Eva raised her own brow, "I could have you calling me Miss B in no time."

With satisfaction, she watched as his expression changed from one of smug assurance to one of pained remembrance of the knee to the balls. She grinned. It was low, but she would not let him keep at her with silly names. "Walker or Aidan will do nicely, thanks, and I'll go with Eva. The B hits a little too low below the belt for my taste."

"Fine, as long as you don't forget it." She

looked over to the floor-to-ceiling windows, taking in the now high-rising sun before turning back to Aidan and breaking the uncomfortable quiet that had engulfed them both. "So don't keep me waiting. Tell me, what have you got planned for my first date?" She gave a little twirl, her skirt floating gently over her thighs.

When she stilled, he stared just a tad too gleefully, as if there was some sort of joke and she was the punch line.

"Nah, I think me telling you will ruin the surprise. I'll just say this: I don't think those little kitten heels are going to be the shoes for you today."

She felt her face drop and the knot begin to tighten in the pit of her belly. Smug bastard. She'd give him a kitten heel all right. One right square up his —

Thankfully the buzzer rang before she could give voice to her emotions.

"I'll get it, hon," Walker said in a ridiculous, sitcom-y style as he once again made himself too at home and went to answer her downstairs bell with an overly familiar, "What's up, C?" indicating he'd indeed gotten chummy enough with her doorman in two days to be on a first-initial basis.

Eva took the moment to silently scream out her frustration behind his back.

156

CHAPTER 10

Okay, now she really *was* going to scream.

Eva looked down from her current perch, twenty feet up in the air, her feet barely making contact with the little notched-out grooves of the rock-climbing wall, her sweaty fingers aching in pain as she held on for dear life. Her oh-so-not-perfect date for the day was about ten feet above her to the left and was currently offering supportive barks of encouragement like, "No pain, no gain!" and "You can rest when you're dead!" to the top of her head.

She ignored the shouting caveman and told herself to focus on her breathing. It would all be fine if she could remember what the instructor, who she hoped had secured her properly into the god-awful, strappy thigh and booty grabber, told her about leaning back and relaxing, releasing some tension, and gliding back down. Down. How was she going to *get* down when she could barely summon the strength to *look* down?

"Come on, Eva, just grab the red hold on your right! Not that right, your other right!"

Eva looked up, wishing more than anything that she could sprint up the wall and grab hold of Trey Stone and knock him loose for barking his stupid, useless orders at her. Better yet, she'd rather get down off this blasted wall and grab a hold of Aidan and shake him for getting her into this date. Fun her ass.

She was over this date almost before it started; the climb up the wall of doom was just the icing on the cake. After Aidan's ominous pronouncement about her heels not being appropriate, the rest of the crew arrived to a flurry of activity. Mitzi gave her a good once-over, along with high marks for the color in her flirty skirt. She then promptly sized her up for a gym ensemble, which she threw into a corporate-sponsored bag, and quick as a whip, they were on their way to awkwardly, oh just so casually meeting up with her prince charming at a waterside fitness club. The whole blasted crew of them.

An avid sportsman and fitness entrepreneur, Trey Stone was co-owner of CroxTrec, one of the hottest and most lucrative new gym chains in the country since cross fit had become all the rage.

When they arrived, Eva was pleased to see that Trey was indeed good-looking, no photoshop trickery, and had a physique that lived up to his vocation, so check and check again. He was muscular, as his photo indicated, but not overly so. Taller than her at a little over six feet in his running shoes. And she saw as she checked out his casual track suit that he didn't dress to make any sort of fancy first-date impression. That was fine. *Not off-putting,* she told herself as she went to change, *but refreshing.* Eva would keep an open mind. *This isn't forever,* she told herself as she looked into his cool, icy-blue eyes. Or maybe it was. She was there to have fun. Who knew? This could work out. Besides, the new Eva wasn't stuck on things like fashion and labels. It was the inside that counted. Image wasn't everything, except when it came to rebranding and rebuilding hers. And she was there to try something new and keep an open mind. She had to remember that.

That Kumbaya feeling of live and let live lasted all of five minutes once she walked past the locker room to the medicine ball tosses, where Trey told her his vision for living a paleo lifestyle. It only got worse during the pull-up session, when he went on about his win in an Ironman competition. The topper came, as he spotted her in a dead lift, when he invited her to his cabin upstate, where he explained he could make her over from the inside out. She didn't want to ask for clarification on what *inside out* really meant, but she sincerely hoped he was talking food and not something else entirely.

Now, as Eva gazed down in utter horror from this ridiculous rock wall, already down two broken fingernails, her head spun out of control while this dude above her yelled nonsense. She reached out, stretching wide to get another hold, as once again Trey yelled, "That's it, girl, slay that beast! Go for it! Kill that dragon!"

At the mention of dragons, her foot slipped, and she scrambled to get back to the wall. So this was what torture felt like. At least now she knew where and what her rock bottom was. It was being yelled at by a maniac while your ass is in the most unflattering position possible and having it filmed for public consumption. Yep, and now she was done. Over it.

She was ready to get down. Get down and get away from his obnoxious barking and everything to do with this gym hopped up on oversized Flintstone vitamins. If she didn't, she would lose all control, and the point of this deal was not to lose control.

With shaky arms, Eva carefully took one hand and shifted it to a lower point on the rock wall; then with the other arm shaking like a pulled wire, she moved it slightly to the right and got a hold, letting out a much-needed sigh. Now for the legs. But of course they wouldn't move. It was as if her legs had decided, *Well, you've got us into this mess, so now we're going to live here forever.*

Eva looked up, and there was Trey, looking back down with his arm outstretched to pull her up. But there was not a hint of warmth in his cold eyes. She'd recoil if she could. But being stuck, all she could do was nothing. Eva swallowed and looked down. Her eyes zoomed onto Aidan. As he had been for most of the day, he silently stared. Just looking and nothing more — arms crossed, legs widespread, expressionless, as he checked out the action unfolding on the monitor in front of him.

She could just imagine what was going through that head of his as he took in all of her uncomfortable moments, her every emotion played out for the camera, capturing her every fear. The image of him with that camera in the greenroom popped into her head, and with it, that same unforgettable rage bubbled up again. Eva sucked in a life-giving breath and, with all she had, used her knees to push away from the wall, at the same time letting loose of the line and rappelling herself down.

She heard Trey's voice from above, and looking up briefly, Eva gave him a small wave and a smaller grin, leaving him no choice but to either stay where he was or follow her. She didn't care — either way, as long as she was on the ground.

Once there, she quickly started to unclasp herself but got tangled in all the lines. In her frustration, she made a mistake of looking over and catching Aidan's eye. There was that sparkle. Damn him, he enjoyed this. Though he tried to appear serious, she could still see the hidden glee in that hint of spark that he just couldn't be decent enough to hide. She felt her own eyes narrow as her brows rose.

"Are you happy, fearless leader? Did you get all you need for the day, or would you like me to do a few cartwheels to round out your footage?"

"What are you talking about? It's not li—"

Eva threw up a hand. She didn't need or want an answer from him. She was sure her fear had given them enough fodder to fill the time slot. Besides, Aidan's darkening gaze was answer enough for her.

She was fully unhooked just as Trey appeared by her side. "What happened to you up there? I thought you were doing great?"

She turned to look up at him. "Really, didn't look to me like I was doing so great. What gave you the clue, my shaking arms or my trembling legs?"

Trey gave her a once-over. "Your legs look fine to me — as a matter of fact, mighty fine. Now what are we going to hit next? We've got the jungle gym or, if you're really feeling adventurous, we can hit the tires."

Eva felt her eyes go wide as she wondered if this was indeed some sort of joke. This couldn't be his idea for a fun date. Could it? Did this ever work on any other women? But looking into his eyes, she could see he was serious. This nice-looking, in-shape, and if his numbers were correct, very-well-off guy was serious. And he really didn't have a clue that he came off like a total jerk — this was, no doubt, the reason he was still single.

She looked around his wacky gym, done up like a Gymboree for adults, and though it was not her thing, it was packed. On paper, you couldn't deny that he was successful. Eva looked around at the gym again, with her professional hat on this time. Despite all the crazy devices of torture, the gym did have one good thing going for it: a bar, and not one of those annoying water, juice, or air bars, but a full-on, drink-like-an-adult whiskey bar. Whoever thought of that little area had been a marketing genius. Eva turned back to Trey, who was looking at her expectantly, and came up with an idea. "So, Trey, how about I buy you a drink?"

Aidan sat behind the monitor staring at Eva's image while she sat on her couch and answered Louisa's questions during her first after-date confessional. Though she tried to hide it with extra powder from the makeup crew and wide arm movements, he could tell the day had worn on her.

"So," Lou started, "how do you think your first date went?"

Eva cleared her throat, and he could tell she was calculating how to best answer the question. The exertion of the day slipped into her expression as her eyes narrowed and her lips drew tight. She looked down, taking in a breath, and when she looked back up, her eyes were brighter, her expression now softer. "It was nice. Strange getting out into the dating world and trying to interact with someone new. After being with one person for so long . . ." She paused and took a moment, looking a little wistful, and then her gaze came back to the camera over Lou's shoulder. She was so polished and natural, it was as if she was talking to an old friend. "I'll admit, I'm a little rusty, and this was quite the, um, physical experience. But Trey was nice. It was good to get out there again."

"But?" Lou prompted.

Eva smiled. It was a sweet smile. Warm and friendly and — somehow he could tell — well-practiced as it never reached her eyes. "But based on one date it's hard to tell. Though I can say, I would think that from his side, he may enjoy a woman who is a bit more physically adventurous than I am." She stopped and seemed to blush at this. "At least when it comes to exercise. I'm more of a regimented, class-taking type of girl. I'm not really one for rock climbing." She tilted her head coyly. "Too much of a city slicker, I guess."

Aidan leaned in. She was good. The ending smile she gave the camera was perfectly endearing without being too put on. She'd made it clear that the muscle dude wasn't for her without tearing him down. The woman knew how to play the game. She

165

even pulled out the sympathy card with her comment about being rusty. She was smooth. He'd give her that.

She'd made it a point to not say anything else to him after coming down from the rock wall this afternoon, and honestly, he couldn't blame her. Just as she was angry with him, he was at war with himself. Maybe he should have given her a heads-up about what today's date would entail, let her know that it would probably be less of a love connection and more of a physical sparring match with Mr. Olympian. But if he'd done that, it probably would have dampened the spontaneity the segments called for. First and foremost, he was there to do a job — and the fact that he'd remembered that would be sure to make his father proud. This was not the time for his head-strong emotions to send him down the wrong path. Still, though, he couldn't help but be annoyed by her attack on him when she'd come down from the wall. He wasn't smirking over the fact that she was struggling; as a matter of fact, he thought she'd handled herself beautifully on that wall. Her coming down showed true courage on her part. But she wasn't ready to hear that from him and was quick to think he was happy over her being put in a fearsome situation.

Aidan ran a hand across his jaw and continued to watch her on the screen as his mind worked over his dueling emotions. For the life of him, he didn't know why he'd insisted on making this his project. Well, of course, he knew why. It was the damned challenge of it. The challenge of her. It was that kiss. She'd pulled him in, and despite the fact that she was right there in front of him and on the show to find her perfect groom, more than anything he wanted to get under her skin. Hell, under her. But it was wrong. It was wrong, and it was dangerous. Her outburst at the gym earlier showed just how volatile she was with him and how at odds they were. But still, here he was — torn, but somehow pulled as if by some invisible force to see it through.

Which brought back his original problem. If he wasn't there to see it through, the show would still go on. Carter wasn't letting this go. Aidan's position as the head boss's son mattered not in this instance. This was out there, and like it or not, Eva's original declaration of intent to find a replacement groom was made on live TV, and that was the shot heard round the world. As Carter said, the public loved Eva Ward, and worse yet, if the numbers were right, the public loved seeing Eva riled up almost as much as he did. Oddly, just as he was turned on, so were they. Still, he had to admit he didn't enjoy putting her in a position where she felt any type of real fear. That crossed the line. It put him over into a sleazy category he wasn't comfortable hanging in. Leave that for the Rick Lancers of the industry. He'd made the decision years ago after doing a story on a hot pop star of the moment, ignoring signs that he should have seen as obvious, and unwittingly ending up filming what would be her final on-air moments. After that he was done, at least with any sort of fluff pieces. But here he was, inexplicably drawn to this woman who'd somehow pulled him back to the world and the memories he'd spent years trying to escape . . .

Not that she noticed, knew, or cared. But just when he was ready to pull her aside in the gym and offer up an apology to smooth things over and give her a chance to end the date, she'd turned the tables on him and literally flipped the script the writers had so carefully worked out. Pulling gym rat Trey aside and drinking with him. The woman was a true PR playa.

"No," Aidan listened, as Eva continued with Lou, "I don't think I'm the sporty type of woman that would be right for Trey, but

I'm sure he will be perfect for someone else, and who's to say never? Not me, that's for sure."

Aidan frowned at her perfect response. Clearly, there was no love connection between her and T-Rex Stone. After all the physical exertion, she'd led him over to the hipster gym's whiskey bar area and let him down easy, all the while subtly explaining that expecting a woman to flip a truck tire or hang from a rock wall may not be the best way to make a first-date impression.

She was so smooth about it, the pumped-up fool didn't even get that he was getting the heave-ho before he'd gotten started. But here she was, doing her thing and doing it well. The viewers would love her. Clearly, she knew all the right PR tricks.

Aidan frowned, recalling her charming tactics. How she had touched Stone's shoulder, leaning in close enough for Stone to reach out and whisper something in her ear the mics couldn't quite catch. How she blushed under his flattery, and then how he'd slid his pull-up-callused hands around her trim waist just at the point where her workout pants started and her tank top ended.

Aidan didn't know why he got so angry. She was perfect. More than perfect, really.

She was doing her job and more than fulfilling her end of the contract. The footage was exactly what they needed. He guessed he was really mad at himself for getting riled over it. So what if he'd shared a kiss — well, two kisses — with her?

What? Was it supposed to have affected her in some way? Because obviously it didn't. Not enough to take her off her game. But it had been more than enough to make him want to take one of those kettlebells and go upside T-Rex's head with it.

Shit, maybe his father had been right. Not for the reasons he listed, but because he would be so much more effective working on something else, anything else. He still had to live up to his commitments to the company and the family, and he could see that just one date with Eva would be more work than he was prepared to put in.

"Did you say something?"

Aidan jolted up at the change in Eva's tone. He looked at the monitor, then over at her. Both she and Lou were now looking not at each other but in his direction.

"Excuse me?"

It was Lou who spoke this time. "Are you getting what you need? We heard you mumbling something over there."

Aidan looked up at their boom guy, Stan,

170

who nodded, then took his eyes skyward. Oh hell. Was he now mumbling his thoughts out loud? He turned to the two women. "I'm fine. You both just continue."

Aidan drew in a deep breath of irritation at his misstep as he watched Eva purse her pretty lips in impatience as once again the light and sound levels were checked around her. It was official: He was in hell. This was what he got for not following the rules and for playing fast and loose with his own privilege. He should have never gone after her. He couldn't believe this slim, unassuming slip of a woman would be the one to have him questioning his lifelong mantra of leap first and look later.

Aidan leaned in closer to the monitor and watched Eva as she tucked a tendril of hair behind her ear. She looked down at her hands, and her full lips pursed a little in annoyance. Then she licked her lips and blinked, that spark jumping back into her dark-honey-colored eyes. She was back, and he was pulled in, remembering that sweet kiss of hers as he narrowed in on the glistening fullness of her ripe bottom lip. Immediately, he wanted to taste it, run his tongue across hers, and take it into his mouth.

Aidan looked away from the monitor, his

head coming up and his gaze going to *her*, not just the pixilated facsimile of her, as she was now spotlit in the middle of her living room. Their eyes caught for a moment as she looked up and over to him in the shadows. He noticed a millisecond of hesitation as her brown depths connected with his, widened for the briefest of moments before she raised one perfectly arched brow, then turned back to Louisa, her smile back in place.

"Yes, I really am looking forward to the next date. Won't you at least give me a hint about him? No?" She feigned a pretty pout and crossed her arms before smiling again. "Oh well, here's to being surprised."

"I think we're good." Lou's voice came over to him sharp and clipped, jarring him out of his thoughts. His head shot up and away from the monitor to find both her and Eva staring his way, Lou's face with a look of impatience and Eva's one of cool indifference. He didn't know which annoyed him more.

He glanced over at Stan, who had been the last to follow them back to her apartment location to get the final wrap-up. Stan wore his usual bored expression, not caring about anything other than if the sound quality was right. Stan gave him nothing more than a silent nod, indicating that he had what he needed and was ready to be done for the night.

"Great. Thanks. Good work. I think we can pack it in," Aidan finally said.

Lou's frown deepened as she shook her head before leaning in toward Eva and unhooking her body mic. He watched Eva finally slump back on the couch, the fatigue of the day releasing on her breathy sigh.

"You okay?" he asked, walking her way.

She pulled herself up, but not before he saw her wince as she reached for her lower back. "I'm fine; nothing a hot bath won't take care of. That and having my apartment back to myself."

An image of her in a steamy tub pulled him up short and had him willing his body not to react.

He noticed Lou's side-eye as she wrapped cords and went about making final adjustments. "Sorry again about the extremes with Trey," Lou said. "But hey, it's the business. We knew he was hard-core but didn't expect him to go that hard. Not on a newbie, at least. But you held your own. Props to you." Eva grinned and gave her a thumbs-up, and Lou gave back a half smile, happily flexing her own muscles as she lifted a heavy box of audio equipment to load it onto a hand truck. When Aidan moved to help her, she stilled him with a firm look. Still, he leaned in and picked up the container. There wasn't time to deal with Lou's power struggles; he was only being nice. Besides, he was the boss. She'd deal with it.

The quicker they were out of Eva's hair, the better for all involved. This had been a long day.

He rose and looked around. Most of the equipment had been stowed or cleared out earlier. They had a few days before the next date, so she would be happily free of them for a while.

"Lou was right, this was good, and you handled things well. And don't worry, on Thursday there will be no tire flipping or rock walls," he said looking down at her still on the couch, her eyes closing and her hand to her forehead.

She opened one eye and looked up. "Promises, promises. You'll excuse me if I'm only cautiously optimistic."

His gaze roved over her body. More than anything, for some reason, in that moment, he wanted to pick her up, carry her from the couch, take her into her bedroom, and take his time wiping that look of contempt off her face. He'd enjoy watching it slowly change.

"So should we wait for you or head to the studio?" Lou's voice from the door way brought his head popping up.

Stan had already made his way to the hall, having moved what he needed to load to the van.

"What?" Aidan asked, annoyed with himself for being caught lusting over Eva and not with his head on the job.

Lou gave him a look that pretty much checked him on his bullshit. Her tiny stature in no way took away from her domineering power. "So you calling it, boss?" The way her "boss" came out, heavy and dripping with condescension, let him know he still had plenty to prove with her.

Aidan let his eyes sweep briefly over to Eva for one more moment before going back to Lou. "I'm on my way. This piece isn't up until Tuesday, so we can get it to editing tomorrow. No need for anything else tonight. Good job. You all go on. My car is downstairs." Lou gave him a brief nod before following behind Stan.

He turned back to Eva and extended his hand, already knowing he should have followed behind Lou and been out of there, but when did he ever do what he was supposed to do? Eva tilted her head, confusion drawing her brows together. "Don't worry.

I'm simply helping you up, Miss Ward. Noticed you had a little twinge in your back earlier."

Her frown deepened, but still she took his hand, and the easy coolness of her slim fingers as they slipped into his produced an erotic tremor — but no, she was the talent. And this was his job. He pulled her up, her body just a little too close, the scent of her soft, lavender fragrance still lingering at this late hour.

Aidan released her and took a step back, clearing his throat. What was his problem? He hadn't been this flustered since he was a kid. "So it looks like we're out of your hair. Thanks again. You did fantastic for your first day. Lou's right. You did really well today."

She turned and walked over to the kitchen island, leaving him with just the memory of her sweet scent before she turned his way again and shrugged. "I did what I needed to do to get through the day."

He watched as she reached into her handbag and pulled out her cell, swiping at the screen, then smiling. For a moment he wondered if that smile was for a guy, but then he remembered the jerk that had gotten her into the situation and knew it wasn't, but still, he was angry at himself for even speculating.

"Is that all this is to you? Something you have to get through?" She pulled up short at that question but didn't answer him. He let out a breath. He was doing this all wrong. "Look, I know you were mad at me over at the gym today, but I want you to know I wasn't laughing at you or somehow indulging in exploiting your fear. I wouldn't do that."

He watched as her gaze softened, and he took a small bit of solace in that. It wasn't much, but at least he got it out. But then her phone pinged again, and she looked down.

"Sorry, but it's been quite a day, and my phone's been off," she said. "I don't mean to be rude."

"It's no problem. I should be getting out of your way anyhow." But Aidan watched as her indifferent expression changed to something else. At first her eyes widened, and then her full lips pulled together, thinning out before she gave her head a slight shake and put the phone back on the counter a touch too forcefully.

She shook her head then. "No, well, yes." Her eyes shifted back to the phone, and she crossed her arms, leveling him with a stare. "I mean, no, you're not bothering me, and thanks for the apology. Besides, what does it matter to you as long as you got what you needed from me?"

"I'm not here to get something from you, Eva. I'm hoping what I'm doing will actually help you too."

She seemed to physically recoil at that, and he held up his hands. "Touchy, huh? Hey, I'm sorry if I overstepped. But I'd appreciate it if you could possibly take me at my word on this one."

She rolled her eyes toward the ceiling. "Excuse me if I'm finding it just a little hard to believe you."

It was then that he noticed she looked more than peeved — in fact, beyond peeved to the point of flushed. Her color was higher on her cheeks, and her eyes were now slightly glassy, showing more distress than annoyance over just sparring with him. Without actually thinking it through, he walked over to her. Walked over, reached out, and took her hands in his. They were cold, and he noticed they had a slight tremor. He didn't know which of them was more surprised. More than anything, he couldn't believe she didn't immediately pull away and out of his grasp.

"What are you doing?" Her voice was a breathy whisper washing over him.

He stilled. What *was* he doing? He should

178

be on the way down to the garage and his own car. But he didn't like seeing her this way. "What's wrong? You were all right a moment ago. Was it the phone? The text?"

She pulled away from him then and lengthened her body so she was taller, as she absentmindedly wiped the hands he had been holding on her skirt. Aidan stepped back and smiled at the nerve of her gesture. It tugged at the center of him to see her as vulnerable as she was. "Okay, princess. I see how it is. You do what you have to do. Go on, keep your tough, 'I'm every woman and have got it all together' thing going. If that's what makes you feel better."

He moved back to the makeshift workstation, picked up his notebook, and shoved it into his bag before looking back up. She had her arms crossed and leaned on the counter, staring at him, no doubt waiting for him to leave.

Fine. That he could do. He lifted his bag onto his shoulder, willing words not to come out of his mouth. Too bad willing doesn't make it so, though. "But tell me this," he started, already knowing it was the wrong move. "That was him, wasn't it? Or something about him? Don't worry, I know it all already. Sorry to say, but he's moved on. Don't you think you ought to too?"

179

With that comment, her chin shot up, and her eyes sparked in just the way he knew or, dare he say, hoped they would. "You tell me: Is being a bastard part of your DNA?" she growled out.

"I don't know, could be. Have you met my father?" He joked. "Now you tell me: Is being completely inauthentic part of yours? I don't know who you're fooling, or trying to fool, but I can see right through you, lady. You weren't all that into the asshole anyway, so why don't you give up the wounded-bird act, at least when it's just you and me? He was simply a prop to you. And worse, he was a prop that failed you, and in a strange twist, his failure brought out the only honest moment we've got of you on film: you having your meltdown and showing your true colors. Just admit it, he was nothing to you. A placeholder. There are no cameras on now. Nobody will know but us."

When he stopped talking, there was silence, which was surprising because he half expected her to scream her head off as she told him to get the hell out of her apartment. But no, she only stared. Stood and stared and looked gorgeous in her anger as she did it.

When they'd come back to her place from the date, she'd changed into a slim black skirt and a lemon-yellow wrap top Mitzi had laid out for her. The lemon yellow was gorgeous against her smooth skin. She had put on her pearls again, and the little seeds rose and fell along with her heavy breathing. She was no longer distressed about whatever it was she saw on her phone; she was now good and heated over his rant about the asshole. The thought of it made a grin tug at the corners of his mouth.

"It's kind of funny, really."

He saw her hands tighten to fists. "What is?" She ground out.

"Your on-air declaration. The fact that you even think you could trade one man for another. Obviously, you've never encountered the right man, or you'd never have made such a statement."

She laughed at that. A pretty, throw your head back, diva-esque, in your face kind of laugh. The kind made to make the one laughed at feel all of two inches tall. When she met his eyes again, it was with a straight-on glare. "And what? I suppose you think you're the right kind of man? I highly doubt that." Her statement was both a dare and a declaration.

And the way she stated it threw the ball into his court. The woman had guts, he had to give her that. At times she showed the type of toughness that would make a warlord squirm. Aidan dropped his bag down onto the floor and walked back over into her space, pinning her in against the counter with his hands on either side of her body. Her intoxicating scent wafted up to his nose immediately, sweet and heady, producing an instant, primal reaction that had a strong sensual heat flaring throughout his body, threatening to burn him from the inside out.

She looked up at him, her eyes sharp and full of flame, nose flaring, lips a tight line.

He leaned down close to her ear, so near the lobe that if he stuck out his tongue the tiniest bit, he'd get a taste of her sweet, diamond-ornamented skin. "Well, you're right about that, princess. I'm definitely not the right man, and I don't think for a moment I ever will be. Though that doesn't stop you from wanting me now, does it?"

He was rewarded with a satisfying shudder that about did him in, and it was all he could do to pull back before things went way too far for both of them.

Aidan leaned back, about to shove off, when she stopped him, her hand reaching out to clutch the hem of his shirt. He looked down in shock, then back up into her eyes.

"Wait," she started, her voice a breathless whisper tickling the edge of his throat and sending ripples down to his center. "If not the right man, what about you being my Mr. Right Now Man?"

CHAPTER 11

What in all that holy hell was she thinking, Mister Right Now Man?

Could she have come up with a cheesier pickup line? And really, what was she doing coming up with a pickup line at all? How ridiculously tacky. Though she could have sworn she heard Cori cheering from across the globe.

Best friend's cheers or not, Eva was panicking, or at least that's what she thought she was doing, or maybe she was just hysterical and having a flat-out, full-on breakdown after all she'd been through. What else could it be? It was probably a reaction to the text about asshole Kevin and his new chick. Well, new old chick, because based on that pic, there was no way he and she were brand-new. That affair had probably been going on for quite a while.

Eva felt her fists tighten as her heart rate sped up when the deliciously masculine

184

scent of an oh-so-close Aidan Walker hit her nostrils. Who the hell was she fooling? She knew she was making excuses. She could put on a mask and lie to her friends, the public, the cameras, and even the barista at Starbucks, but what was the use of lying to herself? She was hot for freaking Aidan Walker. So hot the FDNY would have a problem putting her out right about now.

She looked down at her freshly re-manicured hand, which was twisted tightly into Aidan's shirt. *Lord, since when was she a shirt twister?* Her other hand was placed center on one of his rock-hard pecs, and for the life of her, she knew she didn't want to remove either. All she wanted to do was pull him in closer. Pull him in and let him surround her with all his raw masculinity. Let him take her and make her forget all her silly outside problems and let herself go.

Let go. For once and for good. This whole conversation, fight, whatever it was — she now knew it was an excuse to keep him there, to keep him arguing, because for some reason, when she was bantering back and forth with him, she'd never felt more alive.

It was as if she'd spent the years with Kevin — and, truth be told, the years before him — running on a slowly dying battery.

But it seemed like every time Aidan was somewhere in her vicinity, a spark ignited. Like some sort of sexual — and, God, she hoped not — emotional jumper cables were being applied to her very essence. Around him, her engines finally revved, and she could feel herself coming to life. He was her high octane. But it had to be dangerous to run on that type of fuel when she'd been coasting on regular for so long.

But still, part of her didn't get it. Everything about Aidan Walker went against her well-trained nature. She wasn't the arguing, caught-up, emotional type. She never had been. With her parents and their volatile highs and lows before her father ended up kicking it, literally, with his secretary, she'd always been the quiet peacemaker of their family. The play-it-by-the-book girl.

She had learned early the power of the word *yes,* learned how it made her parents happy, how it brought them peace and, miraculously, a quiet sense of family calm inside their outwardly picture-perfect home. And it was what she relied on to achieve the picture-perfect life she truly wanted for herself.

Early on, Eva had accepted her role as peacemaker and lived it down to her core. She had let it thread into her being and become a part of her. She had learned to squash down her emotions, and the trait had served her well clear through her school years, and especially in her current PR job in the family business. No one handled an overly emotional, in-hot-water celeb like Eva, and because of that her mother was proud of her, for the most part, this latest faux pas notwithstanding. Their "never let them see you sweat" way of living had turned the Ward Group into the go-to PR firm in the city. There was no way she was losing that distinction.

Eva looked down at her hands again and bit into her bottom lip. So what was she doing here now? Why was she going totally against her type and all rational thought? Was it just because she was getting a sexual charge from a ridiculously handsome, dangerously sexy man who infuriated her at every turn?

"You going to make your move, princess, or are you going to keep those wheels up there, spinning, until they come off the rails and you come up with an excuse that will cleanly talk you out of this?"

Shit. Aidan's low rumble sent a shiver through every shiverable part of her body. Eva's glance shot up as if on command, only to get hit with yet another thrill when she looked into his darkly devilish eyes.

"It wouldn't take much thinking to come up with a reason, and you know it," she said.

He stared, his body so close and that damned sexy smell wrapping around her like a spell. She was finding it hard to concentrate. "Of course I do. Shall we list them?" His expression went soft, as well as his voice. Its rich timber vibrated through her, her nipples tightening with his tone. And then Aidan shocked her, leaning in and licking her lightly on the shell of her outer ear.

Sweet, lovely toe curler! Eva's breath hitched, and her body slumped back. *So much for control.* She was grateful to have the counter at her back, or she was sure she would have sunk to the floor.

His voice was deep and rich. "One: We're here to work together, not play."

Eva felt herself nod, though she wasn't quite sure in what direction her head went. Circular maybe?

Aidan then leaned down and kissed her lightly on her collarbone. The ripple threading through her belly went right to her core as her eyelids fluttered closed.

"Two: You're on the rebound, and nothing good can come from a rebound romance."

She nodded weakly as he eased closer, his body connecting with hers, a strong capable hand wrapping around her waist, holding her securely as he leaned over. His lips moved, taking a trail upward, that sexy scruff of his teasing at her cheek.

"Three: You, my sweet little perfect princess, are not my type. And judging by your past track record, I don't seem like I'm the man for you either."

She may have let out a breathy sigh, as once again she shook her head in the affirmative, while his lips took a walk along her collarbone.

Eva swallowed, trying hard to catch her breath as her hand finally unclenched from his shirt and joined the other that was flat on his chest. His hard and steady heartbeat pulsed under her touch.

He paused in his assent and leaned back, looking her in the eye. "So as for being a Right Now Man?" he asked.

Eva stared, taking his hesitance as an implied question. He had put the ball totally in her court. This decision would be on her, insuring no excuses later. He smiled. "Wheels they are a turning. You sure do like to ponder, don't you, princess? Shall I list more reasons for you to back away?"

Eva shook her head, a definite no this time

as she took in that devilish grin, those full lips made to drive a woman wild. Damn, but he was gorgeous. He was gorgeous and sexy and so wrong for her that he'd be absolutely perfect for right now. His list proved that point. He was the perfect get-over-your-last-man man. An ideal way to balance the scales and get her groove back. Hell, Cori was probably somewhere casting a spell at that exact moment, because there were so many rights to this situation it couldn't be wrong. But still, Eva frowned.

It was too bad it was all the wrongs that niggled at her. The wrongs that poked at her like thorns in her side.

The text she'd received flashed across her mind. It was from one of her old friends, the type of friend that firmly belonged in the Facebook "friend" category — the type that had no real substantive connection with you but felt obligated to tag you in every loosely related group shot, evite you to every party, and send you social-media birthday greetings and invites to play games on your phone in order to achieve free likes. This "friend" was a notorious gossip, so Eva knew the news would be spread all over by the morning *if* she hadn't already been the ninth or tenth person to get the text: Kevin had moved on and was now engaged to a hostess at a restaurant they'd frequented many times.

It was just a picture. And if things hadn't blown up as publically as they had, it wouldn't have been a big deal. But they had and it was. It was a photo of Kevin and some chick, one she remembered as being a hostess at one of their favorite restaurants. She was a cute girl, that couldn't be denied, but judging from the photo, Eva could plainly see the woman was everything she was not. Petite and proportioned to be a perfect, curvy hourglass of breasts and hips, the type Kevin had pointed out that Eva was not. The photo showed off the hostess's assets well, framed in a low-cut cropped top and high-waisted skirt that accented her shapely behind to its fullest. In the photo, she was hugging Kevin and smiling wide. It was captioned "save the date for a winter wedding." Just freaking peachy. It was little more than a week after he had broken it off with her, and Kevin had moved on and proposed to a hostess chick.

And, worse, it seemed Aidan had the unique ability to read her way too well. In the short time they had known each other, he'd taken her well-built walls and ripped them down like cheap drywall. The astonishing swiftness and ease of it scared the hell out of her. She told herself that with him it could be so easy, that she could get what she wanted, go in and get out, but was she only fooling herself? Never in her life had someone gotten to her so quickly or so easily. Never had anyone brought out her passions so, well . . . passionately.

Eva looked into Aidan's eyes, this time hoping to see some of that flirtiness, that flash of his, but what she got back was infinitely worse. She saw herself in his smoldering challenge and open wanting, and it scared her to death.

This wasn't right. She should ask him to leave. She needed to stay on task, but more than that she needed to guard her heart. Eva knew from her own family experiences what happened when someone fell too far in love and let it burrow in too deep. It was the type of thing from which you could possibly never recover. She'd seen it happen to her mother, and she'd be damned if she would let it happen to her.

Though Kevin had hurt her to her core, she knew that in time she'd be okay. Her heart, if not her pride, would mend, and that she could live with. But when she looked at Aidan Walker, really looked at him, it was a whole different ball game. With him the rules would have to change. With him staying on task and going with her set list of men, that was the only way.

Eva looked away, shifting her vision from Aidan's eyes to his shoulders and his chest, then down to that tight, trim waist. She swallowed, imagining how tight his abs probably were. She inwardly moaned and felt her center go liquid as Aidan leaned in, his erection hard and ready against her belly.

All thoughts of tasks and right and wrong fluttered right out of her head. *Hey, they were only talking about right now, right now. Right?*

Eva let her other hand venture up and weave through his soft, curly hair. Though shorter than when she first saw him, it was still just long enough to pull her fingers through, which she did over and over. Like an inmate given time in the yard after a week of solitary, Eva let herself stroke and feel with abandon. In that moment, she closed her eyes and committed what she could to the memory of her touch in case she didn't get the opportunity again. She would treat it for what it was — a special treat, only for tonight. And tonight lasted only so long, as the morning would be here quickly enough. With that thought, Eva leaned up and forward and at the same time pulled Aidan's head down to hers.

His kiss intoxicated her and thoroughly blew her mind.

In just the span of a moment, the time it took for their lips to connect, the warmth of his full lips fusing with hers spread throughout her body as he took his hand and pulled her in even closer. Leaning back and tilting her head, she opened her lips slightly to take a breath, and his tongue slipped smoothly between her lips, connecting perfectly, stroking from the inside out, sending a heavy rush of desire throughout her body. Her pulse pounded, hard and fast. It was as if he had lit a long-burning fuse, and, in her mind's eye, she could already anticipate the explosion.

Feeling deliciously wicked, Eva's free hand slipped around Aidan's waist, and then lower still over the back of his jeans, to see if his backside felt as firm as it looked. It did, and she pulled him in even closer, shifting her head, turning the kiss around so that now she sucked on his tongue — drinking him in, tasting his manly essence, gaining energy and power from it. She moved down and licked at his bottom lip, took it between her own, and gave it a nip. She felt his smile as his hairs tickled her cheek.

"So the kitten likes to bite?" he asked teasingly.

Eva pulled back and looked at him wide-eyed. What was she doing biting the man? Especially a man like him. He could destroy her and her work with a simple flip of the switch or, worse yet, the playing of a tape. "I'm sorry. I shouldn't have done that."

She watched as his expression changed, as his eyes went from passionate dark fire to calm understanding. "Done what? Bite me, or started to think about it? If that's the case, then I shouldn't have said anything."

Eva shook her head and looked down. "I don't know, maybe both."

Aidan let out a sigh. "Reluctantly, I tend to think you're right."

Her brows shot up. Wait, she didn't expect that to be his answer. Wasn't that his erection still pressed up against her belly? Still she agreed. "Then it's settled. We'll chalk this up to a momentary lapse of reason."

Aidan laughed at that, the vibration sending a shiver throughout her body. Eva swallowed. "We seem to be having quite a few of those. It doesn't bode well for our working arrangement."

She shook her head in agreement, noticing but doing nothing about the fact that she still hadn't let him go, that one hand was firmly cupped around his ass while another enjoyed the feel of his now thor-

195

oughly tousled hair.

"No, it doesn't," she said as he lazily tilted his hips and swayed. Somehow she found herself mimicking the movement. "Um, I think it would probably be best if we clearly spelled out the terms of our agreement."

It was Aidan's turn to nod as his voice simmered, the heat between them palpable. "I'll agree to anything you put before me right now, Miss Ward."

Her hand shifted, moved from his hair to his waist, going under his shirt and taking in the ridges of his muscular abs. This meeting of the minds, negotiation, whatever it was, was getting all jumbled, and Eva didn't know if she was coming or going. Particularly if she was coming, which was so inappropriate on all fronts. Here she was, supposedly pulling away and getting her crap together, but still her hands were doing the opposite of what her head told her to do. She was delighted when she got a small quiver under the pads of her fingers as a response to her delicate roaming along his abs. "Anything?" she asked. "That doesn't make you the best negotiator."

He smiled, baring those devastating white teeth, the corners of his eyes crinkling as he gave her a hot look that ran down her body, singeing each spot it touched along the way.

"You wouldn't say that if you could see things from my current point of view."

With that, he slipped both hands around her waist and lifted her easily onto the kitchen island. The surprising coolness of the hard granite was a shock to her backside. Eva opened her mouth in instinctual protest as Aidan pushed the phone and her purse aside dismissively, but her protest died before it could be uttered. He leaned over her and tilted her head to the side, raining kisses down her neck and collarbone, lowering himself to the swell of her breasts. He slowly came back up to her mouth to drug her once more with his kiss. Bringing his hands up, he eased the wrap top open and caressed one breast through her black lacy bra, using his thumb to make her already hard peaks even harder. Eva heard her breath hitch as his other hand went lower and trailed up her thigh, trying to gain entrance despite the tight skirt. Eva shimmied and widened her legs, easing his way as her pulse picked up speed.

There was a dangerous spark with his first connection as his fingers brushed against her hard center. Unexpectedly, she bit down on his shoulder to tamper down on her excitement as she tightened her thigh muscles. His head shot up.

Her eyes went wide. "I'm so sorry. Did I hurt you? I won't do that again."

His smile brought a rush of warmth to her center. "Relax, kitten." His voice was a low whisper, soothing her and her racing heart. "It will take a lot more than that to scare me off. Princess, I'm your subject. Use me as you will."

Eva suddenly wanted to laugh at the same time she wanted to scream. This was probably so easy for him. She wondered how many times he'd done this. Gone on a job, bantered a bit, played with a woman's emotions, screwed her, and then moved on. She must be out of her mind. Absolutely bonkers.

But the truth was that, right now, she was also mad and angry and hot as hell for him. She wanted him, and he was here, so why shouldn't she have him?

Just no strings attached.

Now, if she could get her silly racing heart to listen to her rational mind, this might just be the head-clearing experience she needed to move on, so she could think and do what she had to do. The perfect launching off, so to speak, to her new life after Kevin.

Eva sucked in a breath, then she inwardly smiled. *Kitten.* She liked it. He was one for silly names. And regular normal her would tell him where he could take his kitten, and his princess too, for that matter, and shove them, but right here, right now, on her kitchen counter, she felt like donning a cute little cat mask and letting the kitten in her out to play. Right now, being his kitten was just what she needed. It was far enough away from her own persona to make her forget herself and her obligations for a while. Eva let a breath out and looked up at Aidan, giving her lips a lick. "Kittens don't just bite, they scratch too."

It was fun watching his eyes go wide. So much so that she boldly reached for the hem of her top, undid it fully, and let it drop to the counter.

Aidan's breath hitched as he watched Eva make the fluid motion of taking her blouse off, arching her back to show off her slim but still shapely figure to its best advantage, as she dropped the garment behind her. Damn, the woman was sexy as hell in a way that he'd not seen in this lifetime, and he'd seen a lot of women. But there she was, propped up on the damned kitchen counter with what he'd dare say was surprise in her eyes. Could it be the first time she had been on this particular kitchen counter, or any counter, for that matter? One could only hope. If so, that Kevin was more of a dope than even he gave him credit for. But no matter, here she was. In front of him. Wide-eyed but fighting to hide it, up on the counter in her black skirt, black heels, black lace bra, and those white pearls, and sporting an "I'm yours, but just for tonight" smile, looking like every wet dream he'd ever had. She made him rock hard at the same time that she scared the shit out of him.

Aidan felt his eyes narrow as he fought to get control of his breathing. The warning bells in his head chimed like it was freaking high mass in Saint Peter's Square. All the while, an inner duel — his conscience versus his libido — had him practically wanting to blow a time-out whistle. He knew all the reasons to stop. The list was endless. He'd been going over it and adding to it and taking away from it ever since he first laid eyes on her; that's why he could so easily rattle reasons off to her. Hell, he still had plenty more, not the least of which was the fact that he was toxic when it came to relationships, and he knew it. Hadn't he recently almost gotten his entire team killed, the woman he was sleeping with included? If that wasn't proof of toxic, he didn't know what was. Yet here he still was, standing before her with a hard-on that wouldn't quit, ready to sell his soul to the devil for release.

Shit, what an idiot he was. He should have run home after Lou. Hell, he should have left with Lou and the crew, but stupid him, he couldn't leave well enough alone.

Eva smiled, a teasing light coming to her eyes. "I feel like now maybe I should pull out the camera."

He frowned. "What are you talking about?"

"Well," she spoke up again, leaning forward and pulling him toward her with the hem of his shirt. "The great Aidan Walker looking lost. What happened to the cocky, confidant man so full of talk not moments ago? Don't tell me I've scared him off."

He raised a brow. She was enjoying things way too much, or maybe it was just enough. Her teasing smile and sparkling eyes warmed him from the inside out. He reached out and trailed a finger down her neck and along her shoulder, brought it between her breasts and let two fingers slip into her bra and tease her nipple. He watched as her eyes closed and her nostrils flared, while her breathing faltered. His dick throbbed in time with her shallow breaths.

Perfection. The ice princess thaws. She was so beautiful he felt he could almost come just by touching her and watching her like this. It was unbelievably satisfying, bringing that beautiful blush to her maple hued cheeks.

Aidan repeated the motion slowly and steadily, his hands moving in an almost natural, instinctual way as if made to move along the curves of her body. With small circles, he caressed her nipple, while his other hand came up to massage her long, elegant neck. Slowly, she eased back into his caress, trusting him to support her, a trust he so far had done nothing to deserve but somehow wanted to earn. Shifting, he leaned down and added a hot breath to her other breast, delighting when she arched into his mouth, the fine lace, a delicate barrier between her hardened nipple and his insistent tongue.

With a frustrated moan, she reached down and flicked at the bra, releasing the front clasp, springing it free, and pushing the annoying garment out of the way. He filled one hand with her perfect round globe as he happily circled the nipple with gentle fingers and suckled the other one, her perfect peak heaven on his tongue. Her sigh came out almost at the same moment as his groan, sounding like a long-awaited release, almost as if, like him, she had anticipated this too. He felt almost ready to explode, and there he was standing in her living room still fully clothed.

Aidan pushed away from her. He needed a moment. Hell, he needed three. Just some time to gather some sense of control. Around her he felt he had none.

Aidan went to swallow but found the motion as hard as denying his need for release just then. He turned toward the windows and looked at the now-glittering lights of the city against the midnight sky. It was so quiet in the apartment. There was no sound except their heavy, labored breathing.

Turning back, Aidan was somehow surprised to find her still there, staring up at him, a sensual vision in black on a granite backdrop.

Aidan pulled her up, lifting her off the counter. She felt so good and warm in his arms, half dressed with her arms wrapped around his neck and her long legs around his waist, that delicious ass in his hands. It took only a few steps to get to the entrance of her bedroom. But he paused at the doorway and looked down at her. "Stay or go?" His voice sounded strained to his own ears, and it was in that moment that he felt just how hard his heart was beating, how labored his breathing was.

Her gaze went soft. The sex kitten was gone, and so was the ice princess. This woman in his arms was the same unsure, reckless woman he had seen in the studio — the one who took him off guard, the one who sent him running after her. And in that moment he knew why he ran after her. Or at least why part of him did. It wasn't just to film her. Yeah, that was part of it, but it was also because he knew that someone was going to film her either way, and he wanted to be the one to do it. No one else. He wanted to shield her from the rest of them as best he could. If he could. He ran to protect her.

He watched as the question turned in her mind. His stomach did a surprising flip as he awaited her answer, suddenly unsure of what she would say and unsure of what he wanted her to say.

"I'd like for you to stay," she said, her voice holding all the grace as if she were inviting him for tea. Then her eyes darkened and her tone lowered. "For tonight," she added, as if it was both a warning and a promise. He wanted to smile, to jump for joy in his conquest, but something stopped him. It could be the way she made the answer come out as a declaration, or the way she added the "for tonight" — to keep her distance and keep him in his place. No matter. He'd play it her way. Besides, it would seem she was the only one of the two of them who was thinking halfway clearly.

Aidan nodded. "Tonight it is, princess." He grinned. "But only if you promise to keep on the pearls." He saw her eyes narrow at that, and he grinned wider, hoping his smile hid his inner turmoil, as he stepped through the doorway to her bedroom.

Eva was breathless, and her stomach was full of butterflies, fluttering and swirling, doing a magical dance that threatened to send her whole body into celestial orbit.

She swallowed as Aidan laid her sideways in the center of her bed. Leaning up on her elbows, she stared as he stood tall, sexy, rough, and just a little bit dangerous. Her mouth began to water as he reached down and pulled his shirt over his head, revealing more sinewy muscles than should be allowed, and she licked her lips. She almost reached up to wipe her mouth, afraid that she'd out and out drool over so much male eye candy.

He grinned. "You are seriously going to

make me blush looking at me like that, kitten."

She laughed, "I'm sorry, but it's been a minute since I've perused a half-naked man in my bedroom."

He raised a brow. "You mean another half-naked man."

She looked away as the butterflies all bunched up together, forming a knot in her stomach. "Oh yeah. That. Can we just not talk about him right now?"

"Hey," he said, his voice low and throaty. "I'm sorry. It's just that I don't want any games or secrets in here" — he gestured toward the bed — "in between us, with what we're doing right now." Eva felt her eyes go slightly wide with shock over his candor. It was unexpected, but she was grateful for it. And for the moment, she let his honesty touch her heart. But then he leaned, going down on one knee, and pulled off one of her sandals, kissing the top of her foot.

Eva couldn't help the smile that spread as she eased back and the butterflies slowly uncoiled. Aidan reached over and took off the other shoe, paying the same attention to that foot, his strong hands massaging as he went. Eva arched her back. He really had hidden talents, she thought, as his hands trailed her legs, going up her thighs.

Reaching for the hem of her skirt, he shimmied it up, the cool air bringing tingling goose bumps of sexual excitement all over her body. And then there he was, with his hands on both sides of her hips, the flimsy fabric pulling against her skin. The excitement of it all was driving her insane when suddenly he stopped, and she looked up.

He stared at her, his eyes full of a kind of passion she hadn't seen in such a long time. Eva blinked to fight against the pricking wetness where wetness should just not be right now. "Why are you stopping?"

He frowned. "Well, though you may not believe me, I didn't start out this day with some grand plan of seduction. You wouldn't happen to have any condoms, would you? Because if you don't, that's cool, and we can revisit this on another night." His frown went deeper, and for the first time, she actually saw a hint of insecurity in his eyes. "Though I hope that revisiting won't bring you to your senses and have you rethinking the whole thing."

Eva quickly sat up and reached for her nightstand drawer, the side that Kevin usually slept on, but she quickly pushed that thought aside and reached for the condoms. She'd think about the fact that he had insisted on using them long into their exclusive relationship later.

She held up the roll and gave Aidan a grin. "How's this for not rethinking anything?"

"This," he said taking the condoms with one hand and gently pushing her back down on the bed with the other, "is perfect."

And *he* was perfect. He took her hand then, and they both stood and undressed together. Eva thought she might embarrassingly swoon when he reached for the button of his jeans and tugged them off, showing just how perfect he was everywhere.

He pulled her to him and kissed her hard, breaking her gaze. "Really, you're going to have to stop doing that, or you're going to give me performance anxiety."

"Sorry. It's that you're a lot to, um, take all at once."

He laughed. "How about we test it and see just how much you can take, Miss Ward?"

Laying her down, he hovered over her and trailed kisses down her neck, licking around her pearls, going between her breasts, around and under, driving her completely insane before taking a nipple fully into his mouth. Slow and easy. There was no rushing with him. Eva had gotten so used to sex with Kev and him hitting his usual spots that she half forgot what it was like to be lingered over. It was lovely. She felt like a flower blooming to life as he licked and tugged at her gently and reverently.

Normally quiet, Eva couldn't help the sighs that escaped with every new sensation he brought to her body. When he went lower, his tongue dipping into her belly button, she stifled a giggle.

"I like that sound," he said, his voice now a low rumble from between her thighs.

The giggle quickly disappeared on an intake of breath as his tongue flicked across her most intimate, most sensitive of sensual spots. Her eyes tightened shut as her back arched and her hands gripped the duvet. "Ohhh." It came out on her exhale, and her toes curled as he licked her in long, languid strokes. She felt his scruff as he grinned.

"Now *that* sound I love."

He reached up and stroked her torso, going to her breasts, taking a nipple between his thumb and forefinger, squeezing to the point just before pain. He lowered his head, his tongue swirling against her hard peak, bringing her almost immeasurable pleasure.

Eva's toes curled harder. Holy hell. That was really a thing. Her toes, fingers, everything suddenly twisted and folded in as she experienced what had to be the most incredible orgasm of her life.

She didn't know how long it lasted. He was there, and it just didn't seem to stop. But then as the world began to come back into focus and she breathed again, starting to find herself, he was over her, looking at her face with the most fierce, possessive, yet still gentle expression in his eyes.

"My god, woman, you are gorgeous."

Her hand came up to cover her face. Did she really just come like that in front of this man? Her cheeks flamed. "I'm so not. But thanks. A lot."

Aidan pulled her hands down and kissed her fingertips. "Don't ever be embarrassed around me. And please don't thank me." He leaned in and kissed her, at the same time pulling her knees up and getting comfortable between her legs. He reached over, picked up a condom packet, and ripped it open with his teeth, tugging it on and down over his long, thick shaft. Eva wanted to reach out and touch him, give him a little help, but she was practically boneless, and besides, at that moment watching was way too much fun.

"There you go with those looks again, kitten," he said as he pulled her in closer, coming right to her entrance. "Like I said, you keep it up, you're going to have me blushing."

She grinned. "Somehow you don't look like a man who blushes easily."

He cocked his head to the side. "We'll see."

And with that he entered her — swiftly, filling her fully and completely. Any other thought of banter was taken away on a swift intake of breath. The heat from their union radiated from her center throughout her entire body. His strokes were long and languid, caressing her sensuously. The overwhelming sensation made her arch up to meet him as he ran his hands down the center of her body, causing her to rise and fall toward him over and over again.

Finally, Aidan lifted her by her hips and pulled her to him, bringing them chest to chest as he kissed her deep so they fully connected top and bottom.

Eva sucked at his tongue as they found a rhythm, and when she tightened herself around him, he sucked in a groan. "I'm not gonna last, kitten."

"Then let go."

"Let go with me, Eva, please."

His words pulled her up short. He didn't know how much she truly wanted to do it, in so many different ways. But all she could do was follow his physical command, kiss him hard, and come.

CHAPTER 12

Eva checked her cell phone once more, then walked out of her office to her assistant's desk. Yet again. She paced back and forth absentmindedly before turning to go back into her office, paused, then paced back out.

"Is there something you need, Eva? You've been out here three times already. Are you all right?" her assistant, Jess, asked, her dark brows drawn together. "Honestly, you don't look well. Are you sure you're up for your second date tonight?"

Eva paused in her pacing and looked at the young woman. She was sweet. Not long out of school, always on trend with her style, but still professional. Wide-eyed and eager, but sharp and in no way a slacker. She felt lucky to have her. Today, though, she looked at her and felt something different as she took in the girl's appearance. When she had interviewed for the job, Jess wore her long, natural hair twisted in neat dreads that flowed freely down her back. Today the dreads were pulled up tightly into a chignon, mimicking Eva's own style. She remembered admiring the girl's offbeat style, with her asymmetrical skirts and modern tops, but today she wore slim black pants and a cream twinset. The only remaining hint of her true bohemian nature was the delicate nose ring twinkling in her left nostril. Even her shoes were neat spectator pumps that looked like they strangled her feet.

Looking at her now, part of Eva wanted to tell her to loosen up, not to allow the job or the pressure to conform to take away who she was. Eva had settled into her role as a nondescript pleaser long before she was Jess's age. It suited her. It suited who she was and what she did for a living. She played that part well. But she didn't want to have a hand in grooming another stiff, nondescript people pleaser for the future.

"Eva?" Jess prompted. "Did you hear me?"

Eva blinked and made a mental note to figure out a way to approach the subject with her.

"No," she said to Jess, who looked at her with confusion. Eva shook her head. "I mean yes, I'm fine. I'm thinking on my feet about all I need to get together, and the Gardenia account. I hate that their meeting had to be moved because of my ridiculous shooting schedule."

It was an excuse, of course. At that exact moment, she was really pacing with nerves, not over the impending date tonight, but over the fact that she would once again see Aidan. It had been four days since they'd gotten together and made that pact. So yes, she was a bundle of nerves. She was an expert at putting on a mask, but she didn't think she could quite pull off hiding her feelings once she saw him face-to-face.

Jess waved a hand. "Oh, don't worry about them. They were fine with coming in on Monday. Hey, you're the celebrity now. The phones are ringing off the hook. Now that your segment has aired, everyone wants a meeting with you. And the clients understand that you're getting booked up."

Eva grimaced. "Don't remind me. What a disaster that segment was. I looked ridiculous up there on that wall and throwing those balls. Jeez, what a mess."

"Oh stop. It's all over. You looked like a black super hero on that rock wall, and that guy was clearly a jerk, but you handled him perfectly. Now you just relax, and here's hoping that Prince Charming is right around the corner," she smiled. "Or at least on the next date."

Jess looked down, then picked up a file and handed it to Eva. "But if you don't mind, while you wait for your car, can you look these over? They need your signature for the Lush Cosmetics event."

Eva took the file. "No problem. And thanks for taking so much extra work on while I'm dealing with this silliness. When this is over, I'm giving you a spa day. You deserve it."

"Hey, it's my job," Jess said with a grin. "But that is really nice of you."

Eva narrowed her eyes, taking in Jess's sensible pumps; the clunky heels she used to wear were a thing of the past. "And you should loosen up," she said. "Take your hair down. If I've learned anything from this ordeal, it's to be more of myself and less of what's expected."

Jess's smile went wider. "If you say so, boss. Though I don't know what Val would think of that."

"Oh, I know what Val would think, but I'm your boss, and it doesn't affect how you do your job."

Sitting back at her desk, Eva checked her phone one more time before letting out a sigh. Jeez, Cori had not yet replied to her text. She shook her cell next to her ear, then put it back in front of her face and stared at

216

it. No response from her BFF to her cryptic "I've gotten under one" callout, and worse still, nothing back from Aidan since he'd left her apartment. God, was she really being that girl? The thought made her lip curl, it was so infuriating. She was a full-grown woman, and a top, sought-after Manhattan PR exec. She should not be hanging by the phone like a teen waiting on an invite to the prom. And yet here she was. Waiting. Waiting and barely able to concentrate on her job because of the "Will he or won't he call"? sirens going off in her head. But still, it was weird — weird and infuriating — that she hadn't heard a word from Aidan since their encounter.

Encounter. She chuckled to herself. The thought of such a whitewashed word made her think of her mother. Her cool, sanitized euphemism for the completely amazing night of sex would make her mom proud.

But still, euphemism or not, receiving no word from Aidan didn't sit as well as it should have with Eva. She pursed her lips and let out a long breath as she swiveled her chair around, taking in the view of the city stretched out below her.

She guessed that Aidan was following her directions. You couldn't fault the man for that. And he'd proven on Sunday night that

217

he was very good at following directions — Eva got a shiver and unconsciously bit her bottom lip — just about as good as he was at giving them.

"Relax, kitten. I've got this."

The memory of his deep voice was enough to make her cross her legs. Not to mention the memory of how good he looked in his raw masculinity, so sexy as he quickly stripped, throwing his clothes aside without a care for the expensive material and no hint of shame in his body. She couldn't help the unwelcome comparison to Kevin that came to her mind. Kevin was classical in his good looks, but for all his talk about wanting to get so-called adventurous in bed, he never once got half as passionate over her as Aidan had. Never let himself go as Aidan had. And never had she let herself go as she had with Aidan.

Eva's cell phone buzzed on her desk, and her eyes shot open. She blinked, half surprised to be hit by the brightly lit Manhattan view and not her own dimly lit bedroom where her mind had wandered. She glanced at the phone and saw it was Cori finally getting back to her. Her heart sank for a moment, but then it bolstered. Hey, at least she still ranked with her friend. She swiped at the screen.

Sorry been crazed here with IMPOS-SIBLE clients. But love you and will call in the evening my time. I sure hope your "got under" means what I think it means and it had better had been with a new man and not asshole Kev. Because I've already written him out of the friend will.

Love ya. C

The quick note from Cori gave Eva her first real smile of the day. She'd found all sorts of emojis to attach to the text that had Eva laughing out loud. There was a bed, a horse, and cowboy, and for reasons she couldn't get her head around, what appeared to be roller skates. Cori would have to explain that one. But she was still thinking of how happy she'd be when she heard about the under and the whom. Well, Eva knew she'd have to survive on that for a while.

Thinking of surviving brought her thoughts back to Aidan and how she was going to survive without another taste of him. She'd specifically told herself she would not care if he called her. That it was better if he didn't, and now here she was practically losing it, awaiting his call, and for what? All because he'd given her the best orgasm in well, forever, and then repeated the deal two more times. Eva put her head in her hands and once again cursed herself for making up those stupid rules.

There they were in a lovely post-coital haze, with him laying his beautiful head on her breast and her running her fingers through his soft and totally finger-runnable hair, and of course her being her, she couldn't just leave well enough alone. No, she had to go and ruin it by letting her over-thinking mind slip in and snatch away their moment of bliss. It was quiet. He was relaxed, she was satisfied. Why couldn't that have been good enough?

"You know, I meant what I said." The words came out quicker and gruffer than she intended.

"Why is it I know where you're going with this, Miss Ward?"

She took a deep breath. "So we're back to Miss Ward. No Eva?"

"Isn't that where you're about to take me? Back to business? I can tell by your tone."

She thought for a moment. Really, it was for the best. "Well, you're nothing if not perceptive, I'll give you that. I'm sorry, but this can't be more than this. It has to be this one night. No more. Besides, I'd say we've both, to our mutual satisfaction, taken care of what we needed to here."

She thought he may have laughed at that, but he went no further, so maybe she'd heard wrong, so Eva continued, because if she stopped she'd lose her nerve. "There are rules, and we can't break them. The stakes are too high. At least for me they are, and I'm sure you'd like to focus on your job at hand. So what's done is done and can't be repeated."

She was finished. She'd said her peace and for the most part was proud of herself for getting it done without unnecessary, messy emotion. But he was quiet, too quiet, and for a while she didn't know if he had fallen asleep. Until he leaned forward and ran his tongue along her neck in a long stroke, at the same time bringing his fingers between her already damp, swollen folds. His voice was a close whisper in her ear. "Fine, kitten. This is your show. You call the shots. But nothing starts until the night is over, and we still have hours left before the sun rises . . ."

Eva's phone buzzed again, letting her know a message had come through. She looked down and was instantly annoyed that her betraying heart was speeding up. It was from him: She swiped at the phone. And frowned. It was a group text:

Call update: Base Team to meet @ Talent's @ 5:00 sharp.
Team B will meet @ 6:00 @ Bachelor 2-A,

AW

Eva felt her nostrils flare as she re-read the little text for a third time. So now she was "the talent"? She slammed the phone down and ran a hand across her forehead as she tried to look at the figures on the spreadsheet in front of her, but the numbers blurred. Like she said, it was a win/win for him. Fine. If she was the talent, she'd show him just how talented she could be.

Aidan put his phone down and ran his hand through his hair, rubbing irritably at his scalp. Fine, let her take that, and see if it was good enough for her damned professional rules. He'd just gotten out of his third boring meeting of the day and was about ready to snap someone's head off if he didn't get out of this damned office soon. But no, his father had him scheduled for yet another glad-handing session before he could escape.

He leaned back in his chair and turned toward the window. Normally he enjoyed the view that spanned from Midtown all the way to Lower Manhattan and One World Trade. The view used to bolster him, make him think of the city — the excitement of it and all the stories to be told in it, but not today. Today all he could think of was one woman, one story. And how she was so close but still maddeningly out of his reach. He wondered if she was even fazed by the group text he'd sent. Probably not. Why should she be? It perfectly followed her set rules. For all he knew, she might not have even seen it; maybe her assistant was monitoring her phone.

She'd made it clear after they'd made love, though he was sure she wouldn't call it that. Had sex? Gotten busy? Hooked up? Aidan shuddered at all the sayings that paled in comparison to the night they'd shared. No matter, though. Either way, she'd made it clear after they'd handled their mutual, multiple sexual transactions that she was through with him. Aidan shook his head and laughed, though he didn't feel like laughing at all. God, he was really wimping out on this one. What was he doing getting so wrapped up in a woman who couldn't care less about him beyond what would be considered a one-night hookup?

He felt his frown deepen. But really, why was he mad? Was he mad because he wanted her, or was he pissed because he wanted her to want him as much as he wanted her. Again and again. The woman was good in so many more ways than what she was showing on the small screen.

It was days later, and all it took was a thought to bring her taste, her smell, her feel to the forefront of his senses, and he was supposed to let all that go without a backward glance? Aidan shook his head. He could say one thing: That Kevin was a damned idiot, because if given the choice, there would be no way he would have walked away from her.

Too bad he didn't have a choice.

Eva had made her feelings perfectly clear. They were just temporary. A modern-day scheduled booty call with an expiration date on top of that — that is, if he ever even got another chance with her. Aidan felt his jaw tighten. Shit, if he told his boys about his so-called mess, they'd probably tell him to stop his whining — that this was reason to celebrate. Vin would buy him a round of drinks to his success, while Carter would tell him to get ready to saddle up to go out on the hunt for the next conquest. But he didn't feel like going on the hunt or celebrating or any of it. The fact was women like Eva were a rare find indeed.

There was a quick succession of knocks on Aidan's open office door, and when he turned, he came face-to-face with Carter, as though he had mentally summoned him. He gave his friend a quick nod. "What's up, C?"

Carter walked in with an easy smile, looking cool and polished as always. "Just passing through. Wanted to check in and say the first date was eaten up by the viewers. This is going to be a huge win for us." He made a small fist and pumped the air.

Aidan thought he should smile too, but at the mention of the date and the reminder of the one to come, smiling was the last thing on his mind. Of course, Carter was quick on the uptake and noticed it. "What's up? Please don't tell me there's a problem with filming or the next date. Our ratings are booming, and if we keep up this pace and level of interest, I'm hopeful we can take over that top morning spot by the wedding."

The wedding. It was scheduled for only two months away. Eva married to some stranger. Keeping his expression impassive was a true challenge at the moment. But he had to do it. There was no way he was letting any of his true feelings show to Carter and no way he was ruining this opportunity

225

for him or the show. He smiled what he hoped was a convincing smile. "Nah, there are no problems. The dates are set, though I hope they go a little better than the last meathead and we can find her someone to actually connect with."

Carter raised a brow and snorted. "Not likely in the time frame we have, and come on, with her tightly wrung disposition, I don't see us finding someone up to the task of getting her to loosen up without the incentive of liberal booze and/or cash."

At that Aidan couldn't hold onto his temper. "Now that's going too far. We're playing this as by the book as we can. We've already upended her life enough; the least we can do is be on the up-and-up with the guys."

Carter put up a hand. "Okay, sir knight. Cool your heels. No need to get testy. You're in charge, and I'm staying out of things." He shook his head. "Listen, I've got to run. You keep playing the Boy Scout though. It looks good on you. Drinks later this week?"

By way of reply, Aidan answered him with a low grunt and gave him his back. Freaking Carter. If he wasn't his friend and, he knew, loyal to him through and through, he'd definitely want to punch him out. At that moment, Aidan didn't feel like much of anything — not drinking with annoying friends, not sleeping, and definitely not grinning and bearing it through another board meeting and being the perfect face of the next generation at the network. The only thing he wanted to do was the thing he couldn't, and that was to hightail it as quickly as possible back to her apartment and that overly decorated sweet bedroom that he had no business feeling way too comfortable in, and burrowing deep between those satiny thighs of hers, where he had no business feeling way too at home. He had to think of the network and what was best for the show. The fact that they were inching up in the ratings and closing in on their competitors was something even he couldn't ignore, satiny thighs be damned.

Aidan let out a groan as he shifted in his seat. The thought of her thighs had made him instantly, uncontrollably hard. But, dammit, if she wasn't delicious as hell. Just the thought of her thighs, lips, ass — hell, any part of her, even her voice when she was pissed at him — made him hard. It was just her. Not to mention that she shocked him to his core with the way she had laid out on her countertop, offering herself to him in a way that no one else ever had, in a way that he knew was all her, not just giving but taking too. And he wanted that. Wanted to give her a part of him he never had given anyone before.

But it was a mistake, just like it was a mistake trusting that informant, and Aidan should have picked up on it. He should have seen it in the informant's eyes, just as he should have seen in Eva's that he was getting into dangerous waters with the first exquisite dip between her thighs. That was when he should have run while he still had maybe half his senses still intact. But being the fool he was, he didn't. No, he took it all the way. Acting like he had it together. Taking it on as a challenge. Wanting to see how far he could take the ice princess. Well, the joke was on him.

Pearls on or off, she was no ice princess. The woman was as hot as they came, taking him to unimaginable heights with her uninhibited lovemaking. The way she molded and fit to his body made him think ridiculous thoughts, like she could possibly have been made just for him, as if there were any such thing. Yes, she took him all the way, but when it was over she sent him packing. He had gathered his discarded clothes and made his way out of her apartment and into the dawning New York morning, walking on uneasy legs that were not accustomed to a walk of shame. She had used him as a placeholder for all the men who'd pissed her off, and he knew it. He knew it and went with it, and knew that, if given the chance, he probably would do it again. Without hesitation. That's probably what gnawed at him the most, what really pricked at his soul.

Yeah, he'd been screwed and was being screwed in every possible way. But he had to work his way around it. He had to find a way to make this work to his advantage somehow, and maybe the answer was in the rules that Eva had so ingeniously set up from the start.

With a deep breath and a newfound resolution to handle Eva as he would any other assignment — if he was handling it smartly — Aidan stood up to get ready for his next meeting. She was right. Sticking to a plan was the best way. And appropriate distance was the safest choice for both of them. On the way out the door, Aidan reached back and grabbed his almost-forgotten phone, telling himself that checking for incoming messages was only being professional and had nothing at all to do with one Eva Ward.

CHAPTER 13

And still he had nothing to say. Well, almost next to nothing.

Okay, well, that is freaking wonderful. Just terrific, Eva thought, as she smoothed her expression into one of serene elegance and tried her hardest to focus all her attention on tonight's date, a charming financier named Quinton Prescott.

Quinton was everything the gym rat Trey Stone wasn't. And as a bonus, he was also light years toward tilting over into the "just right for her" column, away from brooding Mr. Aidan Walker, who had said all of maybe five words to her since he'd arrived late to meet her and the rest of the crew at their current location. Not that she was paying any attention to him, mind you.

The station had sent a car to pick Eva up at her office and take her to her apartment at four o'clock. With the airing of her first segment, it seemed her popularity had doubled, maybe tripled. She'd expected a bit of an uptick, but nothing like what she'd seen since Tuesday. Her Facebook requests had gone off the charts, Twitter wanted to give her one of those official little checks they gave real celebrities, like movie stars or maybe Kardashians — it was all quite overwhelming. Doing something simple like taking the bus or the subway to work or doing a quick Starbucks run was now a mission to be carefully planned out with tactical precision if she didn't want to be gawked over or mobbed with a thousand catcalls or supposedly innocent questions. She now knew for certain that she had to keep her outward profile low at least until the show was over and she had faded from recent memory. The upside was that with the way the media cycle went, she suspected it would take about three weeks tops after the airing of the wedding.

Upon her arrival home, she'd only had time for a hot shower before Mitzi arrived with a hair and makeup artist to make her look put together, but of course not too put together. She tried to hide her disappointment when Louisa arrived with Stan and only one other guy, with no hint or word of or from Aidan, just a skeleton crew to prep her for her evening at the opera with Quinton.

Still, she refused to ask about Aidan. She wouldn't do it. She guessed he'd taken her at her word and was keeping his distance. And that was fine. Their fabulous one-night stand was obviously enough to put him off her, forever.

Finally, he turned up on the set. Eva frowned as she spied him huddled with a crew member next to the equipment van parked on the corner of Sixty-third and Amsterdam. "Is everything all right?"

Quinton's voice pulled her back his way, and she blinked, coming out of her reverie. Whoops, she'd better focus on her date and the actual task at hand. Besides, it wasn't like focusing on a man like Quinton was a hardship. He gave her a kind smile, and she felt her chest tighten a bit. She wasn't being fair, thinking about Aidan at a time like this. Quinton was a perfectly pleasant man — tall, with a perfectly pleasant face, broad shoulders, and a pleasant smile. Eva could feel her discomfort churn up from deep in her lower belly. What was that? *Pleasant* three times to describe one man? That couldn't be a good sign. *Come on and focus, Eva! You're in PR. You can come up with something better than pleasant.* She moved from his pleasant smile to check out his attire. Well, his suit was sharp. Eva cut herself bonus points for not going for the mental *pleasant,* and she added two more for conveniently disregarding the fact that she was sure a stylist had probably picked out the suit for him, just as her dress had been picked out for her. Better to just go with the fantasy at this point. Either way, Quinton's style was on point, and his well-cut suit set off her red cocktail dress perfectly. What more could a woman ask for on a normally boring Thursday night? Also he was a better choice than the guy with the kid. Eva suspected that Aidan had something to do with Quinton being here in lieu of that guy.

"Excuse me?"

"At first, I asked if you enjoy opera, and then when you didn't respond, I asked if everything was all right."

Eva smiled, smoothing down her dress and giving him her full attention, or at least making an attempt at full attention with a cordless mic attached to her back and a small film army surrounding her. Not to mention the distraction of a certain nonchalant playboy, who was doing his best to ignore her. It was a good thing she was in the middle of New York. At least it seemed she was the only one who thought this situation was in any way out of the ordinary.

Eva slid her arm into the crook of Quinton's. "I'm fine, thanks. Still not quite used to being the center of attention. Normally, I like to leave that up to my clients, and as for the opera, honestly, I haven't been since I was a teenager on a school trip. But I've always wanted to come back. I'm sure I'll enjoy it."

She let her eyes glance briefly Aidan's way once more. This time she caught him as his eyes slid her way and he took in her every movement. She tried to but couldn't ignore the instant heat she felt as she purposefully led Quinton away toward the tall, sweeping arches of the opera house, putting Aidan and their night both literally and figuratively behind her.

Aidan felt his body involuntarily tense as he watched Eva entwine her arm with Quinton Prescott's and look up at him, flashing that smile of hers. Her full lips were painted a glossy red to match her dress, which was the color of a new fire engine. On anyone else the tight elastic bands that were subbing for fabric would probably look cheap, but no, not on her. There was nothing about her that was cheap. The woman was class all the way, from this evening's slightly messy updo to the delicate black satin sandals on her feet and back to those damned pearls.

All that tight, understated reserve of hers had him dying to grab her, flip her over his shoulder like some type of caveman, run off with her somewhere, and have her calling out his name in ecstasy, as she'd done the other night. But at that thought he frowned. Of course, those types of things just weren't done, not by anyone with a lick of sense or propriety, and he liked to think he had both, despite what the gossip tabloids had to say about him to keep their circulation up.

Besides, she'd made it clear as she dismissed him from her bed — later, when both were satiated by multiple orgasms — that he was a quick rebound screw. Looking at her now, and not being some sort of caveman but an enlightened sort, he should respect that and just go with her flow. Sure, it was a pleasant surprise that sexually, little Miss Pearl Button-down turned out to be exactly his type and then some. But as for the rest? As for the two being compatible in any other way? No way. She might talk a good game, but she was ready to settle down into something stable. He could tell by the way she was giving it her all on this date with smooth Mr. Money. She was so dead set on the rule of image being everything and all that came along with it that it was seeping from her pores. She was practically lighting up like the tree at Rockefeller Center with this postcard-looking dude.

Aidan knew, looking at her now, that there would be no way she could make it with him in a relationship that extended outside the confines of the bedroom. She was not the type who could deal with him being on the road and having to go where the stories went. She'd never understand how he lived for the rush of the adrenaline or how he'd hoped to really make a difference with the work he did. Hell, her work was all about putting a best face forward and covering up for A-list celebs and Fortune 500 companies. A woman like that was not for him, and he couldn't let his "for the moment" wild feelings for her take him off of his game.

So despite this twinge of jealousy and this crazy urge — Aidan peered closely at the retreating couple — to forcefully remove Quinton's fingers from the small of Eva's back, just like her he'd stick with the plan. It was a solid one. He would do his time working nine to five. He'd do what he had to do to make his father happy and make his mark with the board, and once that was done, he'd carry on with his life. But it would be solely on his own terms and this time with both his father's and the board's backing, getting them in line to do more programing that mattered and stepping back from pieces like this one. There was no way he'd be permanently tied to a desk or a woman. He was one for the open road, and just like he was filler, so to speak, for her, she, if truth be told, was the kitten that perfectly scratched a particularly annoying itch he'd currently had.

As she turned away with Prescott, Aidan's eyes skimmed over the outline of her perfect, heart-shaped behind as Prescott's hand dared to slide lower. He almost growled out loud as their night together came back, hitting him at full force, and the primal instinct to strike threatened to take over. Jeez, she was almost too much to resist. The woman was going to drive him mad and mess up all he had mapped out.

Aidan's frown went deeper. Their encounter had been frosty when they'd first laid eyes on each other a few minutes before. From anyone else he would possibly have expected it, but from her it came as a bit of a surprise. They should be able to get through this both being cool and adult about things, but as soon as he saw her and tried to talk to her, his voice came out with hints of high school crush that made him inwardly cringe.

"Hello, Miss Ward. You're looking lovely today." *Lovely? Who the hell said that?* Though she did, and it was honestly an understatement. She was gorgeous in the red dress Mitzi put her in for this date, but still, no need to get gushy.

"Thank you, Walker. And thanks for your text update today. Your office is very . . . thorough." Despite the summer heat, her voice could freeze vodka.

"It wasn't my office. I sent it myself."

The look she gave him was equally cool. "I gathered that." She then looked around, landing on Lou, and smiled. "I think I have to go. It looks as if my date for the evening has arrived. Let's hope he makes for better company than my last man."

The way she'd emphasized *last man* had him ready to all but snatch her back and demand to know her meaning. But of course he'd already gotten it, even if everyone else listening to the exchange was assuming she was talking about the gym rat from the other day. Good company his ass. As if he didn't just days ago give her a goddamned, heart-dropping orgasm — a few, as a matter of fact.

But what did it matter? Now he was stuck by the van, watching as she took long, sensual strides on the arm of a tall financier, the two of them silhouetted by the stunning architecture of the iconic opera house and the rushing water of the fountains. Aidan watched as Prescott leaned back, his own eyes taking in Eva's perfect curves. Aidan felt his hands twitch. The memory of her smooth skin, hot to his touch, was still fresh. Prescott grinned wide at something Eva said, and Aidan looked around, kicking himself for not having on a headset yet. Crap. He looked at Eva as she laughed and they made their way into the New York landmark. Aidan's eyes turned to Louisa, who was smiling — a rare sight while she was deep into her work. Hell, this couldn't be good. It couldn't be happening, could it? Week two, ten minutes in, and already Eva had found her Mr. Right? No way would he accept that.

Calm down, man. It would be hours before they were out of the opera; there was no need for him to go inside while filming was going on. He was getting all he needed from the team that was inside. Also, the crew was supposed to be sparse. He had set it up so just Lou and Stan were inside to capture any good moments for the segment if they should happen to come up. They had already gotten a couple of shots of the cast during a dress rehearsal. The two of them could handle the intermission banter fine. In all honestly, he could go home or back to the office for a bit. Show his face, clear off some of the papers piling on the corner of his desk and make his father happy. But who was he fooling? After seeing her with Prescott, there was no way he was going back to the office and getting his take of this date through secondhand footage. No, he'd see how things went with his own eyes and judge for himself if the guy could pull an emotion out of her like he could.

Hanging back in the van, Aidan tortured himself as he watched every moment, listened for every word along with the techs, Mitch and Dave. Eva was stunning as her face filled the bank of monitors. She elegantly sat in the chair Prescott pulled out for her in one of the opera house's side luxury boxes, as if this sort of thing was an everyday occurrence. From where the cameras were set up, her face glowed, as though it was lit by soft candlelight, with high and low depths from the illumination of the stage. Her eyes sparkled, and her cheeks held a beautiful rosy glow, giving her an ethereal quality. She seemed to shiver a bit, and he watched as her eyes slid left and the camera smoothly panned to Prescott's well-manicured hand; the overly perceptive ass had picked up on her discomfort and rubbed his paws over her bare shoulder and down her arm in what anyone could tell was a veiled attempt to get his hands on her.

Prescott leaned in, and Aidan heard his voice come through his headset. "Are you cold? Would you like my jacket?"

"Yes, thank you." Eva's voice was low and breathy. It was way too close a reminder of the breathy whispers and deep moans she have given him the other night. Stirrings of desire churned up in Aidan's belly, and he fought to calm them down.

Aidan turned to Mitch. "Are these levels good? I can hardly hear."

Mitch put down the gyro he'd picked up from the food truck outside with an annoyed sigh and looked at his control panels. "They're fine. And really, why are we so worried over every word here? It's not like this segment is going to run longer than three minutes." He shook his head, then shot Aidan a look before taking a pull of his soda that let him know he didn't like having his experience questioned, potential head honcho or not.

Aidan shrugged. He got it, and Mitch was probably right, but still he wanted good audio as he watched Prescott remove his jacket and place it around Eva's shoulders.

"Thank you," she said and gave him an easy smile, leaning back. The two watched the performance in silence, with barely any action until about forty-five minutes in when Prescott shifted. It was as if he'd had his move timed to go with the action on the stage, so that his little move happened as the music went to a full crescendo and the action on the stage became particularly dramatic. Sword fights, swooning sopranos, banging drums, and clashing symbols were all a backdrop for the casual Casanova to slide closer to Eva and slip his hand into hers at the right moment and bring her hand to his lips, kissing her fingertips. Lou made sure every movement was caught on camera and, yes, Mitch was right, the sound levels were perfect. Everything was on tape — from Prescott's maneuvering to Eva's surprised reaction as Prescott leaned in close to her ear. "It may be in Italian, but I think some things are universal."

Aidan couldn't help his eye roll and was thankfully bolstered when both Mitch and Dave burst out laughing. "Was that corny or what?" Mitch cackled out, wiping at the lettuce that threatened to escape his mouth and hit his precious console.

"It sure as hell is," Dave said. "But I've got to give it to him for going for it. It's no telling with women. Look, she seems to be eating it up."

Aidan's blood heated as he watched Eva smile warmly and nod Prescott's way. She really couldn't fall for a stupid line like that one, could she? He watched as she turned back to the stage but now leaned in a little closer to Prescott; meanwhile, the actors played out a bloody fight scene, signaling that the intermission would be starting soon. There was a boom, and then the sound of symbols that were so loud both techs winced, pulling away their headphones. Aidan remained transfixed and didn't even flinch. He watched, stoic, as the curtain went down and Eva slipped her hand from Prescott's, joining the others in a thunderous applause.

Oh hell. He really should just go. Why torture himself? Leave her to Prescott and the rest of the dates and go about his business. He had no real business being here anyway. This had nothing to do with his plans or his endgame. Still he stared at the screen, watching as the couple got up and the camera went in and out of focus, and for just a moment, he saw her let out a breath as she stretched her back as if she'd been holding it stiff for far too long. That tiny movement, when she didn't feel she had to be on, and her faced relaxed reminded him of their night and what she could be. Aidan stepped out of the van and headed toward the concert hall.

People crowded the atrium, everyone stunning and smiling and generally happy to see and be seen. Aidan wanted none of that. He scanned the intermission crowd, looking for his crew. He spotted Prescott over by the bar, gathering drinks, then he quickly shifted right and looked up to see Eva. Honing in as if trained on a signal from her red dress, he saw her going into the ladies' room. There was no sign of Lou or Stan, who had probably had enough small talk for their tiny segment and were now getting ready for the next setup, when Prescott would return with the drinks. For reality TV, things on this show were pretty well scripted out. But now Aidan, fueled on complete irrationality, headed up the grand stairs and waited for her.

What the hell was he doing? If anyone saw him there, that would be their first question, and though he was usually a quick thinker on his feet, he had no answer. He couldn't very well answer, "I'm waiting for the talent to come out, so I can just be close to her for a moment, get a rise out of her, and remind her of the mind-blowing sex we had the other night." All were true, but all were unacceptable answers. Aidan looked at his watch and ignored the odd look he got from a pinched-faced woman with dripping diamonds as she left the ladies' room. *No worries, ma'am, I'm not casing the place.* He hoped his nod to her said that, but based on the way she practically sprinted away, with her clutch held tightly to her chest, he didn't think it had worked. Where was Eva?

Finally, she walked out. She held her head down at first, but when she looked up, he couldn't deny the instant sexual charge he got as her eyes widened and then narrowed at the sight of him. He put his finger to his lips, stepped forward, and leaned in close to her delicate ear. "Don't talk," he whispered, "the mic will pick it up." She pulled back and glared. He could see her color rising and the fact that she was fighting to keep it in check, as throngs of people milled around them. He could tell she'd just realized that she'd forgotten to turn off the mic when she'd gone to the bathroom, and now the rest of the crew had heard her use the toilet.

Not that they cared or paid any real attention. When it was a crowd of this size, all murmuring at once, they weren't looking for those types of sounds. Aidan took in her features — her eyes on fire, nostrils flaring, ready to rant — and in that moment, it was all he wanted. He looked around and saw a side exit, grabbed her hand, and pulled her in.

The door closed behind them with a satisfying click. Aidan instantly went down on his knees in front of her, delighted by her sharp intake of breath. He reached up and lifted her dress up to her thighs. The delicious scent of her right in front of him had him wanting to close his eyes and bury his face into her. But no. He flipped her around quickly and reached to the back of her dress and switched off the mic before turning her back around and coming to his feet. Eva opened her mouth wide, about to let go, when he leaned in and kissed her, hard, pulling her into him and taking all he could in the seconds he had. He felt his chest expand as his dick hardened when, rigid at first, she finally relented and kissed him back, her lush body going soft against his. She opened her mouth, and once again he tasted that sweet honey, and he felt like he could happily feast on it forever. Finally, he pulled back and breathed in deep. The silence between them hung loud and long as they stared at each other. He moved in close to her once again, and this time she backed up, pressing in hard against the wall. Aidan remained still. He held up his hands and leaned in again, so close to her ear only she'd be able to hear, mic or no mic. He didn't want those outside to know they were there. "I want you. Please say you'll have me tonight."

He pulled back and looked at her.

Eva just stared as the quiet loomed between them and she gave him a look that simmered with both desire and rage. Then suddenly the lights flickered, even in the stairway, indicating intermission was over. Once, twice. Aidan turned her around again to go back to his knees to flip her mic on. "You know, there is an easier way to do that," she said. "My dress is pretty low in the back, and it has a zipper. You don't have to go down that way."

Aidan looked up at her. "Maybe I like it when you have me on my knees." He saw the hint of a smile as she shook her head, then pulled the dress down, but she didn't answer him. He came up as the lights flicked again, and she kissed him before whispering in his ear.

"I don't even like you like that, Aidan Walker."

Aidan closed his eyes briefly, then leaned in to nip at her ear and answer her back. "Oh yes, you sure as hell do."

She laughed and pulled out of his reach.

"That's what I'm afraid of," she replied before disappearing back into the venue's hallway.

Eva slipped back into their box after refreshing her lipstick and gave Quinton a brief apology.

"Are you okay?" He asked his eyes full of questions she had no intention of answering.

She pasted on a well-trained smile. "I'm fine. I needed an extra moment in the ladies' room away from the crowd. I've come down with a sudden headache, so I took a few aspirin. Nothing to worry about. I'll be fine."

She sat in her seat and looked forward, though somehow feeling the heat of a thousand eyes on the back of her neck. Once again, Quinton placed his jacket around her shoulders. She turned, giving him a nod of thanks. But still, she could feel another presence hot and insistent on her swollen lips, making breathing difficult and concentration almost impossible. She turned and looked at the camera; it was as if he were right there. Watching her every move. Honing in on her every emotion. She was a fool for having had that night with him. And a damn fool for thinking she could have it and then they could both just get over it like it was no big deal, while he watched her go on orchestrated dates with other men like their night had never happened. Eva's heart was racing with the thought of him on the other side of the camera, just out of her reach, picking up on everything she said and did.

Eva looked past the camera to Louisa, and she was hit with the woman's tight jaw and jutting chin. The narrowing of her eyes told Eva she didn't buy her excuses about a headache. Not at all. There was a reason she had this job. This woman was no dummy. But no matter. There was no way Eva would cower or lower her eyes and give herself away any further to any more of the crew. She looked at Louisa straight on and gave her a smile. She indicated the empty chair in the corner of the box. "Why don't you take a load off, Louisa? You have to be getting tired yourself."

"No need to worry about me. I can do tired when I'm dead." Louisa narrowed her eyes, turned, and grabbed a tissue. She reached out toward Eva's neck. As Eva pulled back, Lou leaned in close so only she could hear her. "I'm fixing your makeup. You seem to have smudged lipstick onto your neck . . . somehow."

Eva felt the heat climb up her neck; she hoped it didn't show in her face. As calmly as she could, she snatched the tissue from Louisa's hand and wiped at the side of her neck. For the briefest of moments she let her eyes drift back to the camera and gave it a glare before turning to face forward toward the stage once again.

She hoped he was watching. Something in her told her that of course he was.

Damned Aidan. As if her life wasn't complicated enough, he had to go and complicate it further.

More and more, she regretted the day she had stepped into WBC's studios. Or at least that was the line she was telling herself.

CHAPTER 14

Aidan should have regretted going after Eva, but for the life of him — and after that kiss — he couldn't drum up enough reasons on the regret side of the board to get behind that particular emotion.

The feelings were too strong, the taste of her way too good, so much so that he knew he'd do what he had to do to steal what moments he could for however long he had.

And yeah, sure, she'd given him her directives about it being a thing for that one night and all that, but if her response to him in the stairway was any indication of her feelings, there was definitely room for negotiation in that area of their verbal agreement. He may have been temporarily thrown by her initial declaration and followed her advice, staying away from her as she'd directed, but that was only because his head was a little fuzzy after their amazing night together. Thus he had made the

251

mistake of blindly following her lead.

But that time was past.

He was never one to blindly follow anyone's lead, and now he felt the fool for listening to her and talking himself into believing she was right about it being the best for both of them. All that chatter went out the window when he looked at her face-to-face. And to think he'd wasted four perfectly good nights, tossing and turning, with nothing but memories of her, when he could have been between her delicious thighs making memories.

Aidan grinned, pleased with his decision and logic and the fact that all it took was a kiss and the spark was there again. The veil had lifted. Little Miss Ice Princess couldn't fool him. Hell, she could barely fool herself. She had a tell, and it was written all over her face in every hot, angry look she shot his way.

I don't even like you like that.

Those words, though, caused Aidan to pause in his walk back to the van. She said she didn't like him, and yet she yielded to him and kissed him with a passion like none he'd ever experienced. Aidan licked his lips. She didn't like him? Most of the time she probably wanted to throttle him, and the rest of the time he was sure she wanted to have sex with him. So what was it now? Was what she was feeling closer to pain or pleasure? She might call it something closer to pain, but that pain was passion, and he knew it. Aidan shook his head and ran a frustrated hand through his hair as he made his way back to the van, rare niggles of doubt gnawing at him that he desperately wanted to sweep away. Dammit, if he wasn't right about her feelings, then he was the pompous jerk she'd pegged him to be.

Aidan made it back to the van and looked at the monitors, seeing her wipe the corners of her mouth, then hit him once again with one of those scorn-filled glares. It was a perfect shot right to the center of his gut.

He grinned.

"Damn!" Dave said. "Did you get a look at that? Talk about looks killing. What the hell's gotten into her now? No wonder the other dude bailed. Can you blame him? She may be gorgeous, but, hell, a look like that could freeze a man's dick off."

Aidan should cut the guys off. Their talk was unprofessional, bordering on inappropriate, but who was he to talk in that moment when he couldn't quite keep a straight face? All he wanted to do was smile, and he was having trouble keeping down a roaring erection. He stared at the screen.

That look was everything he never knew he wanted — heat, passion, a warning, and an invitation all rolled into one. It said so much without saying a thing. In her dark, fire-filled gaze he saw himself and knew he was caught. He also knew that somehow he'd find his way back to her, back into her arms and into her bed, before the night was over.

Aidan's brows drew together as he watched Prescott once again smoothly sidle up to Eva, easing his hands into hers. The camera zoomed in as if they really needed yet another close-up for their short segment. Aidan's chest felt tight as he barked into the control panel's intercom so his voice would be heard over the crew's headsets. "I think we have enough," he growled out. "We can make sure the next location is ready. Tell the talent we're cutting this short."

"Huh? What do you mean cutting it short?" Lou's voice came out as a loud, sharp rap over his headset.

"I think we've gotten all we need here. No need to stay for the finale and hang on their every word. The segment is short. Why draw this out? We can head to the next location and have the car bring them along."

He was met with silence, and in that silence, Aidan could feel Lou's questioning reproach.

Finally she spoke up. "Come on, Aidan. You know it's best to have more footage than less. We're in the third hour here. With her social media numbers, the viewers will clamor for more — web extras and all that. They sure as hell won't be tuning in for yet another mommy makeover. Besides, you never know what may transpire without us watching. And the laws of reality TV say that if something will happen, it will probably be when we're not watching, so we have to keep watching all the time. Besides, she's got a nice chemistry going with this guy. The viewers will love him."

That comment drew him up short. Of course the viewers would, but did she really have chemistry with him? Aidan stared at the monitor. With Eva it was hard to tell. And Lou was right, something could happen when they weren't looking, but as tense as he was, he wasn't in the mood to watch.

He ran his hand through his hair again. Dammit, he seriously needed to get some perspective on this thing. It was bound to bite him in the ass in the long run if he didn't play it right. He looked at the screen again, watched as Eva leaned ever so slightly toward Prescott, not a lot but enough to show she was interested and not being off-putting. It was just enough to give him the go-ahead signal, so he now extracted his hand from hers and let it smoothly trail up to slip around her shoulder.

"Fine. We'll split the crew. You don't need all of us, and you can handle things here without me. I'm going to check in with Mitch here at the restaurant," he said, speaking of the first grip. Still, there was a bit of a long-drawn-out silence, and he was about to take off his headset and leave when Lou's voice came back over.

"Okay. I'll see you there."

"Great. I'll make sure everything is at the ready." He tried to bring a bit more easiness to his voice. This wasn't that deep. It's not like he was in a war zone or out on a jungle trek. This was an easy piece, but though it was light, it was important to Louisa and the rest of the crew. He couldn't let his personal shit get in the way of her or anyone else's job. "And thanks for being on top of things," he said by way of a sign-off before removing his earphones and getting some much-needed distance between him and Eva.

Well, distance for now. As for later, he made no promises.

After the opera finished, Eva could barely make it through the dinner with Prescott she was so preoccupied with Aidan's surprise, out-of-the blue, sneak attack.

The man was incorrigible, and she now knew she needed to find some way to deal with the problem that was Aidan Walker once and for good. During her dinner with Prescott, Aidan had played his laid-back observation game and hadn't said a word to her directly. She was starting to get his deal and understand his style of working, at least in mixed company, and at least with her. It was brood from a distance, while giving all his directives to Louisa or to one of the other crew members on staff. He spent an inordinate amount of time talking into his headset or looking at the monitor and had barely spared her a glance. It was ridiculous, and it was driving her mad, which she thought might be his ultimate objective. Well, it wouldn't work. His clear and obvious avoidance of her, though it made it that much harder for her to concentrate on the work at hand, made her that much more determined to put all she had into doing a good job and putting on a hell of a show. This ordeal for the cameras would not be in vain — not if she could help it. She'd come out on top and have her reputation and her life back. Her name as well as the Ward name and company would stand for come-backs.

Over a light meal of after-opera tapas and drinks in what she was sure would have normally been a romantic eatery, given the right circumstance and company, she and Prescott played their parts well. Though sadly, now that they were one on one — minus the crew — he was doing the ultimate date dull-down trick of going on about his net worth, how most women were concerned with his bank account, and what he could do for them if they wanted to reciprocate in kind. Whatever the hell that meant, and honestly Eva wasn't sure she had the energy or the interest to even unpack what she was afraid it meant.

She was trying her hardest not to go there, but with all his talk about money and figures, she was getting the distinct feeling he considered a night out a down payment for sex. She fought not to fidget in her seat and really focus on what he was saying. Thankfully, he shifted gears and now asked her about what she did.

"My job is really not all that exciting. Mostly looking for ways to make popular people even more popular. Or putting out fires in the media made by those popular people or some unthinking company big-wig."

Prescott flashed a smile that, upon critical study, Eva could honestly say was charming. She leaned in a bit closer, hoping to feel a connection and at least get a fizzle of a spark that would tell her he could be the one that she could at least come to an arrangement with, if not a full-on romantic connection. He really was a nice guy, nice enough if she gave the "reciprocate" comment a pass. It was kind of amazing that he was still single. "So putting out fires. Is that what you're doing here now on this date?"

She pulled back and gave him a teasing look. "Are you implying there's some sort of spark?"

He shook his head, took a long pull from his drink as he adjusted his tie and gave her a deep gaze, then leaned back and licked his lips as if he were imaging how she would taste. Eva felt her lips tighten in response. She bet that look probably worked on lots of women. "Honestly, up until this moment not so much. But now you have me intrigued. It was that hint of fire during your on-air tirade that got me to apply for the show. Though I will say you weren't at your best. But it's okay. I like a little fire in my women." Eva's brows went up as Prescott leaned in close to her ear. "Always that much more fun when I break them."

And bingo. The reason he was still single was revealed.

Eva wrenched back in her chair, crossed her legs and arms, and gave him a hard stare as she tilted her head. *What the ever-loving hell?* And then, as if by some invisible force, she looked past him to the camera that was set up in the back corner of the restaurant before bringing her gaze back to Prescott. "Women, you say? Isn't that interesting? Well, I'm glad you have more than one who will go along with your foolishness. Because this one is not a horse or any other such animal that needs to be tamed or, God forbid, *broken.* That sounds quite," she tilted her head before taking a sip of her cocktail, "harsh."

Prescott's brows drew together in a somehow not all that surprising flash of anger as he shifted in his seat. But he took another long swig from his drink and then looked back at her with a slightly calculated smile. "Hey, I was only kidding around. Just joking, you know? No need to get your panties in a bunch because you bring out the beast in a man. Besides, one woman's broken is another's blessed."

Eva coughed, the drink going down the

wrong way. She looked over at Prescott, staring with a way too smug and confidant expression for a man who had just delivered such a line. Eva laughed. "Did you practice that?"

His brows drew together again. "What are you talking about?"

"Because I can't believe that crap rolled off your tongue, and you really say such things to a woman on the first date?" She looked around, taking in the lighting and the crew, catching a glimpse of Aidan in the shadows. He probably got a real kick out of this. She shook her head. "And on camera, no less."

"Maybe you're being uptight. Have you ever stopped to think you might need to loosen up a bit? There are things I see in you, hidden depths that I know I could bring out in you." His comment, though made off the cuff, suggested too many shades of Kevin wannabe and hit Eva where she was already hurting.

She nodded and stood. "Thanks for a mostly lovely evening. Good thing it's on the station and you won't need to worry about how bunched my panties happen to be, and I won't have to worry about owing you any reciprocation for the bill. And for the record, I'm fine just as I am and definitely don't need a man like you to bring out any hidden depths. And side note, just because there was a popular book that eluded shades of bondage, not every woman fantasizes about being broken. It's called fiction for a reason. I'd suggest getting a new line. Good night."

Eva felt a storm raging in her brain as she fought to hold onto what little control she had left. The nerve of that ass! How many men would unjustly and, mind you, unrightfully accuse her of being uptight and then have the gall to act like they had some duty to turn her out sexually. As if!

She was just making her way toward the coat check area when Aidan caught up with her.

"Are you all right?"

She sucked in a deep breath, then let it out slowly.

And here comes another one. Another man who thought he knew her so fucking well but only knew what she let him see. Why couldn't he lay back and leave her alone? She didn't need him catching her in yet another emotional moment, storming off. "I'm fine. As if you really care. Sorry to disappoint you, but you're not catching me in another meltdown. I've got it perfectly together."

"Of course you do," he started. "And I'm not here to catch you in another meltdown. As I told you already, you can trust me."

She raised a brow. "Really? And we saw earlier at the opera house how good you are with keeping your word."

Aidan's brows drew together as he pulled her in with a long stare. His gaze moved from her eyes to her lips, causing her to unconsciously swallow and lick them to quell the sudden dryness.

He laughed, which pulled her up short and made her want to smack the smug look off his face. "As if you are always one hundred percent truthful. Don't try and play me, Miss Ward. Now, how about we go ahead and film your confessional now." He looked down toward her hip. "Seeing that you're all mic'ed, and it's been a long day."

The reminder of the mic and the fact that she'd just hinted at their time in the stairwell wasn't lost on her. She let out a long breath as his gaze went back to hers. This time it was filled with so much heat she felt she would ignite right there in the restaurant's vestibule. "That way we can get you in a car and home in bed, sooner rather than later."

Eva's brows went up at his mention of her bed and the challenge in his stare. Just as she thought, here was another man thinking he could somehow change her life with the magic of what he had between his legs. Unfortunately, though, the heat of his gaze had her nipples hardening, and she wanted desperately to jump him then and there. She frowned and shook her head. "Point me to the camera. The quicker I get this over with, the quicker I can get home."

CHAPTER 15

Eva briefly looked down and adjusted the drawstring on her sweatpants, then pulled down her tank top before opening her apartment door.

"You weren't seen, were you?" she said, blurting out the first words that came to her mind when she saw Aidan in the hallway. Well, to the credit of her impeccable filter, they weren't the very first words, because if that were true she would have opened the door and said something like, "Get in here and take me now, you sexual beast." So her query about not being seen was a lot more in line with her mother's fine upbringing. Score one for her filter!

Aidan raised that brow she was coming to both love and hate and shook his head. "Only by your night doorman. It would seem the paparazzi aspect of your story has moved onto the teen queen cutting it up and showing out at every club in

265

town lately."

"Thank goodness for that," Eva said. "If she was my client, I'd have her sit her ass down for a minute or at least learn the power of panties if she insists on taking an upside-down tumble every night. But she's not, so it's no problem of mine. Still, why did you go past the doorman? I distinctly told you to go around the back. I gave you the code."

"You are a bossy one, aren't you?" he said, his eyes going toward the ceiling. "And here I thought you were good at your job. Don't you think I'd be calling more attention to myself when I came up on the doorman's security monitors? A guy who doesn't live in the building, skulking around and coming through the back entrance? Relax, it's all cool. I chatted him up a bit. He saw me earlier and the night before. I told him I had more business to attend to with you. We're now old friends. Oh, and he and his wife are getting tickets to a studio taping of *Price Busters*."

Eva felt her lips tighten. Dammit. She hated that he was right. Again. She should have thought about the surveillance cameras at the back entrance, but she was used to fielding situations for others, not for herself. And she definitely wasn't used to setting up her own clandestine, late-night trysts. It had her thinking out of her own head.

"So, are you going to let me in so that we can conclude our business, Miss Ward, or shall we talk out here so that your entire floor can be in on it? Again."

She felt her face flame but covered it by stepping back and shaking her head as she let Aidan enter the apartment.

Eva closed her door and leaned her forehead against it for a moment as the resounding click of the latch went through her. She pushed back off and collided with his hard body. Jumping, she turned around. "What are you doing?"

"I'm standing here. Are you all right?" Eva nodded.

"Now, princess, do you care to voice why you texted me, or should we just skip ahead and take this where it's inevitably going to end?"

Eva felt her face flame as she pushed past him and headed to the kitchen. She knew that text had been a bad idea, but still she couldn't stop her thumbs from tapping away across her keyboard. Now here he was, throwing it back up in her face, talking about where they'd inevitably end up. She leaned against her kitchen counter when suddenly the memory of what they had

267

done together on that counter came back to her in a rush. Eva pushed away from it as if burned, wandering over to hang by the living room window instead. "You really are a jerk. I did text you to come here. But to talk." She crossed her arms tightly over her chest. "Now, what the hell was with that kiss today? I thought I'd made myself perfectly clear the other night."

Aidan swiped his hand through his hair as all the playfulness left his gaze and he let out a frustrated breath. "You know, you're a piece of work. You could have called me to chew me out, but you're clearly not ready to be honest with yourself or with me. You know as well as I do that there is something going on here, but you're not ready to face it, and you're using me and this continuing argument as an excuse."

He shrugged as if he was done with the conversation and done with her, and in that rising of his shoulders, Eva felt her anger rise too. Her eyes narrowed at she opened her mouth, ready to fight back, but he stopped her with his chuckle. "Like I said, a total piece of work. You like the fact that I piss you off and get you all riled up. I'm clearly your sexual venting post, and hey, if that's what turns you on, princess, then it's fine by me. I get it. I saw what you were used to dealing with, so I don't blame you. Mr. Pocket Square looked like a total bore. He couldn't get a woman like you to break a sweat if he tried."

Eva opened her mouth once again but couldn't come up with anything quick enough. Shit. He was right. Sex with Kevin had gotten dull, as had most things with Kevin — dinners, conversation, life.

Aidan continued, though this time there was no joking, no laughter, and no ire. Just a dead-serious calm that rooted Eva where she was. "We're both adults, and like you said, we both have jobs to do. Either we have fun while we're doing it and both get something out of the deal, or I say goodbye and walk out the door, and come back tomorrow to do my job. Just my job. Not that I'll be happy with the latter. I think it would be a lot more exciting to play while we work, but still, we'll both get something out of things if we walk away from option two." Eva saw the hardening of his jaw and his resolve as he said his next words. "And you don't have to worry. Whatever your decision is won't change how I work with you or how you're portrayed on the show. I made a promise to you to treat you fairly, and I intend to keep it as you hunt for your perfect man. But you need to know I do want you. I am attracted to you, but I'm not in the mood to play these back-and-forth games with you. It's too tiring, and honestly we both only have a limited amount of time to make up our minds — well, your mind, in this case. It's all up to you right now, but just know that after tonight, depending on your decision, I'll no longer be available to play your games. Tomorrow is a workday for both of us."

Eva stood stock-still, because she didn't know what to say. The last thing she expected was for him to come in here, turn the tables, and be angrier than she was. Who the hell did he think he was? And, worse, why in the hell did he have to be so right? When she sent the text, she didn't think of it as playing any type of game, but honestly she didn't look at it from any point of view but her own. And from her view it was him and all others of his sex whom she was fed up with, while at the same time she was frustrated to no end because she knew part of her still wanted to be with him. There was something about him that was stirring up feelings she didn't even know she had, but only read about or heard about from, in her mind, overly emotional or hormonal women who, frankly, she frowned upon for not being able to keep themselves in check.

Eva looked at Aidan now as he stood at the far end of the living room, totally out of her reach but staring at her, his scorching look hot enough to practically burn her from clear across the room. Still, she tried hard to stand firmly where she was. She didn't want to move to him. He'd given her the out she needed — spelled it out and made it plain and clear that the relationship between the two of them was purely sexual to him, and was one that would last for as long as the show did and would end when she found her groom.

So what was the problem? She'd called him. He came. They could have sex, and tomorrow they could continue on as they had been. Eva reached for the couch, readying herself to take a step forward, when she stopped, aware of the hard thump, thump, thump of her racing heart. Oh, there was a problem all right, and it wasn't in the man across the room but within her. Could she really go through with this and have the type of affair that seemed to roll so easily from his lips? Her head, her raging hormones, and, somewhere on a luxury yacht, her BFF were all screaming, "Hell, yeah!" she could. But her stupid heart was telling her something entirely different. Her stupid heart was telling her to take a step back and not forward. To run the other way and not look back. It was telling her that if she took that step, her heart would end up in pieces, possibly never to be repaired. If she took that step, he had a real chance of being the one to turn her inside out, take her to heaven and back, but in the end, leave her to live with the hell of knowing he never was hers. He could possibly be the one to emotionally devastate her, as the rest of the world thought Kevin had done. He could be the one to leave her the bitter woman she was running, so far and so fast, from becoming.

She looked at him, those dark eyes taking her back to one of the most glorious, most freeing nights of her life. Her stomach did a little flip, as butterflies of excitement began to flap their wings, and her hand involuntarily went to her belly as she fought to hold them down. Maybe it was meant to be just that one night. Some people don't even get that in a lifetime. It was best if she didn't take that step, best if they turned and went their separate ways.

Eva lowered her gaze at the same time as something inside her began to close up and fold over on itself. She watched as Aidan's boots shifted. She was sure he was turning toward the door, but her breath hitched as he took a tentative movement toward her.

That one small movement was all she needed for her heart to race again as she followed his lead and ran into his waiting embrace. She crashed into him with an "oomph" and wrapped her legs around his waist as he pulled her to his lips.

"You had me nervous for a while there," he said.

"So did you. I thought you were leaving."

"I thought you wanted me to leave."

She pulled back and looked him in the eye. "The night is still young, and we've got at least seven hours until morning."

Aidan raised that brow, and her nipples responded in kind. "Well, then, I suggest we put them to good use. I'd like to reserve at least six for myself and one for my beauty sleep." He started to carry her toward her bedroom.

Eva bit down and nipped at his ear.

"Ouch! You don't want me to go to work with a bruise tomorrow, now do you?"

"Oh, you'll be fine. You can say one of your many women gave it to you."

Aidan stopped in the hallway and looked her in the eye, his voice doing that low, serious thing. "Not this. When it's you and me during this time, it's just you and me. No one else. I'm not like that. Cool?"

The possessive way he was holding her up

— with his hands gripping firmly around each of her cheeks and looking at her as though he was somehow making this temporary thing feel like forever — had Eva ready to melt into a puddle of yes in his arms. "Cool."

He smiled then, a smile that was both warm and ridiculously sexy as he squeezed her in close to his hardness. "Fantastic. Now let's get going, princess. The clock is ticking, and it's not like you texted me for nothing. I believe I have work to do."

Why didn't he ever listen to his own advice?

Aidan knew he was lost as soon as he walked into her apartment — hell, as soon as she sent him the text, and he answered, and he freaking knew it was wrong. Wrong for his head, and especially wrong for his heart. Eva would surely chew him up, and instead of spitting him out, he set himself up to be swallowed, devoured, and then unceremoniously eliminated when the next better prospect came along. And stupid fuck that he was, he'd be the dumb ass delivering the next better prospect. What. The. Hell?

"But come on. Get your shit together," he silently told himself as he stood there like a schoolboy waiting to hear if the most popular girl in the class would say yes to him about going to prom. He really should be happy about this. In all honestly, it was the perfect arrangement. Hey, on paper it would probably sound like a great deal to any other guy, but something poked at him. It was as if he'd seen the end before the show even began.

The worst part was that he was directing it. And that part he could see no way out of, no matter her answer to his question after her declarations. If he was smart, he'd turn and leave, admit that he was wrong and she was right, count his losses, and go. Maybe even give up the job altogether. There were other execs, and really he could pass it all off into Louisa's capable hands, making both her and his father very happy.

But he knew that he wouldn't do it. That he couldn't do it. There was no way he'd break that promise to her and not see it through, and shit, if truth be told, there was no way he was giving up being near her during this time.

He looked at her standing there, beautiful and defiant, still determined even in her obvious state of confusion, and he knew then he couldn't leave her side. At least not yet. He would see this job done and leave only . . . Aidan paused, stilling his thoughts.

He'd leave only when her heart really convinced him the time was right.

Aidan stared at her. She knew she was good-looking, that was a given, but he bet she didn't know what it did to him to see her as she was now — stripped of her perfect social mask, fresh-faced from the shower, with her hair pulled back and wearing a tank top and those loose sweats, which he was sure were designed to, in some way, be off-putting but did just the opposite and turned him on all the more. Part of him said he should have just taken the easy way out. When he got to her door, he was all ready to do it. But one look at her and that plan went out the window as the events of the day came flooding back and she tried to come at him, lumping him in with every other asshole she'd been with or been around. Sure, he was no prize, but he'd be damned if he'd be categorized as just another chapter in her book of jerks. No way. He'd stand out or get no pages at all.

Looking at her now, he wondered why it was so important to him to stand out. What was it about her that had him speaking without caution and going totally against his nature to an end result where he knew neither one of them would be a winner? The thought of the question with no answer left him feeling lost and paralyzed with an uncertainty that he couldn't quite stomach. One thing he did know was that he'd had enough with sparring for one day. Right now, he wanted to know once and for all where she was comfortable with letting this go and for how long.

Their few days apart had been far long enough for him, and at that moment, all he wanted was to get her back in his arms, taste her sweetness again, and know she was his, for the moment at least. He watched as her chest rose and fell, as her breathing slowed and her shoulders slumped with something that looked like despair. In that moment she pulled at him as if with some invisible tether, but in her pride she looked away, closing herself off and shielding herself against the weight of his stare. Her face took on a placid quality, letting him know she was just as exhausted as he was with the whole situation. When she looked at him, her eyes were glassy, and she blinked as if she was actively trying to hold back an emotional dam that could break at any moment.

Aidan let out a breath and took a half step back before rushing forward, thankful that she was meeting him halfway and covering her mouth with his own. What was he doing

277

to her? To himself? He blocked the questions out and focused on her. The delicious honey taste of her, the amazing perfect fit as she jumped up and into his arms, her soft behind feeling like home in his hands.

Eva pulled back and looked into his eyes, the wet tips of her lashes making his heart literally ache. "Tell me we can do this. Tell me it will be okay and we're not making a huge mistake," she asked. There was no hint of the angry and defiant woman from the opera and nothing of the seductress from the other night. Here was simply a woman looking to him for assurance that he could somehow work everything out as she wanted it to be. He'd never before had so much responsibility, and for a moment something like real fear gripped at him as he stilled.

"We can do this, and I promise this can be whatever you want it to be. I'm here at your will. I won't do you wrong. You can trust me." His heart raced, and he hoped like hell he wasn't screwing her over with words that were foreign to his lips.

She smiled weakly at his promise, something about it letting him know she believed him about as much as he believed himself.

"I bet you say that to all the girls."

He let out a small laugh. "You'd be surprised at how few, princess." Eva raised a brow, and he could see her wheels turning. "Okay, now, don't you start calculating in your head. You have a bad habit of doing that."

"I like to know I have things in order."

Aidan pulled her in close, cupping her lovely ass and grinding her center against his growing erection. God, he wanted — no, needed — to be inside her, and soon. "Baby, nothing about us is in order."

She gave him a hard stare and then licked her lips. Everything south of his belt jumped in response. Suddenly, he wanted so badly to taste where she just licked. "I think that's why I like it."

Unable to resist, he leaned down and kissed her. "I know that's why you do. And it's cool. I can handle it. Like I said, I'm here for you. For whatever."

Her gaze shifted as she looked away. Aidan could suddenly feel her hesitancy, her need to pull away, and the thought threatened to send him into a panic. Now that he had her, he didn't want to let her go. He reached to her chin and gently forced her to look up as she began to speak again. "Are you sure this is good for both of us? I'm going through with this show, and, Aidan, this has to be just what it is: the two of us having fun. I don't want you to worry."

Aidan felt his eyes narrow as he leaned back, giving her a hairsbreadth of space. The investigative reporter in him suddenly had questions, lots of questions. But the man in him told him not to go digging for the answers he wasn't prepared to hear. He had his own agenda anyway. "Like I said, I will do and be whatever you want me to be. No one has to know about our arrangement. We can do what we want for the next seven weeks, and when the show is over, so will we be too. No attachments, no responsibility. Will that make you happy?" He'd be damned, but saying the words set a rock in the pit of his stomach.

He watched for a reaction from her, a hesitation, a flinch, anything. But he got none.

All she did was lean up and kiss him. Soft and sweet, easing him in by twining her tongue with his in a sensuous dance, twining and stroking against his, a sexual precursor of what was to come. When she finally pulled back, meeting his heavy gaze with a sexy smile, she shocked him by cleverly leaning back and pulling her tank top up and over her head, then letting it ease from her fingers to the floor. "Well, then, I think we'd better get started. Seven weeks will go by pretty fast and seven hours even faster."

CHAPTER 16

A shaft of sunlight hit Eva's face, and she winced, turning away from it and then stretching her foot out. When her toe hit a hairy leg on the other side of the bed, her eyes popped open wide to a smiling and possibly way too smug Aidan Walker. Well, this was different from the morning greetings she'd gotten used to with Kevin and way different from her close-to-normal days of waking up alone. But instead of enjoying the moment, Eva couldn't push away the feeling of panic that invaded her senses.

"What the hell are you still doing here?"

"I'm watching you sleep."

"Well, what are you doing that for?" she shrieked as she flipped over and looked at the clock, her heartbeat racing at the sight of the display showing 7:15. "Have you gone mad? Why didn't you get out of here last night, or at least earlier this morning? Jeez, Aidan, do I have to type up a set of rules

281

for you and attach it in an email? What if one of the crew comes early or something? What if you're seen leaving my house by a photographer? There are so many things that could go wrong here, and the situation I'm trying to diffuse could blow up in my face. It's not like you're actually low profile yourself."

"No, it's not like I'm not, but the crew is not due here until ten, so we should be fine. I'm the only early riser, and besides, you wore me out. Can't you give me a break over the fact that I practically passed out when you were done with me last night?"

Eva turned, a look of disbelief on her face, while a small smile threatened at the corner of her lips. "I really made you that tired?"

He kissed the tip of her nose. "Oh, stop fishing for compliments. You already know you did. Now who's being full of herself?"

Eva grinned wide and did a mocking gesture of brushing her shoulders off.

Aidan laughed and kissed at her bare shoulders, going lower and licking at the ticklish spots on her side. She kicked at him and couldn't hold back her laughter, sobering up quickly when it hit her that it had been a long time since she'd let go and laughed with a man, let alone laughed with one while naked in bed.

The thought gave her pause, and she grabbed the sheet and attempted to wrap it around herself and shimmy out of the bed.

"Hey, relax. We still have time. This is fun. Work will be all day. Let's stay here and play a little more." Aidan pulled on the sheet and drew her back down on the bed and into his arms. He tucked her into him as she was spooned, her back to his front, as he whispered low in her ear, the sexy, growly sensation setting her into a shiver she tried hard to steel herself against. Shivering was for the night, and today was a new day.

"Oh come on, kitten, don't go baring your claws just yet. I know it's morning, but the day hasn't quite started. Is this really how you are without any coffee in you?"

She gave him an elbow to the gut, and he laughed. "This is totally how I am without coffee. Get used to it." Shit. Did she really just say that? Eva's heart started to race as panic hit her once again.

"Good to know," Aidan said pulling her in tight. "I guess I'd better get right on it." But instead of heading to the kitchen, Aidan leaned down and kissed her shoulder, slowly tugging at the sheet, easing it down as he kissed further down her spine, adding small licks as he went until he got to the top of her behind, where he flipped her over and started the same deal on her belly and breasts. Eva had never felt so exposed, with the harsh light of day blazing on her, but still she was enjoying the moment. She focused on him and how he was taking his time worshipping every inch of her as if she was something to be adored. What did it matter that he was still there and they were playing a dangerous game of beat the clock? She was going to relax if it killed her and enjoy herself for once at seven AM on a workday. Well, a date day, but what did that matter?

Suddenly he stopped and his head popped up, abruptly releasing the nipple he'd been so gloriously teasing. "What happened?" she asked.

"Princess, you have got to stop thinking so hard. I can practically hear your wheels turning. Now, please relax." He leaned down and extended his rather amazing tongue and swirled it in the most tantalizing circle around her nipple. "If you just lean into it with me, this won't take too long at all."

She couldn't help but laugh then. "Lean in? Really, you're going with that?"

His head popped up again, and she saw the playfulness in his eyes. "I'm going with that. It's your bed. You call the shots. Now, lean in and tell me what to do, boss lady."

She shook her head as Aidan went back to work. What was she going to do with him? They'd broken all the rules by going on and now had to totally rewrite the rule book. She turned and looked at the clock. Shit, they really didn't have much time. "Aidan, please. You've got to go soon. We've got my third date today, and I've got to get ready for it, plus the crew will be here soon. You don't want to get caught."

He stilled mid-lick and looked up at her. "Okay, fine. But only if you join me in the shower."

Eva tilted her head, looking down at him. "And how will joining you in the shower speed up anything?"

Aidan grinned as he leaned back, showing off his wide chest, amazing abs, and what was now a rock-hard erection. "It probably won't, but I don't think I'll be able to work today if you don't join me."

Eva let out a long breath. He was incorrigible. Completely and totally infuriating. He drove her mad and got on her very last nerve. She then looked into his eyes and caught the wicked flash. He was also the very best time she'd ever had in her life. "Okay, but you'd better not get my hair wet, or I'm cutting you off." He pulled her up and against him. "Well, at least cutting you off for the rest of the week."

He pulled her in and kissed her hard. "Trust me, kitten, I promise to get everything in that shower wet except your hair."

Eva had never felt more ridiculous in her life. She sat in a dirty boat in the middle of Central Park, trying to look like she belonged there while wearing a silly straw hat with an organza flower on top of it no less. Her dress today was a flowy one in a tiny floral print more suited for an English garden summer wedding and definitely more suited for some petite English rose of a girl and not a grown New York woman like her. She didn't know if it was the flower that set her nerves on end or the floral print dress. It didn't matter; either way, she knew she must rein them in or risk it all showing on camera.

Besides, it was a beautiful day. She had that. And the night would come soon enough. She now had that too. Her mouth quirked up into a smile as she thought once again of her morning excursion with Aidan. Maybe the hat wasn't so bad after all. At least at the right angle it could hopefully shield the blush she was sure was rising on her cheeks. She had to get it together, get her mind off Aidan and on the date in front of her. But damn if it wasn't hard. Aidan had indeed kept his promise and her hair hadn't gotten wet in the shower, but the prolonged time she had spent up against the steamy shower walls with Aidan behind her did little for its previously smooth appearance. The network's hairdresser was in a right tizzy when she arrived at her apartment along with the makeup artist, not twenty minutes after Aidan finally departed and she got a look at how frizzy her hair had become overnight.

"You're looking like you're finally enjoying yourself. One would think you were meant to be on the water."

The voice brought Eva's wandering mind forward, and she once again focused on today's date. Walter van Wetherton III gave her a Cheshire cat grin as he rowed her around in his Bermuda shorts and blue, crested coat. As Eva looked at him, she sincerely hoped it was Mitzi's wacky hand that had gotten to him too and he didn't consider his outfit everyday attire. But sadly, something about him had her suspecting it was his style, and that brought her down. Tall, dark, and indeed handsome, he was the kind of man her mother would surely approve of. But his attire and affected way of talking had her instantly knowing she and he would not be a match.

It was kind of a bummer, though. He was from a well-established African-American family and pretty well known in society. Old money, as far as old money went in the black community. And in the span of their already short, cute meet and greet at the park's carousel, where she took a reluctant and embarrassing ride for the cameras, he gave her the rundown of his complete résumé. He had gone to Yale and from there to Oxford. Was a lawyer and also on the board of his parents' company. He summered on the Vineyard, where they had a home, though at times, he'd slum it and rent with friends in the Hamptons. Which was said as if he were doing the Long Islanders a favor or something. He was also on the board of several city conservation projects that bore his family's name. Oh, and he was an avid skier. As if.

His comment about her change in expression took Eva completely off guard. He was right — she was out of it and, yes, rudely thinking of hot sex in the shower and could give a flip about skiing in the Catskills — but at that point, she had completely tuned him out, expecting not to have to contribute anything to today's conversation and, after the boat ride, to be able to strip off the hat with the offending organza flower and get the hell out of there.

She cleared her throat and looked around. "I will admit it is beautiful out here. The view of the city from this angle is breathtaking. I've walked by here so many times but never thought of what it must look like from this angle." Eva looked around and took in the tourists gawking at her from the other boats, as well as the other people watching from the edge of the little pond. The film crew, with their two cameras and long-range lenses trained to capture every word, were on the edges of the pond as well, with all lenses pointed in her direction. She could bet Aidan was having a good laugh at her expense. He couldn't hide his mirth when he saw how Mitzi had her done up. And when he had gotten a look at Walter this morning, the edges of his mouth quirked up and wiggled so much Eva almost went over and gave him a swift kick. She would have punched him in the arm if she didn't think he would have gotten a good laugh out of it. Part of her wanted to laugh too, but there was no way she'd give him the satisfaction. She told herself she'd keep it professional when the sun was up, and that's just what she intended to do. No matter how boorish or silly the date, or how sexy and provoking Aidan was, it mattered not. She still had her mission, and she was determined to see it through.

Then, as if by some cosmic reminder, the cell phone in her purse rang, and she practically jumped out of her skin at the surprising intrusion, sure she had put it on silent since they were filming. She quickly looked toward the shore, breaking character (which felt odd since she was the character she was breaking) and caught the disapproving glare of Louisa and the head shake of Stan as he put his finger to his ear. Aidan stood with his legs wide, muscular arms folded, and shook his head. "Sorry," she yelled as the phone squealed again. She looked at Walter as she reached into her purse and caught his raised brow. The better part of her wanted to tell him not to get his ascot in a bunch, but instead she swiped at her phone. "Mother, I can't talk. I'm filming."

"Hello, dear. I wanted to see how it's going. I won't keep you. Just checking on today's date. What did you say his name was?" It was as if her mother didn't even hear her as she went off onto her own ramblings.

"I didn't, and I will have to call you back." There was a long pause. "Please do. And remember what's riding on this. You know how important this is. You have a part to play, and you must play it well," her mother said, going on as if Eva hadn't just said she'd have to call her back.

Eva looked over at Walter. Once again, she thought he'd probably be perfect to play the part her mother had in mind. She could see their initials monogrammed on stemware. Or cashmere throws for their ski house. It was that type of thing her mother would eat up. Just then a bee buzzed around Walter, and he waved his hand dramatically, making the little row boat rock violently. Eva frowned and looked back at the phone. "Of course. Now please, Mother, like I said, I really have to go. It's rude to talk on the phone while I'm on a date. I should not have answered."

"You're quite right, dear. I don't know why you did," her mother said sharply. And with that, Eva was left with a click and silence. Nice. Eva rolled her eyes as she turned the phone off and looked at Walter, then toward the shore. "I'm sorry," she said to Walter. "I'm sorry," she said, lower this time and leaning down toward her chest, knowing the whole crew could hear but not really knowing what she was apologizing for. Probably for being a pain in the ass and getting them all into this in the first place. If not for her, they could all probably be doing some much more important work, like those "I lost half my body weight, so now aren't I a much better person?" makeovers the morning shows loved to push so much. At least there weren't goofy location shots and faux yacht captains with those stories.

Once again, the boat rocked violently, and Eva looked over at Walter. It would seem the bee had brought along a friend, and now both of Walter's hands were flapping. "If you ignore them, they'll probably go away," she said calmly.

"I can't ignore them. I'm allergic," he said, his voice rising.

"Okay, how about we row back to shore and get out of here then?"

But it was as if Walter wasn't hearing her. He was going into real and true panic mode, flailing his hands about and attempting to stand.

Eva put her hand out. "Um, Walter, why don't you sit. I'll row. Don't worry."

But he wasn't listening, the attempt to stand now a full-on "I'm getting the hell out of here" jump up. All six feet plus of him got to his feet as his arms flailed, making the boat scarily unsteady.

"Don't do that. You'll make us tip over!"

292

Eva yelled. "Here, you sit. I said I'll row." Eva rose as she attempted to swap places with him, and in his panic, Walter turned quickly, and there it was, she was gone, right over the side of the little gray wooden boat.

"Dammit!" Eva yelled as she came up out of the murky water, her big floppy hat in hand, the organza flower a ruined mess.

The water wasn't deep at all, and she ended up swimming past the boat and Walter, who seemed to have calmed, so she guessed the bees had gone on about their business. Lucky bees, she thought, as she made her way to the shore. Her dress was a sodden mess, sticking to her legs. One of the PAs was kind enough to wrap a towel around her shoulders as she came out of the water. Aidan had come running up to her and stopped, looking her in the eyes. She could imagine how she must look. Soaking wet, dress all sticky with New York Central Park pond water, hat in hand, makeup runny.

He reached out and swiped some of the hair away from her face. She watched him intently as the corner of his mouth quirked up. "And you were worried about getting your hair wet."

This time she did punch him in the arm.

■ ■ ■ ■

The next two dates were less eventful than the infamous rowboat date, but still Eva's public momentum kept growing right along with her passion for Aidan. She learned to play shuffle board from a guy named Paul, and in a terrible twist of fate, she ended up with a dog after the studio thought it would be a good idea if she had a rental dog from the pound for her doggy date with Doug the dog whisperer. She may be the ice princess, but even she wasn't so cold as to give the cute little fuzz ball back after spending an afternoon with him giving her the full-on charm eye.

As for Doug, the dog whisperer, she didn't have any problems giving him back. It was almost tragic, if it hadn't been so annoying. He made a point of ending all his sentences as if they were commands. "We're stopping here for coffee. Now." And instead of asking if she wanted to sit and take a rest on a park bench, it came out as, "Let's sit, Eva. Sit." She was hoping she would get a treat or something at the end of each of these requests slash commands, but being the expert trainer he was, Doug taught Eva early on that all treats were reserved for his dog, Lucy, who clearly had his heart and was the reason he was probably still single. The man only had eyes for Lucy, and though he was tall, dark, and good-looking, he was completely oblivious when it came to the opposite sex — or any sex, for that matter. It was as if he walked through the city wearing dog-colored glasses and was blind to the abundance of approving stares he got as he and his pooch walked down the street. Cute guy with a cuter dog. Instant in. Hell. Eva was sure he'd not have given her the time of day that afternoon if she hadn't had her rent-a-pup by her side.

But enough was enough. Time was ticking, and she was fast becoming certain she would end up choosing the best from the worst at the rate she was going, or have to end up admitting defeat. Which was clearly not an option, unless she planned to never deal with her mother again. Or go out in public in New York. These stupid segments had made her more of a personality than ever, bringing even more attention to the fact that she had to somehow make it work.

"What are you thinking about so hard now?" Aidan said from behind her, where he had her snuggled and warm, her backside to his front, cuddled on her bed. This easy, familiar thing they were doing and the little after-snuggle was way too fast becoming the best part of her day, and frankly, it terrified her how much she looked forward to it. She knew there was a definite expiration date on these feel good feelings, so she was a fool for letting herself enjoy them so much. Sex was, for the most part, replaceable, but comfortable, intimate feelings like this she knew she couldn't replace. They'd fallen into an odd pattern of seeing each other, though not quite. He'd come to her place two or three nights a week, and if it had been a filming night, he'd trail back around a half hour after the crew left, usually bearing some sort of late-night snack for two from the twenty-four-hour diner a few blocks over. He joked that he needed his strength since she was wearing him out, but she'd come to love his seemingly infinite appetite.

Truth be told, it was she who needed the extra sustenance. She felt more tired, though at the same time more stimulated and alive, than she'd ever been in her life. Just about the only thing she had true motivation for, though, was meeting up with him. On the nights he didn't come by, she tried to bury herself in her work, which there was plenty of, but she had trouble focusing, she missed him so much. This was just what she had been afraid would happen.

Aidan nudged at her back. "So?"

"So what?" she asked sleepily, not wanting to deal with his questions, just happy to lie there next to him and pretend these few hours were actually something real, something that could be her normal, her forever.

Aidan let out a frustrated sigh, and she could feel him tense behind her. "Fine, if that's how you want to play it. I can go with it."

Eva couldn't help but stiffen too. She fought not to give into it, but she did. The way he'd been reading her body in the short time they'd been meeting, she knew he'd pick up on her signals right away. It was her own fault. She'd quickly fallen into the relaxed habit of letting her guard down too much around him, and she knew that was a dangerous thing. She had done that with Kevin, and look how he'd played her. Eva closed her eyes and mentally willed her body to relax. Then she turned to him and smiled, pushing at his shoulder and playfully leaning forward for a kiss.

"Now, come on, stop being so serious. You know we don't do that here." She grabbed his perfectly curved ass. "Once those pants come off, so do all of our outside stresses. Now relax. There's nothing to worry about.

297

I was just stressing about the last few dates and my mother."

"Your mother? Why?"

Eva shook her head. Stupid. She'd opened herself up for that one and probably shouldn't have even brought it up. This was more of a conversation to have with a friend, not your designated layover on the way to Relationshipville. "You don't need to hear about this. It's not anything for you to worry about."

Aidan's brows drew together, and he put his hands up and close to hers. "Wait a minute. I'm calling a time-out here."

"What are you talking about?"

"I'm calling a time-out. This deal or whatever it is we have — as lovely as it is, it's not working. Call me crazy for saying this, but we can't work together all day, do a minimal amount of talking, and then jump in bed to screw our brains out without any talking in between."

Eva's top lip curled, and he laughed, as she wiggled against his stiffening erection. "I don't know what you're laughing at. If we were really going to go through with this long term, it would probably make for the perfect relationship," she said.

He rolled his eyes and shook his head. "Play fair, kitten." He held her hips steady.

"Okay, you're right . . . but still. For most men it would. But humor the reporter in me. I always need to know the full story." He leaned down and kissed gently at the swell of her breasts. "And no matter how tantalizing you may be, I want to know what's the deal with you and your mother? So spill. I'd really like to know what's going on in that head of yours."

Eva frowned again and let out a breath. More about her? What for? What good would letting him in do? It would just be more to miss when this was over and he stopped taking her calls, bringing her off her diet of midnight greasy fries and back to her normal, boring three squares and two healthy snacks and probably routine sex with a guy who filled out a suit well but barely fulfilled her.

Besides, what he was asking went against the rules. Neither of them needed to get that close. Talking and sharing? Crap like that took intimacy to a whole other level. And that made the stakes too high.

Eva stared at him, wondering if she could indeed pay that high a price. She did want to talk, and she thought, as she looked into his rich chocolate eyes that at times held a deep melancholy and caused her breath to hitch, part of her wouldn't mind knowing what was going on behind his dark depths. "Fine, I'll give a little, but not all. It will be like when we have sex. Even all the way. Let's make this a game of give and take, but make it question and answer. That way we'll both be satisfied."

Aidan grinned, but his eyes turned even darker as he took in the ramifications of what Eva had proposed. "You really are a little witch. I knew it when I first saw you. Don't ask me why I ran after you in the first place, because the only answer I've got to that one is I'm a glutton for punishment."

Eva laughed, snuggling closer to him. "Good. That's at least one question down. Wasn't that easy? Now you give me one."

His stare was hard and made her wonder if agreeing to this was a good idea after all. He was a reporter and could cut pretty deep. But then he opened his mouth and sealed the deal. "Why would you settle on marrying anyone, when in reality you don't even want to get married?"

Fuck. Go straight for an artery, why don't you? Suddenly Eva couldn't breathe. Shit, this really was a mistake. Just like when he was making love, Aidan knew how to go for all the sensitive spots, and even though this was supposed to be just a game, the man didn't play around. Once again, all this

300

proved was that not going with her gut had gotten her into trouble. When would she ever learn?

CHAPTER 17

Her settling? Not want to get married?

Eva was sunk, and she knew it. She should have shut up while she was still ahead of the game. They'd each had a fairly decent day. Had a late dinner, then even later lovemaking, and were now full and satisfied. Why did she have to go and push it into the ruin column with her overthinking and chatter?

Everything in her told her to lie. To say something about it really being her dream all along to get married, yada, yada. It was right there on the tip of her tongue. She could spin this to the gods. Hell, she was a spinner extraordinaire.

But in the end, she couldn't do it. Just when she was ready to say the words, start the wheels turning, they got all sour and sticky and went back the wrong way down her throat. Eva coughed and looked down, picking at a loose thread on the end of the sheet. She frowned. Sheets this expensive shouldn't have any loose threads. She cleared her throat again. "You're right. I think in his own way Kevin did me a favor. Not that I didn't want to marry him. Because I did. At one point," she swallowed, "But now that feels like it was such a long time ago. I think I loved him. I don't know, maybe it was the idea of him or what he could be. Maybe it was what we could have been together." She shook her head. Ashamed of the sound of her words. "I guess it was my own stupid pride that made me say what I did in the studio. My pride and my anger. And after it was said, I couldn't back out. I had to save face for myself and my family and go through with it." She lowered her voice, "Honestly, I can't bear to disappoint my mother. That's the problem I'm having now. Letting her down is just not an option."

God, it sounded ridiculous to her own ears as she said the words out loud. She could only imagine how it sounded to him. Eva felt her face heat up and resisted pulling out of his embrace and running to hide in the bathroom until he finally gave up and left. Left her alone to wallow in her embarrassment and shame.

But he only stared at her, at first wide-

303

eyed in what seemed like astonishment, and then his lids became heavy, as if a pang of sympathy and comprehension dawned all at once. "I understand," was all he said.

Eva pulled back, momentarily shocked. "You do? You don't think I'm some sort of pathetic loser?"

He leaned forward and kissed her lightly. "You, princess? Come on. How could you ever be anybody's loser? And of course I do. I met your mother, remember? She's pretty formidable. Reminds me a lot of my father, and those types of people are not the easiest to disappoint. No one that you love is." His words pulled her up short in surprise. He didn't seem the type to be talking about familial love. Or maybe he was, and she'd just categorized him unfairly that way. "Besides," he continued, "I'm sure being the only daughter and heir must not be a picnic."

She made a face. "No, it isn't. But I learned early on how to cope, and really she's not all that bad. I know she wants the best for me. She's worked hard and has been through a lot to make our company what it is today. Doing that on her own in this town is something to applaud. And I understand, though I didn't growing up, that in her own overbearing, controlling way, she's only been trying to protect me. Making it easier for me than it was for her. Even if in the process she's driving me crazy."

He pulled her in close. "Is that what the whole getting married on television thing was? You coping? You doing it all for her?"

Eva thought for a moment. She didn't know how much she should tell him, but part of her wanted to get things off her chest. What would it really matter anyway? It wasn't like they were the real thing or that she even really mattered to him. This could be like therapy. Well, therapy with a twist, so to speak. She shimmied up against him and felt him harden against her.

"Don't try and dodge the question," he said.

"Who's dodging? But remember, you'll owe me, and I'm not taking sex as payment."

He laughed at this, and it felt good. Made her smile in a way that somehow felt deep, true, and easy. It was the type of smile she hadn't experienced with any other man. "As if you could afford me."

She chuckled. "Now you're pushing it."

"No, but I will be later." Aidan nipped her on her shoulder. "Now, back to the show. Was that you coping?"

305

Eva shrugged, then let out a long breath. "Not really. And I may be a lot of things, but I can take my own lumps. I'm not pinning this on my mother. This is my bed to lie in."

Aidan cocked his brow, and she snorted. "Don't start. Now, Kevin and I were together a long time, and like I said, I loved him, or parts of him, or maybe it was the idea of what he and I could be. You see, we used to be good together. We had our thing down. Us taking the next step was inevitable, and the show getting involved seemed like a wonderful twist of fate that would be a boon for our family business. We were doing well but getting staid with our clientele, and when one of our younger associates said she'd heard about the casting for the show, part of me thought it would be great for PR. My mother agreed. She thought the buzz would be fabulous. We both thought it would be the high-profile thing we needed to take Ward to a new level. Having the Ward name mentioned once or twice a week on a national station seemed, at the time, a small price to pay for loss of privacy with a wedding that had been part of my plan all along."

His brows drew together. "And where did Kevin fit into all of this?"

Eva bit her lip. This part was hard. Where did he fit? "Honestly, I guess that's where I failed. Kevin was always there, happily on the rise, right along with me. I'd invested a lot in him, and I think he was fine with it. We met in school. I helped him through, made sure he passed the bar exam — well, the second time around. I even gave him the makeover he needed to get him the position he currently has at one of the best firms in the city. But really, deep down, now I'm not sure I was what he wanted, even back then." Eva swallowed the words that were now the toughest to say, and Aidan ran a reassuring hand easily up and down her bare thigh.

"Maybe I was a settle, a step up the ladder for him. Who knows?" She shrugged. "I thought I was doing all the right things and all he needed was a little nudge. It's sad, but I was the first one to bring up marriage when I brought up the show. He probably would have been happy going on as we were indefinitely, or at least until he was ready to settle down with the woman he really wanted."

After that declaration, Eva looked down and away. She didn't want to see the pity that was no doubt in Aidan's eyes. No one knew she was the one who had brought up marriage to Kevin. The running official story was that he had proposed in the most perfect way, getting down on one knee during the ending credits of her favorite movie, *Love Actually.* It was her story, and she was sticking to it. The reality was that he'd ended up saying yes, sure they could get married after she'd laid out her plan and agreeing that being on the show would be beneficial to both of them. Of course that yes came after they'd had sex on her couch, something she called a rare treat for him since she was usually strictly an on-the-bed type of girl. At least the *Love Actually* part of the story was true, since his yes came during the rolling credits, their lovemaking lasting no longer than the end of the movie and the end of the credits. After Eva had laid it all out, Kevin thought a bit and decided to go with the ring, promising to take her shopping the next day, and then flipped the TV to SportsCenter to end the talk and wind down for bed. Eva felt like a fool now, thinking of how it had all gone down and the ridiculous fairy tale she'd spun around him. She was a real ass for ever going for him and, worse, for her own bullshit in the first place.

Aidan let out a long breath as his reassuring strokes now moved onto her back.

"That's about as real as it gets, but I asked. Still, I don't understand. Why did you settle?"

Eva looked up at him, not quite understanding why he didn't get it. He was such a man. She shook her head. "The thing is, I didn't think it was settling. Kevin was a good catch. A handsome, good-looking lawyer from a decent family and with no kids. And back then, he was mine. Well, at least I thought he was. We were in a long-term relationship, and he told me he loved me. In between video games and Sports-Center, he still said he loved me, and that's not so easy to come by, and if you go by my stats, the odds are not in my favor as a single, soon-to-be-thirty-year-old woman. I always knew that eventually I wanted to have it all — the man, the marriage, and, yes, even the kid — before it was too late. I was making sure it happened. Now may not be the perfect time, but it's the only time I have."

Aidan's brows drew together, and Eva could feel his judgment simmering toward her. "Hey," she added, "as a man you can push it to fifty or sixty, lose your hair and get a gut, and you'll still have better odds of getting married than a woman does."

Aidan let out a whistle.

309

"Yeesh, that's a sobering thought."

"You're telling me. But hey, it's not like I'm down on myself or have low self-esteem or some such crap. I'm laying it out there. Men don't want to commit, but women only have a certain viable prime-time shelf life when it comes to work and family. Sometimes you have to do what you have to do. And if that's settling, yeah, maybe a little bit I freaking settled, but I truly didn't see it that way. I thought I could turn it into my happy ending. The happy ending my mother never got, I was — well, *am* — going to make."

Aidan stared, and she felt her stomach clench. Oh hell, had she gone too far? She probably had. She had gone against code and spilled the tea on what truly was. Shit. She should have kept the mask on and remained the kitten in bed he wanted. The kitten or the ice princess or anyone but this woman who was a settling, manipulating wreck and who was desperate in his eyes.

"So is that what you're doing here, with me, what you have to do?" Aidan finally asked.

Eva's brows shot up as she felt the familiar spark of anger ignite. Men. She would pity them if they weren't so crazy making. She let out a sigh, then looked Aidan in the eye

310

and spoke slowly. "How is what I said even about you?" She went to push him away, but his supposedly easy grip was surprisingly firm. "I swear you men are all alike. I thought we were talking about me, but you want to make this about you." She let out another long breath. "With you, no. With the show? Yeah, I'm doing that because I have to get my life back. I have to save face. Save the image of my and my mother's company. It's up to me to clean up the mess I've made. I will not go skulking off as the scorned woman without a man. The picture just looks too sad, woe is me, and all that. So yeah, I'm doing what I have to do. But as for with you, no."

Eva looked at him. His strong jaw, his dark, dangerous eyes, his wide expanse of chest. He was more than she could even dream of. A man so out of her realm and off her deviated plan that, no, she'd never think of him as something she'd have to do. This time with him had quickly become a living dream that she didn't want to walk away from. Eva bit her lip before starting again. "With you here, when we're alone, for once I'm doing what I want to do. Like you said, no attachments and no responsibility. I've never had that type of freedom."

It wasn't as if Eva expected Aidan to rant

311

or rave, but the long stretch of quiet was almost unbearable. Eva knew he was thinking over her words, letting them sink in, and probably trying to plot his exit. Fine, it was done. He could do with her revelation what he liked. It didn't really matter one way or another. They only had a handful of weeks left, and they would be done and going their separate ways. She tapped him on his side and brought his attention back to her.

"So I spilled my guts, now it's your turn," she said with a raised brow. "There is no way you're doing this gig for the love of my story. What got you stuck on this ridiculous beat and not out roaming the globe? And don't lie, because if you do, I'm kicking you right out of this bed."

Aidan chuckled at what he hoped would be the easiness of it, calming the churning in his gut. Why did he ever say those words? *No attachments, no responsibility.* Coming from her, though, the words raked over him like fine glass. But he covered his feelings by giving her a grin. "Shit, you got me, woman. Is it too late to make this truth or dare? How about I take a dare instead?"

She smiled back but still narrowed her eyes. "No way. I did my part, so you're not getting out of this. Spill it."

He let out a sigh and then began. "All right. I'm embarrassed to say my reasons are not far off from yours. I'll just say you weren't all that far off with your first assessment of me when you accused me being assigned to you as some sort of punishment."

When she shot him a look, he quickly reached out and squeezed her leg. "Only you were definitely not part of my penance — or, should I say, rehabilitation."

She mumbled under her breath.

"What?" he said. "I didn't quite catch that."

Eva looked him in the eye. "I said, that's what happens when you play around and act like an overgrown boy."

He raised a brow and poked her in the side, causing her to jump. "Well, well, well. Look who's clawing up. Easy there. Sounds like you've been hanging on Google again. I would have thought that with your job, plus the dates," he trailed his hand along her thigh now, "plus our extracurricular activities, you wouldn't have time to troll the internet."

Her eyes went to the ceiling. "You'd be surprised what I have time for."

He chuckled at that. The woman was a constant thorn.

"Trust me," she continued. "I don't. I

usually filter out seventy percent, and if I leave thirty, in your case that's still enough to burn up my screen."

"Damn, you're tough. Now shall I talk, or let you?"

She twisted her mouth but looked suitably guilty for her assumptions. "I'm sorry. This is your story."

He kissed her, then pulled back. "It is. And you're partially right. You always were. As I started to explain, I am here for a certain amount of rehabilitation. On my last assignment, I made a call that I should not have." He coughed then, a lump bubbling up in his throat out of nowhere. "And if it wasn't for me, my crew and I never would have been on the trek we were on, and we wouldn't have gone, inadvertently, across the border where we did, following after my false lead. I put lives, our lives in jeopardy, and after that, it was time to come back home and reassess." She reached out then and rubbed a gentle hand across his head, letting it glide down to his shoulder, where tension had knotted up out of nowhere. He gave her what he hoped was a convincing smile. "It's not all bad, though. After a tense few days when we were all pretty much scared shitless, the network paid what was demanded, and we all made it home. There are quite a few relieved families who are grateful for that. And the ordeal made my father adamant about me taking my place in the family business. I guess my near-death moment made him consider his mortality. That's not something I meant to do, and I'm sorry for it. For putting him, my mother, and so many through so much."

When the lump knotted up in his throat again Aidan just wanted to be done. Done with talking and the session of over-sharing. Though he didn't feel any of the expected waves of judgment coming from her direction, he still felt the weight of them on his own heart. He knew he shouldn't have crossed the line with her. It was safer all around keeping things as they were, staying in the space where she wasn't looking for anything from him and he wasn't looking for anything from her.

Aidan leaned in then and rested his head against her warm skin. For just a moment, he took in the dangerous feeling of calmness and content as she continued to lazily massage his tight shoulders. It was a content he didn't rightfully deserve.

"It wasn't your fault, you know."

At the sound of her voice, smooth and easy, he lifted his head. "I was the lead. It was my call. Of course it was my fault."

She frowned. "What was the story?"

"What does it matter? The fact is, we didn't get the story but got our asses handed to us."

She leveled him with her gaze. "Humor me."

"Fine. We were looking for an encampment of child soldiers while following up on a lead about sexual exploitation."

Eva sucked in a breath. "I'd say that was worth any risk. And as for your team, they knew what they were getting into when they took the job. The fact is you all made it home."

Still Aidan couldn't take it in. "That doesn't matter. I spent long enough being the guy you heard about. Before I covered more serious issues, I started out doing hard-hitting celebrity news. My interview was the last one the night before a young pop star died of an overdose. I'm a magnet for trouble."

Eva pulled back at the same time she pushed at him. "Wow, you really think you're a special snowflake, huh?"

"What are you talking about?"

"Just how much of the universe do you really think you control?" She laughed. "Sorry, but it's a bit much."

Aidan wanted to offer a comeback but

couldn't. She'd gone and tossed his guilt aside like it was nothing. And for the first time in a long time, that guilt started to feel a lot less like a boulder on his shoulders. He honestly didn't know what to do with the feeling. But Eva leaned forward and kissed him sweetly, her lips a balm to his confused soul. When she pulled back and looked at him and he took in her gorgeous cinnamon skin and those delicious full lips, even plumper now from all his sucking and biting this evening, he was once again instantly hard. Aidan then looked at her straight on and got a glimpse of those pretty brown eyes and wanted to kick himself all over again. Though some of his anxiety was eased, how far had he really come from the guy he had been back then if he was currently in her bed when she was going to marry another man in just a few weeks? Aidan swallowed and looked away.

He studied the tidy bedroom that was so her. Light and sweet. Prim and ladylike. It's hard to imagine a man ever truly inhabiting this space, ever sullying her and making her less of the princess she was at heart.

He looked at Eva, now hoping that when she looked back at him she'd see the remorse and the truth of his heart in his eyes. He hated the person he used to be. For a while, after the pop star's OD, he had had some pretty dark years, but it was Carter and their friend Vin who had brought him back from the brink. He also hated what he'd done to his crew, but he couldn't change it. Thankfully, he could fix his mistake when it came to her. He could see this process through and make sure she was protected and would at least be shown in the best possible light. Though she tried so hard to act strong and as though she had it all together, he knew there was a vulnerability to her that kept her just on the edge of breaking. He didn't want any part of the process to expose that. But still, at the same time, he couldn't, at least not right now, walk away from her and protect her from himself, and that scared him more than anything else.

Eva pushed up and kissed him gently, the feeling so soft and tender he wanted to lean into it and breathe it in deep, pretend she was his and would be a part of him forever. "Hey, it's okay. You have to forgive yourself for your crew and for your past. Like I said, your crew knew the risk when they took their jobs, and as for your past, we all have one that we need to let go of. It's called the past and not the present for a reason."

He lowered his eyes and then looked back

at her. "You say that like you're almost convinced of it yourself."

She smiled then, and he knew he'd had her. "Okay, you caught me. I guess we both could do with easing up on ourselves. But it's so easy to say and hard as hell to actually do. I even go back to when I was a kid and wonder if I had been perfect enough for my father, could I have kept him with my mother? What kind of sick mess is that?"

Aidan nodded. "Okay, you win on that one. Woman, even a real princess couldn't have made that happen." He leaned in and kissed her again. "You had nothing to do with your father and your mother not making it, and for the record, you damn sure had nothing to do with that dumbass breaking up with you. The fact that he was an idiot is on him."

"If you say so."

"Oh, I say so. But I get it. I still feel responsible for so much, even though part of me itches to get back out there. That's pretty jacked up, isn't it?"

She grinned. "Yeah, it is. But you know what I think? I'm not surprised. There are times when you can't hide your restlessness, when you're behind the monitor and we're on location. I see you looking around. You want action, and watching me play the not

319

quite match game is boring you to tears. Action is in your blood. I think you need to find a way to bring the two parts of your life — the road and your network responsibilities — in line so that you can be happy." Eva tilted her head. "You do deserve to be happy, you know? You can't give up on that."

He grinned at her then and leaned in for another kiss. "I could say the same thing to you, you know."

Now she was the one who didn't have a comeback. Instead, she nodded, and he continued. "But like I said, I'm working this from the inside out. I have no problem doing my part. My dad is getting up in years. He's done his time, and I'm here to help, so leaving right now is not an option. For now I'm stuck."

Her brows came together. "Lucky me."

He pulled her in close to him. "Oh, baby, it's not like that. With you I'm the lucky one. It may not seem that way for you, but this is the best part of me being back."

Eva smiled then, her lovely lips spreading, her gaze perfectly relaxed and sincere. "Don't worry. I'm not that fragile. I totally understand, and thank you, but you don't have to stroke my ego. Going back to where we started, this is not permanent, so what I think or understand really doesn't matter now, does it? Don't let that worry you in the least." She turned away, then onto her back, for the first time leaving his arms and leaning up against the headboard. She looked at him squarely. "But I am wondering what you're doing working on this show? You could be doing anything with the network, things that are a much better use of your time."

Aidan shrugged, trying his best to appear nonchalant when in reality he was anything but. "Don't worry. I do a lot of things when I'm not chasing behind you. But the truth is, I like chasing you. Something about you does it for me, if you haven't noticed by now." He waggled his brows at her in an attempt to lighten the moment. "You pull me in. You did from the first moment I saw you, and then for sure on the day you ran off the set, right before you told your ex what you really thought and made that declaration."

"Don't remind me," she groaned.

"Well, I thought it was glorious. Crazy but glorious. Then and there I was drawn to you and wanted to know you more." His voice lowered and became slightly hitched. "That's why I ran after you. It wasn't about humiliating you. It was because I wanted to know you, see what made you tick."

She pulled up short. "What, like some

strange social experiment?"

He shook his head. "No, of course not. It's because I was drawn to you. I didn't want to see you go. Yes, you were the story. For good or bad, that's how I am. It's in my programming to go where the story goes. That we've sadly established. But it was you too. I didn't want to see you walk away. And then you kissed me. Well, that was it. From that moment I was a goner. Smashed balls and all."

Eva twisted her lip as she stared, and he just let it all sink in. Like a guy in a confessional waiting to find out what his penance would be. But really it would seem they were both imperfect and doing what they were doing for all the wrong reasons — out of anger, obligation, and circumstance. And now they were here. He couldn't be mad at that. In fact, having her with him right now, tangled in sheets and looking oh so sexy made him want to give the evil hand of fate a high five.

Aidan heard a small sound, like a light shuffle, as Jester, her little dog, came over to the side of the bed and stretched up on his hind legs, staring at them with his big brown eyes. He let out a little whine, indicating he wanted either some attention or a walk or food. Aidan really didn't know what the dog was after, but there he was, all eyes and fur. Yet another consequence of their circumstances that could not be ignored.

Eva looked back up at Aidan. "You really probably shouldn't have chased me, you know."

He leaned up and pulled her down so she was once again flush with his body. Instantly, his body heated. Then he kissed her, his tongue twining with hers, stroking her deep until she softened, her body becoming liquid as his went rock hard. It took all he had to pull back when Jester let out another whine. "Okay, so maybe the dog wasn't one of my better ideas, but chasing you is not one I'm going to regret."

CHAPTER 18

As they walked, Eva could not help but notice the side glances Aidan got from many of the passing women. To his credit, there were none of the slick glances back their way when he thought she wasn't looking, the way Kevin used to try and unsuccessfully do. No, he seemed totally and completely focused on her and Jester. Like they were some sort of little city family unit, and the scenario filled her with panic.

It was still early morning, and she didn't know what had gotten into her, perhaps coming off a lovemaking high, but Aidan had talked her into joining him to walk Jester and grab some breakfast out. It was Saturday morning, and they didn't have to film. Eva was clad in easy shorts and a tee with a baseball cap and shades worn low to cover her features by way of disguise.

As for Aidan, he, too, wore shorts and a baseball cap, though, at least according to her, hiding his hunky features was a lot harder. Even with his cap and shades, she felt she would be able to spy him out from blocks away. And the fact that he had the nerve to be this hunky guy walking a ridiculously cute little mutt did nothing for them going incognito.

"I don't think this is the best idea," Eva said, again, as a jogging blonde almost bashed into a tree after tripping over Jester's leash while she was busy breaking her neck double-checking Aidan. Eva pulled a frown, while Aidan played it cool and stayed totally focused on saving Jester from disaster, sidestepping the blonde as she embarrassingly skipped away. Eva could tell, though, that he was furrowing his brows behind his shades over her comment. "It's fine. We're just two colleagues out walking a dog and picking up some breakfast. If we're for some reason questioned, this is a business breakfast — the business being, I've got to get some food in me because you have worn me the hell out, woman."

At his joke Eva couldn't help but laugh. And when she did, he leaned in and nudged at her shoulder, and for a moment she thought he might actually kiss her. She quickly stepped back and frowned up at him.

"Ouch, princess. Your wounds go deep."

"And you are playing with fire. We've only got a few weeks to go. No need to mess up now."

Eva saw his full lips thin. "Of course, no stopping a woman on a mission."

She let out a sigh, then looked up as they reached a restaurant with outdoor tables where they could eat and sit with Jester. "Come on, don't be like that. We're out, right? This is our time. Let's just enjoy it, have some food, and then get back to real business." She gave him a bright smile that she hoped held no indication of the turmoil she was feeling over just taking a stroll with him outside. Over just taking a few moments to play with the idea that in some alternate universe they could possibly be a couple. The teaser of it was torture. She should have never let him talk her into this. It was a huge mistake, and their relationship should never have gone any further than her apartment door. Her stupid heart couldn't handle it.

Back home, she shielded herself behind her bathroom door as she tapped at her cell phone.

E: I'm in trouble.
C: Oh hell. What's up? Do I need to call in

326

reinforcements?
E: I think I've fallen.
C: So I take it it's not for any of your
intended matches?

Eva stared at her phone while she leaned
on her bathroom sink and thought of what
to text to Cori. Finally she typed.

E: No. It's A that I've fallen for.
C: Is that really so bad?
E: It is.
C: Oh honey, I'm sorry. I wish I were there
to tell you this in person. If you've fallen,
you've got to get the hell up!

Eva took one look at Miguel Diaz and let
out a low breath. She didn't mean for it to
come out so loudly, but one glance Aidan's
way and she knew her mask was momentarily dropped and she'd blown her cover.
Yeah, he must have heard her if his steely
eyes and tight jaw were any indication. But
damn, who could blame her? This Miguel
Diaz looked good.

Once again she was wrangled into another
date at another fitness center, but this time
her date was nothing like over-pumped iron
man Trey Stone. Yes, Miguel was tall and
muscled, but that's where the similarities

ended. His muscles had a longer, lither quality. He had inky black hair cut shorter at the back and sides, with a nice wave that swooped over in the front, highlighting the most gorgeous, sparkling green eyes. She would have had to be half blind to not notice his good looks right away. The guy could be a model — hell, a soap star, maybe even on a telenovela, where the guys really have to be all-around hotties.

And that wasn't the half of it. He greeted her by lightly taking her hand, raising it, giving it a soft kiss on the knuckles, and then saying smoothly, deeply, and almost musically, "Hello, Eva. I have been so looking forward to meeting you," with a sexy accent she just about swooned over. Hell, even the hardened Louisa sucked in a breath, and Eva definitely sensed a few of the PAs, both male and female, flutter.

How could they not? The man was walking sex.

"Hello." Eva fought to get her cool back. She was on camera and still had to be on task with getting her image back on track. *Get in the game, girl, you can do this. The world is watching.* She swallowed as she slowly pulled her hand away, purposefully ignoring the prickles on her neck that let her know how hard Aidan was staring. "It's so nice to meet you."

It was then that Eva looked around the room where they were meeting and had her first letdown of the day. The room looked like your normal workout room. It was a neat, well-lit room and mirrored on three sides, but hooks hung from the ceiling with long swaths of fabric. She suddenly got even more prickly as various BDSM images jumped into her head. Just how far were they trying to push the envelope with this morning show?

She tried to make her voice sound light as she looked at Miguel. "So I hear you're a yoga instructor?"

He smiled, hitting her and the camera with the full force of his devastation. Eva almost laughed out loud. Yeah, there was no way this guy was really looking for a wife on this show. He was definitely in it for the fame. She let out a breath and smiled. Oh well. He was good-looking, and who could blame him? Maybe when this was all over, they could take him on as a client. He definitely had star quality.

"I am. I teach Ashtanga and Kundalini."

And once again the mask fell as Eva giggled with the way he rolled his l's, making the word *Kundalini* sound positively dirty and made her want to both strip and at the same time cross her legs. She looked over at Aidan's stern expression and burst out laughing full on.

"What is it?" Miguel asked.

But she couldn't stop laughing at the unlikely absurdity of it all. Here she was, secretly sleeping with one man who, for the record, just hours earlier, had performed his own version of exactly what Miguel had her thinking about while she was eye-banging him. There was no way Kevin could accuse her of being a prude now. She was a social misfit and an emotional mess, but a prude she was not. Just the thought cracked her up even more, and the laugh came from somewhere deep in her belly.

"Are you okay?" Miguel asked again, placing a hand on her shoulder.

She nodded her head and shook her hands out. "Pull it together, Ward," she inwardly told herself before telling Miguel, "I'm fine." Eva looked over at Lou, who now was looking at her like she had grown two heads, and purposefully didn't look Aidan's way. "I'm fine. Sorry. Let's begin."

"Great." Miguel continued. "I heard you like yoga." Eva nodded again, feeling more together and infinitely more relaxed after getting that laugh out. "Good, because today we're going to do something a little

330

different. I plan to make you fly."

Her usual self quickly snapped back into place at the threat of something different. She instantly looked up at the hooks and the fabric hanging from them. "I'm not doing anything kinky, darling. We've only just met."

Miguel laughed. "Don't worry. Kinky is reserved for my personal silks at home."

And there it was. His tell that pushed him into the first disaster column.

Eva's frown deepened, and she looked Aidan's way. He was looking at the monitor now, but his head came up, and his eyes met hers. "Uh, I'm not sure I know or like where this is headed."

"So you've never done anti-gravity yoga?" Miguel asked.

Eva blinked, giving a small head shake to a stoic Aidan, who looked like he was ready to take one of the silks hanging from the ceiling and strangle Miguel with it. *Uh oh.* That wouldn't do. Though it would make for exciting TV, it definitely wouldn't do. She then looked up at the hooks with the large swathes of blue fabric attached. Trying to keep her voice light, she spoke. "Why would I like to do anti-gravity anything? Gravity is a good thing. It keeps us grounded. Without it, we'd be flying off into space."

He grinned. "So I take it you're the type who likes to stay grounded."

Eva raised a brow. "Nothing wrong with that."

Miguel shook his head and made a sort of "tsk" sound that annoyed her to no end.

"What's that for?"

"Oh, it was nothing. I'm sorry."

Eva crossed her arms. "You were judging me, Mr. Silky Swing."

Miguel put his hands up. "I was not. There is no judgment here. None at all. I was just hoping you'd give it a try. You never know, feeling weightless may be something you like."

Eva felt her brows draw together tight, but finally she uncrossed her arms. "Fine, Silky, let's go at it. I won't have it said that I'm not a team player." When she looked over at Aidan this time, his expression had miraculously changed from one of barely checked rage to one of barely concealed enjoyment. Now she was the one who wanted to jump across the monitor and wring a neck.

Aidan was pissed. He was pissed and growly, and if that smooth, silky gigolo ran his hand up Eva's thigh one more goddamned time, he was going to go over there, kick his ass, and hang him by the balls, using his own fucking silks. How could he ever have thought this type of date was a good idea? Thought it would be amusing, no less. Showed what he knew about fun family programs.

He watched as indifferently as he could while the good-looking charmer took Eva through a series of sensual moves clearly better suited for the bedroom than for the mixed company at hand. Things started out well enough with the usual sun salutation and downward dog, which they did separately on their respective mats. But then the guy had the nerve to step out of his lane, come over, and lift Eva by her trim waist and smoothly place her in the makeshift scarf swing that hung above her, taking the fabric and easing it gently around her buttocks. That was when Aidan crossed his arms and locked them tight around his chest to hold them in place for the safety of all involved, and he hadn't uncrossed them since.

Aidan watched as Miguel told Eva to trust him as he put her into something called a "monkey pose" and asked her to lean back into him — way back, letting her head fall all the way to the ground so she ended up supported only by her crossed legs and the silks wrapped around them. Aidan's jaw dropped at the sight of her heart-shaped behind on display in such a way. It only got worse when Miguel told Eva to trust him further and had her spread her legs wide, while he held her balanced and stood centered between them. With a gentle push to her outer calves, she swung forward and back toward his groin. Aidan couldn't help it and groaned aloud at the sight as he finally unlocked his arms and ran a frustrated hand through his hair.

Louisa shot him a look, and he gave her one right back. Fuck it. How in the world did this guy get into the mix? He was billed as a yoga instructor, not some new age holistic gigolo. To calm himself, Aidan considered all the heads he planned on rolling over this particular pick. Shit. Dammed if that didn't reek of something his father would do. But he didn't like seeing Eva pawed over in such a way, and even worse, he hated that he cared as much as he did about the whole situation.

But care he did.

After their talk, he had felt even more twisted than before. And worse, he was more attached than ever, doing what he told himself not to do. Never to do. When you

334

got emotionally attached to a subject, your judgment was off, and here clearly his judgment was off. He closed his eyes briefly and then decided to look at the screen instead of at the scene in front of him. At least he could let the HD version take the place of watching up close and give him a bit of emotional space.

Be objective, he told himself as he watched Miguel bring Eva back up. She smiled, and her soft brown cheeks took on a rosy glow. He smiled to himself. Despite it all, it was nice to see her looking happy. This was the first date on which he had witnessed her smile like that, the first on which she had that glow that he now knew came from deep within, and if the silky swirler did that for her, then he had to accept it and be happy for her. He knew her. The smile he saw now wasn't her fake "we're rolling" smile, and it wasn't the smile she gave him either, the one that was genuine and real but hidden in the way back, behind the depths filled with that hidden sense of regret that she thought he didn't detect. Seeing her now — smiling, laughing, and genuinely having fun while swinging with this dude — he felt happy for her, though it ripped at his core in a way he wasn't prepared to deal with.

Eva stepped out in front of the silks and

was led by Miguel to go behind them and lean forward, front first, into a downward dog but with her feet in the air. Aidan's mind instantly went to how he'd love to have her in that position himself. As if reading his thoughts, she looked his way for a moment right before her head went forward. He gave her a grin he knew she couldn't see from where he was behind the monitor. But still her mouth quirked up at the corner anyway, as if they were in mental sync, and he couldn't help but shake his head and make a silent promise to her to send her flying as she'd never flown later that night.

CHAPTER 19

"We've got a problem."

Aidan tore his gaze away from the monitor and his view of the couple frolicking in the water and instead aimed his gaze toward the sound of his friend Carter Bain's voice. *What the hell is he doing here?*

It was the weekend, and Eva was on yet another date, this time a beach affair. Aidan couldn't help but laugh when he saw his friend looking so out of place as he made his way across the sand of Rockaway Beach in his corporate getup. But he gave him props for trying to make it work by rolling his suit pants to his calves and carrying his loafers in one hand and his jacket in the other.

"I guess we do have a problem for you to come all the way out here. What could possibly tear you away from your desk and out of your Guccis?"

"Trust me, I wouldn't be here if I didn't

have to be."

Aidan shook his head. "You are so full of shit. Now that I think of it, you were probably dying to get your ass out of there and get your feet in some sand for a change." He looked to the left and tilted his head. "Besides, knowing you, you're probably looking to bum some food off Vin."

Looking for a change of location, the crew had ventured outside once again, though this time they had taken to the coast and gone out to Rockaway Beach so that the latest bachelor, CJ Pace, a competitive surfer with his own line of clothing and gear, could showcase his talents, not to mention promote his merchandise, in which one of the network execs had a small stake.

It rubbed Aidan wrong, as nepotistic as it was, though it shocked him not at all. Not to mention the fact that he had to, once again, look at a scantily clad Eva get pawed all over by yet another fitness hunk. He should have specified they put at least four suits on this list and stay away from this lineup of wannabe Captain Americas. Today's date looked okay enough on paper, but honestly Aidan should have looked further, checked the fact that the popular surfing champ had a fan base that was mostly women; there was a reason he was constantly tapped to model for lifestyle campaigns. As if anyone would believe that the perpetually tanned, ambiguously raced stunner with the piercing green eyes was really out here looking for a wife and that wife could possibly be Eva. Come the hell on. They could sell a lot, but there was no way they could sell that this dude would want to give up his playboy lifestyle.

At least he got to see Vin today. It had been way too long since he'd hung with his old friend. Vin was doing good and looking great, frankly better than Aidan expected since the sudden loss of his mom. Vin had always been a bit of an outward brooder to the lay person, and his mother's death had only brought out more of those traits. It had devastated Vin, and Aidan felt like an ass for not being around more for his friend during these past few years. But recently he and Carter had gone in with Vin, investing as silent partners in his restaurant idea, an offshoot from the original beachside shack he and his mom had founded years ago.

Still, investment or not, it was a surprise to see Carter out on the beach today. He wouldn't complain, though. It was good to have the three of them all in one spot. Hell, getting Carter out of his expensive loafers, well, that was almost worth the cost of seeing Eva cozying it up with another dude. Almost.

"So what is this problem you're talking about?" he asked, directing his question to Carter while still keeping an eye on Eva and the overgrown surfer boy. Really, how old was this dude? Aidan's brows drew together, and he instinctively moved forward when Eva fell off her board and briefly went under the water, only to be pulled up and into the bronzed arms of smiling CJ. His white teeth practically reflected the sun, hence his toothpaste contract. "Pretty shithead." Aidan mumbled under his breath.

"That right there," Carter said.

Aidan looked around, then back at Carter. "What the hell are you talking about? Come on and spit it out. It's not like I have time for your game playing. Some of us have real jobs to do. You know, the kinds that call for actual work."

"Just cut it," Carter said, shielding his eyes from the sun. "Take those headphones off, and come on, buy me a beer."

Aidan took another glance toward Eva and then signaled Lou before taking off his headphones and walking with Carter over to Vin's food shack.

"Don't worry, it's not like he'll be able to swim off with her while the whole crew is watching."

Aidan raised a brow but wouldn't give Carter the satisfaction of an answer to his comment.

"What the hell? Am I being audited or something?" Vin said, turning his muscular body away from the grill and coming around to shake Carter's hand and hug it out as they walked over.

"Cut the audited bullshit. And make me a taco, you ass. Some of us like to dress like an adult. We can't all live like you — the overgrown teenage bad boy in your cutoff jeans and tanks."

Vin cocked his shaved head to the side and narrowed his eyes on the slimmer Carter. "Aww, honey, you've missed me. Well, I'm right here where you left me just waiting for you to come home." He then gave Carter a wink, after which Carter gave him the finger, and Aidan inwardly noted that though the years had gone on, nothing had changed in the relationship he had with his old friends.

Aidan shook his head and laughed. At least he could say that this bit of good came out of his forced grounding.

It had been too long. Vin pulled two beers out of his fridge and served them up. Then he went to the grill to work some magic, coming back with a few of his famous shrimp tacos. His little beach shack was only a front for the much larger restaurant behind it. Vin had done well for himself since the old days of bumming with them. Aidan knew his mother would be proud. And one taste of his food and he knew his investment was secure. As part of the sad but profitable neighborhood gentrification, Vin had done his part by securing a space from an older, established restaurant that was closing, and he just expanded on cuisine his mom had taught him to rustle up for hungry beachgoers. He was quickly getting a rep with the hipsters who were moving in, but doing it on his terms.

Aidan bit into his taco and looked at Carter. "So, you going to spill what brought you all the way out here? Besides our friend's excellent cooking, of course?"

Carter took a long pull of his beer, then leveled Aidan with a hard look. "I came to ask if you're actively trying to sabotage this project."

Aidan's brows pulled together. "Why would I do that?"

"I don't know. Why would you?"

Aidan let out a breath. "What the hell are you talking about? Like I said, I don't have time for this. If you're going to keep talking in riddles, I'm going back to work."

"You mean you're going back to gawking at your girlfriend."

"She's not my girlfriend." Aidan picked up his beer and took his own pull.

Carter shrugged. "Okay, I'll give you that; maybe she'd not your girlfriend. Are you trying to sabotage this project by making a fuck buddy of the talent?"

Aidan's beer slammed down hard and fast but gave Carter just enough time to jump out of the way of his oncoming fist. Vin let out a bark of laughter, and Aidan turned on him, eyes blazing. "What the hell are you finding so funny?"

"Damn, man, way to show and tell. You used to be better than that. Carter pulled that out of you in one move. I saw him playing you from a mile away. I mean she's fine and all, but I had you called from the moment you all walked up. Honey's got you whipped."

"And you just admitted it. Like I knew you would," Carter said. "Not that you needed to. Your little early-morning dog walk did that for you." Carter pulled a piece of paper out of his breast pocket and slammed it on the counter. It was a clipping with a picture of Aidan and Eva walking Jester. She was looking up at him and smil-

343

ing. They definitely looked like a couple.

He gave Carter a sharp look and saw he was now smoothing his hair and reaching for his beer again, no longer afraid of getting knocked out since it was clear he had played Aidan just to get a reaction. "We were having a business meeting."

Both Carter and Vin laughed in unison.

Aidan shot them both hard looks. "Either way, you had no business talking about her like that."

"I know," Carter said. "And it won't ever happen again. I just wanted to get straight to the point of what was going on with you. Now, I'm sure she's perfectly lovely, but like Vin said: You're whipped."

"When have I ever been whipped?"

Vin and Carter looked at each other, then turned to him in unison. "Now!"

He threw up his hands and shook his head. "You're both wrong."

Carter chimed in again. "If you say so, then I really hope so. You know I have a lot riding on this. We all do. She needs to walk down that aisle in a few weeks, and it needs to be with one of these guys. I can't have you metaphorically, or literally, screwing this up for me. Some of us aren't grandfathered or fathered into the board. I can't have two of my segments bomb, especially not twice in a row."

"Don't worry. She will walk down the aisle," Aidan said through gritted teeth as he watched Eva try to balance on her board while holding CJ's hand.

Carter frowned. "Now, why is it that I don't feel too convinced?"

He turned and raised a brow to Carter. "You don't want to keep pushing me on this."

Carter raised the hand that held his beer and tipped it to him. "Fine. Just get it done. I'm trusting you. I'm sure the right man for her will come along soon. Like you fought so hard to convince me when you insisted on taking over this shoot, we owe her the happily-ever-after she came to us for."

Aidan turned away to walk back to his crew. As he did, he saw Eva fall right into CJ's arms and heard Vin, behind his back, mumble some crap about having it bad. Fucking friends. What did they know?

Eva lay on her side, counting the seconds until the display on the digital clock turned over. 1:45, 1:46, 1:47.

Aidan was uncharacteristically silent after their lovemaking — well, actually he was even beforehand. When he had come by her apartment around midnight, she knew right away that something was off with him.

Opening the door, tired from the day on the beach with bachelor CJ, Eva instantly perked up after taking one glance at Aidan, looking sexy and perfectly delicious in his jeans and body-accentuating tee. All she wanted to do was get her hands under that tee, run up against his warm body, and feel that sexy scruff of his as it scraped along her neck and made its way down to in between her thighs. Really, she should be ashamed of the outrageous woman she was becoming, but she couldn't muster up the self-righteousness to do it. She'd spent enough years being perfect for everyone else and then making that outward perfection her profession. She was good and well going to enjoy these nights of letting go while she had them.

Aidan stepped in silently and kicked the door closed behind him. Leaning down to give her a long kiss, he captured her mouth and cut off the funny greeting she was about to give him. The words became lost to her memory as his tongue entwined with hers in a slow and sensual coupling that had her feeling slowly drugged and slightly breathless, and then he finally pulled back and her eyes blinked open.

Her gaze went from his chocolate eyes to

his full sexy lips, and then finally to the takeout bags in his hands. She broke out in a wide grin as she snatched the bags and headed for the kitchen counter. "Oh good, I'm starving. I barely ate on the beach today, with the wind kicking up like it was. I don't know whose idea it was for us to eat out there anyway," she said, raising a brow his way. "I mean, really, who likes eating on the beach? And what a shame. That food, at least the one taco I got down, was delicious."

"I'm glad you thought so. Vin, the chef, is my boy; we go way back."

Eva paused mid-unpacking. "Oh, really, how so?"

Aidan shrugged. "It's not anything worth talking about," he said, dismissing her question as he walked into the living room and sat on the couch. Her mind instantly went into overdrive. *What the hell?* Why even bring up the guy is your boy and then say it doesn't matter? It wasn't like she brought it up.

Eva watched as he took a look at the leftover equipment in the corner of the room, and she couldn't help but notice his stern expression and the tension in the way he held his shoulders, straight and high up by his ears. Eva dropped the tin containing an order of what was, probably at this hour, a wilted salad on the counter with a thud.

She let out a short huff as she stared at the back of Aidan's head. So he wasn't in a chatty mood tonight. Duly noted. She paused and thought over his earlier, on-set persona. Now that she thought about it, he really hadn't been himself after Carter Bain had stepped onto the set that afternoon. Sure, he was never the most congenial guy on a date day, and she'd gotten used to his brooding, but with Carter there he was markedly tenser, and she noticed how he'd made odd requests to add more shots of her and CJ in the water frolicking together. Walking along the beach, he even had Lou suggest they walk down to the arcade and do a silly bumper-car ride. It was totally ridiculous. Normally, he was content with letting Lou, for the most part, run the show and only giving the occasional comment, and he almost never pushed her into more intimacy with the dates. This totally went against his character. She took out another container, this one with what looked to be overcooked pasta, and grimaced, continuing to unpack. Suddenly she paused. Could it be he was setting her up for their inevitable end? Now that they were weeks into the project and past the halfway mark, was he already halfway out the door and her bed?

"Why would it not be worth talking about?" Eva asked as nonchalantly as she could, trying her best to ignore the gnawing thread of dread churning in her belly.

Their time was quickly passing, and standing there as she looked at the back of Aidan's head, waiting for his reply, was a sharp reminder of that. Finally, he ran his hands across his face in an exhausted gesture and rose. He came over to her and took the aluminum container out of her hand and placed it on the counter, as his other large arm snaked around her waist.

"I know you're hungry, but can it wait? I want you now."

"But —" The rest of what she was about to say was cut off by his kiss. He lifted her easily by reaching under her behind and grabbing her ass with both hands. Her legs, as if on instinct, smoothly wrapped around his waist. "Dammit, Aidan. I know what you're trying to do. I want to eat and talk, and you're trying to avoid it."

"Good," he said nibbling at her neck and totally ignoring her words.

The worst was that her body was totally ignoring her words too, not connecting with her brain as her nipples hardened and wetness immediately flooded her center. The food was immediately forgotten as Aidan carried her to the bedroom. As if ravenous, he quickly tore her T-shirt up and over her head, barely taking time to look at her before he reached for the edges of her panties and pulled them down, going to his knees.

As with every time they made love, Eva was lost, her mind dissolving along with her body as everything went to goo under his hungry kisses and soft caresses. She wanted him so much it scared her. She thought that by now some of the newness or novelty of it would have worn off and they would have settled into a nice routine of mind-blowing, could-be-counted-on orgasms, which she enjoyed but wouldn't have a problem walking away from. Right now she was feeling anything but in the mood to walk away from the feelings she was having. They were mind-blowing, that was for sure, but they were also filled with scorching-hot passion that sent her heart racing like nothing and no one ever had before.

But Eva knew she couldn't hold onto that thought, because if she did, the fear of it would paralyze her. It was something too close to love, and if she went there, she knew there would be no coming back. Already she felt herself slipping too far, going too close to the edge and scarily slipping out of control.

Pulling away and out of his embrace, Eva lifted herself up and nudged at Aidan's chest, pushing him back. Enough of this; it was time to get back into control. He came up, licking his full lips and looking at her with a daze that seemed sort of like a wild hunger. She let out a frustrated sigh and briefly looked away. Shit. No one in her life had ever looked at her like that, and in that moment she had a feeling that no one ever would again. It both made her bloom with power and also want to shrink away with dread over the fact that it was fleeting and would soon end. Just two more dates and she'd have to choose, narrow it down to the best of the mediocre and take it to the next . . . her mind paused over what to call what she was doing, and all she could come up with was the next whatever with whoever would be her groom for the moment. Images suddenly flashed through her head as she flipped through the guys at a rapid-fire pace, shuf fling through them like a deck of cards of potential grooms. But where it all ended up did not really matter.

None of them were Aidan.

Her belly seemed to seize and knot, and Eva closed her eyes against the useless thought.

"Don't do that," Aidan said, as if reading her mind.

She looked at him again. Damn him for his ridiculous mind-reading abilities. And damn this whole stupid situation.

Suddenly her anger at Kevin for humiliating her hit her anew. Eva knew it was irrational, but if only he hadn't done what he did, in the way that he did it, she wouldn't have met Aidan and be stuck unpacking these feelings. If only he'd been a man and at least told her his feelings beforehand, or, at the worst, gone through with it and let her down after the show, she wouldn't be in this mess, stuck falling for a guy she should have never even encountered. Hell, Kev the coward still hadn't even picked up his things. The box she had packed for him was still waiting, untouched, with the doorman. It would seem, after she'd received the text about him and that girl, that he'd fallen off the freaking radar, flown the coup to who knows where, and was lucky enough to not be followed by a TV crew of paparazzi. His reputation was fine. It was hers that had ended up in shreds.

Aidan ran a hand slowly along the length of Eva's arm, and in that moment she stiffened under his touch as she thought of

Kevin and his betrayal, the fact that there was no closure, that he'd done what he'd done to her with no explanation. It still stung like the devil. There was a part of her that still itched as a result, like a rash that hadn't cleared up.

She stared at Aidan, her confusion mounting even in her fuzzy clarity. She knew what he was doing with tonight's seduction, with his refusal to talk about even the most superficial of things, like his friend's food on the beach. His eagerness to just come in and screw her and get it over with. And silly her, she jumped in with two feet and went right for it. She was already so tangled up with him, both physically and emotionally, that there was no way she'd say no. But there it was. Aidan was doing the same thing she had done earlier on in their "let's not call this a relationship, but keep it only a sex thing" arrangement. He was distancing himself, seeing the end and making space for it, making a door that would be easy for them both to walk through. Though it hurt her to her core, at least he was being the smart one. A painful smile pulled at the corner of her lips. She could and should take a cue from him.

Eva looked down at her empty left-hand ring finger and thought of her ring still tucked away in the drawer where she'd re-hid it. She swallowed, then brought her gaze back to Aidan and smiled full on. "You're right. What's the use of talking or thinking when there's much better things we could be doing with our time. Now let's get you out of that shirt and pants. I think you're terribly overdressed for this party."

CHAPTER 20

Aidan lay in the quiet darkness for a while, holding Eva while listening to the calming sound of her breathing in her sleep, relaxing to the mellow rumble of her low and steady snore, something he was sure that if he told her about, she'd surely deny. The thought brought a reluctant smile to the corner of his mouth. He was turned on his side, holding her back to front, a position he'd come to find way too much comfort in. But she fit perfectly, tucked under him with her head resting on his arm. He knew he could stay for a few more hours and leave around five or even five-thirty, before the day-shift doorman came on, and head to his apartment to shower and change for work. He wanted nothing more than to stick with their usual routine and do just that, but today changed all that, and he knew it was time for him to head home now.

They were sunk. And it wasn't because of

what Carter had said. Hell, he couldn't give a damn about what Carter said, and if truth be told, the pic from the paper didn't bother him all that much, but he knew it would bother her. A lot. And he also knew that for all that Carter had said, the pain in the ass was right. Aidan didn't need the distraction or the entanglement, and neither did she. She'd mapped out the plan from the beginning, so why was he going around it and playing out some waste-of-his-time, midnight-to-daybreak, happy-hubby fantasy, and possibly jeopardizing both their reputations in the process? Shit, if he wanted to bet on a sucker fantasy and gamble at the same time, there was pay-to-play fantasy league football. He didn't have to fool himself with this pretend game of daddy's home that they were playing. Besides, she wanted a husband, someone to complete the perfect picture she had in her head, and he wanted his freedom, a chance to move on and pursue his stories with freedom and no fear of entanglements. They both deserved to have what they wanted. So this had to come to an end.

Eva yawned and stretched a bit, wiggling her behind and causing his dick to jump to attention once again. Damn, it was amazing how he responded to her, though. He inwardly groaned and his fingers flexed. He was aching to reach out and grab her thighs, pull her creamy mocha skin closer to him and just bury himself in deep, go on and get lost in her sweetness one more time. Instead Aidan leaned down and softly kissed her shoulder, before easing his arm from under her head and slowly turning over onto his back and lifting up in order to put on his clothes. He was bending down to pick up his boxer briefs when her sleepy voice floated over to him.

"You're leaving?" Her tone wasn't angry or accusing. No, it was worse, soft, low, and full of sad disappointment.

She turned over to her stomach and now faced him.

"Yep, I'm going to head out and get an early start."

Eva turned away and looked at the bedside clock, causing him to look too, even though he already knew the time. 1:48.

"Does it really matter now? Can't you stay? Wait until morning?"

Aidan looked toward the window at the darkened sky and the never-quite-dark view of New York below. So many of her neighbors' windows were still lit bright and blazing against the midnight sky, so much so that when you looked up you couldn't see a star if you tried. As it was, the almost-full moon had to fight for its share of attention. It was so different from the calm skies he'd seen from the most devastatingly war-torn countries.

Aidan turned back to Eva. God, she was beautiful. Looking at her now, with her tousled bed hair and her half-sleepy eyes, all he wanted to do was get back in the bed with her. There was something about being here with her, while the rest of the world was blocked by a layer of concrete and steel, the haze of her being made him somehow feel — maybe, just for a few brief moments — that there was not a tense world living on the edge, ready to blow that sweet haze away. But there was, and at some point they'd both have to face it. He might as well be the one to make the leap and do it now. She gave him a smile and crooked her finger, beckoning him to come back to bed. Yeah, he needed to be the one. If not now, then he might lose his nerve, and his delay could turn into never. At least this way he wouldn't have to watch her find her perfect mate on camera and play the part of an innocent bystander in the train wreck that was sure to come.

Aidan leaned down and kissed her, enjoying the sweet honey and cream flavor of her that he'd come to love so much. He drank it in, getting his fill before he pulled back once again. "I'm sorry, princess, but I've really got to go."

Eva didn't say a word but just looked at him, her eyes glistening, and his heart did a flip and something in his gut twisted.

It didn't take him long to dress, and he did so in silence. When he was ready to leave, she spoke. "I would walk you to the door, but I'd rather stay here. Let you remember me this way when you're sitting at your desk today." She was doing that light thing she did with her voice, but he detected a falseness that he'd hadn't heard from her in a long time, at least not in the hours from midnight to six AM.

Aidan laughed at that, his throat uncomfortably dry. "Okay, Miss Ward. I'm sure you'll be on my mind all day as you are every day."

Eva's eyes narrowed. "You're not even out the door yet, and already I'm back to being Miss Ward?"

Aidan leaned down and kissed her, then pulled back and looked into her now-sharp eyes. "I'm practicing for work. Making sure I have my lines right."

"Are you now? Because if you ask me, it felt like you were saying good-bye. Good-bye for good." She laughed nervously, and Aidan couldn't help but look away.

She took his hand, and he looked down at her. "Stop being silly. We have work to do. It's not like you won't see me again." He leaned down and quickly kissed her once more and smiled, letting go of her hand and quickly squeezing her beautiful thigh. "One thing you have to know about me is I always finish my jobs."

What am I supposed to do now? Eva thought as she swiped at her cell to check for incoming texts, knowing good and well the answer to the question before the swiping. *You're supposed to get your act together, find your groom, and move the hell on!*

It had been a week, and she missed Aidan terribly since he'd left her last week feeling unsettled, though completely sexually satisfied. She'd somehow managed to get to sleep around three-thirty AM after tossing and turning, her mind going over the little bit of conversation they had had more times than she could count. What did he mean he always finished his jobs? The question was, had he finished with her?

When she had been hit with the newspaper picture of the two of them, she had called him immediately, only to have her call returned by Carter, who said that Aidan was out of town for the day on business, but he was on the case and not to worry about that photo. It was nothing. They were just two colleagues having breakfast. The fact that Carter had used Aidan's exact words infuriated her and gave her more answers than it hid.

She needed to just go ahead and admit what she'd known as soon as she'd opened the door and seen it on his face last week. He was through. With her at least.

But now here it was date night once again, and the crew was here, though quite scaled down, as it would seem they'd gotten the process streamlined to a bit of a science. And surprise of all surprises, this scaled-down crew didn't include Aidan. Once again.

That was it. He was now in full-blown avoidance mode. He had sent her a couple of texts over the past week about being swamped with work and using that as an excuse for getting out of their late-night trysts. And for her last date, Peter, a shy but surprisingly engaging literature professor and writer, whom she met for coffee and a stroll uptown at the Cloisters museum and gardens, Aidan was a no-show as well, citing another work commitment and leaving

Louisa as the point person in charge.

Eva tried her best to hide her disappointment over not seeing him that day, and for the most part she thought she'd done well. It was at night, when she was alone yet again, that it really got to her. When midnight came around, and there was no buzz at the door, or when she looked up and realized she was hungry because she'd neglected to eat, since she was hoping to share a relaxing meal with him, then fall off to sleep in his arms after making love. Yeah, that's when the fact that she was alone — and not just alone, but without him — really hurt.

And now here it was, the day when she'd have yet another date, the last one before it was time to narrow down her options, and he wasn't there again. Dammit. This time hiding her feelings was almost impossible to do. It took all she had to not ask Louisa or Stan or even to whisper to one of the PAs and find out where he was. Had he flown the coop for good? Given up on her and her segment all in one fell swoop, without a word? Her mind began to spiral, though she tried to act all unaffected and nonchalant when the makeup artist happened to ask Mitzi where "that hot Aidan Walker" was today. But with the tension in her lips, and the rigidness of her spine, she was sure it was a dead giveaway.

It was Louisa who chimed in. "He's being pulled in a lot of directions, from what I hear. He has some high-priority assignments for the network, so he's asked me to step in and take over where I can."

Eva blinked and felt the muscles in her eye twitch.

Her eye twitch did not escape Lou's notice. She quickly came over and gave Eva's hand a pat that was not entirely comforting, but Eva knew it was a big step for the no-nonsense Louisa. "You don't have a problem with that, do you? Because I assure you I can handle the job. You're in safe hands with me. You can trust me."

Safe hands? Trust? Eva felt the floor shift beneath her feet at those words. They were eerily similar to Aidan's, and look what had come of that? One last night of passion and then a no-show. She looked sharply into the petite powerhouse's eyes and from the all-knowing look she got back, she knew with every fiber in her being that Louisa knew too. She could feel the moisture threatening to well up in the back of her eyes, and imagined pinching herself in order to make it stop. She blinked and smiled softly at Louisa while willing her voice to remain steady. "Of course I don't have a problem. I'm sure you've been doing most of the work anyway. I know how these suits are."

Louisa continued with her hard stare for one beat and then another, and then one beat too long after that. "I do what I do. It's my job."

The makeup artist took Eva's chin in hand then and lifted it higher to the light, coming at her to swipe more blush onto her cheeks. "And I've got to do my job if we're going to keep on schedule. Can you turn my way and give me a smile? I need to rosy you up a bit. Add some color to those cheeks. All of a sudden you're looking a little washed-out."

Eva nodded as she waited to be done with makeup. Washed-out wasn't the half of it. At that moment she felt washed out, used up, and wrung out. Makeup finally done and her fake smile feeling like a clay mask that could too easily crack under the pressure, Eva headed to the bathroom, where she'd change into her dress for the evening.

That freaking bastard! Eva hung the black sausage dress on the back of the bathroom door and paced, cell phone in hand. Frustrated with the confined space and starting to feel like a cloistered criminal, she finally gave up and leaned hard against the edge of the vanity, staring at the phone and contemplating texting him. More than anything, she wanted to not just text but call and give him a piece of her mind. But the little entourage was just outside her bathroom door, and it would be certain they'd hear her heated exchange. And what would she say anyway? Would she yell at him for not being there? Accuse him of being a wimp and avoiding her? Or would she throw it all to the wind and beg him to come be her groom, get her out of this mess, take her in his arms and never let her go.

Shit. Well, that wouldn't do at all now, would it?

These were all questions and requests that Eva knew she couldn't ask and really didn't have a right to. They were over the line and broke the rules she'd put in place when she'd started this whole thing. And really, besides the annoying avoidance, he wasn't doing anything wrong. It wasn't like they were a couple or exclusive or had any type of claim on each other at all. During the course of their murky meetups, that much was abundantly clear.

Eva bit at her bottom lip as her hands began to shake and her eyes watered. Freaking crap. She couldn't cry. Not now. Not when her makeup was already done. She put down the phone and fanned at her face while she jumped up and down, fighting for control. Then she picked the phone up once more and hit her contacts, texting Cori as she looked at the dress hanging on the back of the bathroom door.

E: So I took your advice and got under one. And now look where I am. About to squeeze into a Léger dress worth more than my rent and I can't stop crying. Remind me to never listen to you again!

She found the emoticon with the crying non-smiley face and hit SEND. She knew that with the time difference it would be a while before Cori saw it and responded. In the meantime, she might as well go on with her next date.

Tonight she was meeting some hotshot lawyer for a more traditional, casual dinner type date. She didn't remember the name of the guy. They were honestly all starting to blur together. He was some last-minute replacement by the matchmakers, but she was at least assured that tonight's date didn't involve any climbing, acrobatics, water, or outdoor activities of any kind. With that, she was already ahead of the game.

Eva let out a sigh, thinking about having to make a choice soon. She guessed that if at this point she had to choose — and hell — she did. It would be either Opera Dude or the Surfer. She frowned. Scratch Opera Dude, he gave her the creeps with all his breaking talk as if she were a runaway horse, and Surfer, despite the sand and the physical extremes, made her laugh quite a bit. Also, how wrong was it that his rigorous travel schedule spelled an amiable marriage for all involved?

Eva let out a long breath. It really was pointless. Probably in a couple of weeks she'd be admitting defeat on national television and falling on her proverbial single-in-the-city, bound-to-be-a-spinster-girl sword.

This whole idea was ridiculous anyway — a modern-day, shotgun-style wedding, and she'd set it up so she was essentially her own jury and executioner.

Eva grabbed her dress and shimmied herself into it, overshooting the mark and pulling it up high under her breasts, then smoothing it back down over her hips and adjusting her breasts so they sat up on the built-in booby display shelf in just the intended way. She scrunched up her face and rolled her eyes. Hell, you didn't see guys going through all this bullshit. There aren't any cock amplifiers built into pants.

Bring back the codpiece!

It was then that Eva's phone pinged, surprising her and causing her to jump. She picked it up and swiped.

C: Dammit woman all these years later and you choose now to start listening to me? You know I don't have no good sense. Shit!

Eva snorted and sent her friend a kiss emoji by way of answer. She then picked up her pearls and gently clipped them around her neck, the coolness tickling her softly, bringing her mind to Aidan's gentle, feathery kisses. Her pearls looked good against her skin and the black dress backdrop. But still her brows drew together as she looked at her reflection. It's not like he would be on the other side of the door to admire them, as she'd foolishly gotten used to. Eva paused as she reached for the bathroom door handle and looked herself in the eye. "It doesn't matter," she said to her reflection. "You started this by yourself, and you can end it that way."

She quickly picked up her phone once again and swiped at the contacts before she started typing.

You said you always finish your jobs. You, Mr. Walker, are a liar. Good day.

Aidan looked at the screen, then slammed his cell back on his desk.

"What the hell, man? Now I know you never had to worry about money like the rest of us working stiffs, but come on, breaking cell phones can be an expensive habit. Especially if you're out of contract," Carter said by way of greeting as he entered Aidan's office.

Aidan looked up from where he was seated and leveled Carter with a sharp glare. "I'm not in the mood right now, C," he said in hopes that Carter would get the hint and leave him be.

He didn't.

Instead, Carter ignored the cue and walked straight into Aidan's office as if invited. Shit, just what he didn't want, Aidan thought as he shrunk down the board email he'd been forwarded from his father. But what was Carter's interruption really? Just another unwanted interruption to add to his list of life interruptions. He hadn't planned on being at the station for any real length of time, but this was ever so stealthily turning into a full-time thing. Strangely, he was actually starting to think he might

369

need to invest in taking the time to hire a full-time personal assistant for when a gatekeeper was needed and not just some temp from HR that was always a no-show. The young woman they sent, Monica, was more interested in who was coming in for casting than what his schedule was, and his schedule was getting increasingly more demanding. At this rate, who knew when he'd get back on the road?

Aidan let out a frustrated sigh, then regretted it. He really should be more patient. And possibly a little more charitable, but, dammit, he was rubbed raw. Who was she to call him a liar? The woman was the queen of bullshit cover-ups and masks, and besides, he was only following her orders, the ones she had set for them back in the beginning.

So why was it he felt so unsettled? So off, and like a fraud for not being by her side as she got ready for her date tonight. *Her date.* That was why. Right freaking there. The whole thing filled him with dread. It was cowardly, but after last week, something had turned. Turned as in had gone sour, like old milk. And it wasn't her, it was the process, what they were doing and the fact that he knew where it was heading.

He just didn't have it in him to watch her

up close and personal as she auditioned another potential mate. And she was just as crazy as this harebrained idea if she thought he could, night after night, stand by and watch her do it without it ripping him to his core. Like tonight. How was it he was supposed to watch her have another dinner out at a restaurant with some guy, when though they'd shared every sexual intimacy imaginable, he'd yet to even hold her hand in public? Aidan groaned. And what? Was he twelve, dreaming of holding a woman's hand? Shit, he really was gone over the bend. Tonight's date was supposed to be some replacement hotshot lawyer they'd found when the predetermined hedge fund manager fell through. On paper, the guy seemed right up her alley. But enough was enough. There was only so much a man could take before he blew. And as Carter had pointed out on the day of the beach shoot, his emotions were already becoming transparent, so the farther away he was from her and the set right now, the better.

Carter took a seat across from him and crossed his legs. "What's got you in such a snit? You bit the heads off every executive manager in that last meeting. Damn, man, even your father isn't that tough."

Aidan felt the tension in his shoulders

tighten. "That's because my father doesn't mind wasting time sitting and listening to endless bullshit. I don't have to rehash things that don't matter, or go over and over a point ad nauseam. It's a waste. I'm not here to build up egos. And I'm sorry if that means you too."

Aidan picked up a file and started to flip through it, hoping Carter would once again pick up on the dismissive vibe. The file was the proposal for a promising new feature, and it was the first thing that had come across Aidan's desk that had sparked his interest. At least he could absorb himself in one show that looked worth the money it would take to produce. They were looking into sending a news team deep into Sudan to research women's rights after a recent rash of underreported kidnappings. He wanted like hell to get back out in the field, and if he couldn't do it himself, at least he could manage a team from here and hopefully make a difference, bringing awareness where it was sorely needed.

"You know, tonight is the final date before she makes her decision, right?" Carter said by way of pulling Aidan's focus back his way.

Aidan looked up at him slowly, trying hard to keep his gaze impassive. "And you're telling me this because?"

Carter shook his head. "Shit, I was afraid this was going to happen. I just didn't expect it to be this bad or this real."

Aidan let out a snort, then leveled Carter with a hard look. "Stop trying to talk about something you don't know about. Real? What are you, tripping? You must be falling for your own sappy TV hype. I don't have time for real. We have a job to do, and time is precious. See, that right there was your problem in the meeting. You and all your executive cronies spending too much time flapping your gums and living in the clouds." He threw the file at Carter's chest. "See, this is what's real. Not your bullshit date piece that serves nobody. This is real news and real life. Not what you're doing with your puff pieces and definitely not in the boardroom wasting time in useless pissing-contest meetings."

"What?" Carter said. "Are our pissing contests disturbing your on-the-road, Superman-wannabe lifestyle, or is the problem that we're keeping you from your precious getting-a-piece-of-pearl-draped ass time?"

Aidan jumped up, and before he knew it, Carter's collar was balled in his hands and his face was pulled in close to his. "Don't you ever let me hear you talk about her ass or any other part of her anatomy ever again. I thought we got that shit straight on the beach."

Their eyes were locked. It was a complete flashback to an old-school, ten-year-old back-in-the-college-days standoff. Aidan felt for sure this time he would take Carter out. And then his friend's lips quirked up at the corners, and he shook his head. "Yeah, that's what I thought."

Aidan felt his eyes narrow as he fought to get control of his erratic breathing. He shook his head and let Carter go. The man only slightly swayed as he smoothly brushed at his lapels, straightening his suit. "What the fuck are you talking about, man?"

Carter shrugged. "Like I said, it's what I thought. You're in way over your head. No matter what you say."

Aidan let out a growl and slumped back down in his chair. "It doesn't matter. None of this matters. We're not compatible. She wants this sham marriage thing. She doesn't want to be one of those unmarried statistic women that we keep doing all those sensation stories about." He paused and looked at Carter, letting that sit for a moment. "And the fact is, I don't. I know that life isn't for me. I'm made for the road. Not for settling down with a socialite ice princess like her. She'd never be the type to get up and go with me. Besides, why would I even expect her to? You see what the life I want is like. It's dangerous. And not one in which you can make attachments. The smartest and the best way for me and for both of us is to go our separate ways."

Carter gave him a look that turned him inside out and back. "So you say. But you're wrong. Plenty of top reporters make it work. Both male and female."

"Well, they are not me," Aidan said by way of feeble answer.

Carter gave him a confused look and shook his head. "Yeah, but she still hasn't chosen a groom. Looking at the videos, it doesn't seem as if there are sparks between her and any of the guys."

All their amazing nights of passion suddenly flooded Aidan's mind, and he had to fight to keep his body from responding. "Well, that may be partially my fault." Aidan studied his desk, really taking in the confined edges of the solid expanse of wood. "This is why it's probably best that I step aside. Let Lou finish the job. She's more than capable."

"Yeah, especially tonight," Carter said low under his breath.

Something in Carter's tone forced Aidan's head to shoot up. "What and why?"

Carter looked down, inspecting his loafers.

"Bain, I wouldn't test me if I were you. What is so special about tonight that you don't think I should be there?" Aidan asked, his voice full of steel.

Carter sat up straight and looked him in the eye. Aidan knew him well enough to know that his firm gaze was all false bravado. "Well, I may have gotten a call from her ex, and we may have landed a great idea for a final date."

Aidan felt a low growl come from deep in his throat. "You have got to be fucking kidding me." He felt his blood run cold as he looked at his old friend and imagined Eva seeing Kevin once again under the watchful eyes of the television cameras. He got up and grabbed his cell and his keys, going for the door, but first he turned to Carter. "If I didn't think of you as a brother, I swear I'd beat the shit out of you."

CHAPTER 21

She was going to kill him. Which him, at this point Eva wasn't sure. Maybe one, maybe the other, could be both. Either way someone was in serious freaking trouble.

Eva could not believe that once again she was being taken for a fool, and on camera no less. She felt her throat close up, and it was as if a fire had ignited deep in the pit of her belly. At first, just like before, once again Eva thought, maybe, just maybe, it was all a joke. But of course not. It wasn't a joke the last time, and it wasn't one this time. She'd come to learn the hard way that Kevin didn't do jokes, and it would seem now that neither did Aidan.

That was, unless the joke was on her. Now there was the joke. Sleeping with her. Turning her inside out and making her feel . . . Eva sucked in a short breath and stopped the thought right there, putting a pause on the pain.

No way. She wasn't going there.

There was no need to think about whatever it was Aidan had made her feel, because right now he wasn't here. So feelings for him were not to be dealt with. She might as well put a halt to that. Let the dull, hard lump of misery currently in her belly hang out on its own. Push it aside or bury it, or hell . . . she took a long look at Kevin standing before her, a tall, dark picture of her own manufactured perfection.

He really cut a good figure with his smooth-burnished mahogany skin, close-cropped hair, not a wrinkle out of place on his probably custom-made suit. She let her eyes rake over him slowly from top to bottom and back up again as she picked up the glass of white wine to her right and quickly drained it. The waiter should really have left the bottle.

"Hey, beauty, I think you want to slow down there. You know how quickly alcohol goes to your head," Kevin said by way of a greeting in the trendy karaoke bar the network had picked for their date night. Though she had had no clue about Kevin, she wasn't surprised by the bar, since Lou had spent a good portion of the evening trying to convince her that belting out a tune would really be the way to America's hearts.

The idea filled her with dread, and she had no intention of going through with singing, so she and Lou settled on her rocking back and forth with a hostess, and that was it.

By way of answer to Kevin, Eva frowned, then signaled for the waiter by holding up her glass and giving it a tap, indicating that she was ready for another. She then turned back Kevin's way and gave him an acidic smile, knowing full well that the cameras, though not up close and right in her face, were trained on her every word. Her mic pack, which she'd become used to, suddenly dug into her back, and the boom mic hung overhead like an ominous big brother waiting to pounce. "You care to tell me why I should give a crap about what you have to say about anything?"

Kevin put up his hand in surrender and gave her a soft smile, the same smile she'd come to know and hate so well. "You're right, of course. I have no right to give you advice of any kind. I was just looking out for you. Caring for you is something I can't help doing. It comes naturally to me."

The snort came out before Eva could stop it, and she looked up at the boom mic with a roll of her eyes. Yeah, that would come off great for sound engineering. She then looked back at Kevin with a raised brow.

379

"Really? Oh, please. I don't have time for bull, Kevin. Now why are you really here?"

Kevin took the seat opposite her, then reached forward, taking her hand. The feeling was odd after so long, and her instinct was to pull back because it was so cold and foreign, after so many nights spent linked, warm body to warm body, in Aidan's arms.

"I'm here to plead my case and win you back. I'm here to apologize and tell you how wrong I was. I'm here so we can still have our dream wedding like you always wanted."

With that, Eva did pull her hand away from his and wrapped it safely around the stem of her glass. Part of her wanted to laugh at the absurdity of it all, while another part of her itched to throw the drink in his face. She looked around, half expecting to see Aidan there, scowling at this whole exchange as he had with all of her dates.

But he wasn't there. There was only Lou, Stan, and the rest of the crew, watching her expectantly, their eyes wide in hungry anticipation for one of two things — either a tearful, heartfelt reunion to end this little series and make America happy or another crazy meltdown on her part, and still America would be happy. Either way, America won, and she'd be the loser.

She stared Kevin straight in the eye. "So

you're not here for much, huh?" She laughed at her own joke before sobering. "But what made you come back now? The last I heard, you were off with a hostess. Engaged, no less. I thought that was your new deal."

Kevin shook his head. "That was just some foolishness."

Eva raised a brow. "Smooth talker, aren't you?"

Kevin shook his head. "Eva, I was a total idiot, and I take full responsibility. I think I was overwhelmed with the show and work, and things seemed to be spinning out of control. But when I got a call from the execs of the show and we talked things through, I knew this was the right thing to do."

Eva felt her eyes shoot up before they narrowed. "You got a call. So this wasn't your idea?"

She knew the moment Kevin realized his mistake, saw the hint of fear and hesitation in his eyes. "Baby, of course it was. I knew when I heard from Walker's assistant that this would be the best way to get to you. Now you know that if I had called, you wouldn't take my calls, and if I had showed up at your apartment, you'd probably have me on the 'do not let up' list."

He was right about all those things, but

Eva couldn't see past the point of him saying Aidan's assistant had called him for this. She looked around again, suddenly finding it hard to breathe, as well as difficult to focus.

How could he go this far? How could he betray her in this way?

The waiter came by to take their order, but Kevin stepped in and spoke up before Eva could say anything. "She'll have a glass of water, and I'll have whatever you've got on draft that's dark."

The music got louder, and a couple of male hipsters were now onstage and, she guessed, finding it ironic to belt out "Material Girl." She noticed that one of the cameras swiveled and was trained on them, while the other was on the scene between her and Kevin. In that moment, Eva wanted nothing more than to punch everyone in the face — Kevin, Lou, the PAs, the rest of the crew, the karaoke hipsters, and most of all Aidan.

Kevin reached out and took her hand once again. "Believe me, Eva. I really am sorry, and I want to do all I can to make it up to you. I've seen each of your segments, you on your dates with all those guys, and not one of them is right for you, and not one is worthy of you."

Eva almost snorted again, but even in her two-glasses-of-wine buzz she knew a second snort would be over the top. "And you think you are worthy? What a joke."

Kevin shook his head. "Hardly. But if you give me a chance, I hope to be someday." He then picked up both her hands and brought her fingertips to his lips. "Please, let me do all I can to make it up to you. Even if it takes me a lifetime."

Eva stared, her fingers feeling numb, almost dead. Not a hint of the thrill she had stupidly became used to. She felt like such a fool. Still, she could admit the words were good, and she could give credit to whatever writer had fed him such amazing lines.

Her mind began to swirl as she thought of what to say. She had no lines prepared for this meeting. All that had been gone over and prepared was now moot, thanks to this blind-side setup. How could Aidan do it? How could he set her up like this and then run away and not even be here to witness the devastating carnage?

But then she felt it. A stirring down where that boulder was. It started down deep but moved and swirled, traveled, and heated up in her chest. Her breath caught, and Eva turned.

There he was. Just beyond them. Once

again, in the shadows, watching the whole uncomfortable exchange.

Eva felt her anger quickly ignite and burn fast as she wedged her hand away from Kevin's grasp. "I need a minute, please."

She walked the long way around, going straight for Aidan and smiling when he seemed to pull back a bit as she lunged forward to whisper in his ear. "Don't worry about it. You never have to worry about your balls again around me."

"Eva, stop, please," he said reaching for her. His large hand grabbed hold of hers, the sizzle instantly fizzing up her arm and radiating through her body. But she jerked out of his grasp as if shocked and brushed at her too-tight dress. She straightened it as she forced herself to take wide, confidant strides and head for the stage. On her way, their eyes locked, and she gave Louisa a hard look and nod. If they wanted a show, then a show they would get.

Eva took the stage to the whoops and hollers of the crowd. There wasn't time for nerves, at least not many. The few she had she took care of with the quick shot of Jack the waitress handed her on the way.

The spotlight was an instant reminder of the red light from the infamous dumping scene. It made her want to rethink the song she had picked and start in on a chorus of "Hit the Road, Jack." She laughed to herself and felt a little woozy as her eyes searched for him in the crowd, but she couldn't find him against the beam of the harsh lights. No matter, this was all for show anyway. She cleared her throat as the familiar soulful ballad began. In no time, she had the crowd going right along with her, singing about good and bad times and staying together. The soulful classic was a surefire hit. Part of Eva wanted to laugh even as she wanted to cry. This was indeed quite a show. The ratings would be great. Her mother might not agree with this unorthodox method, but she knew it would win over clients, and all would be well. It mattered not who she sang to or what she really wanted. She was living up to her obligation and getting the job done. She looked to her left, and there was Aidan watching her, just off to the side as he'd always been, his jaw set and rigid, his dark eyes blazing with smoldering fire.

Eva finished the song, and as if on perfect cue, striding through the glaring lights, there was Kevin, walking toward her. He smiled and clapped as he walked up to the stage and opened his arms. Eva knew what he wanted, what they all wanted, and her heart ached. She looked over at Aidan, and still he didn't move. She looked back at Kevin, took in his perfect smile, good looks, and dark eyes that told her nothing but to see it through and get the job done, and with that Eva stepped down into Kevin's arms and kissed him.

Aidan looked at the TV monitor in his office with simmering anger as he fought against the urge to go running down to the studio to catch up with Eva. She and that asshole were being interviewed on *The Morning Show* live about their upcoming on-air nuptials, and it would seem everyone one was in a tizzy. It was as if WBC was hosting their version of the royal wedding or something. They actually cut in with live questions from viewers who were hosting morning watch parties. Some were so excited that Eva was getting her happily-ever-after — finally, after kissing so many frogs. As if that ass who had broken her heart in the first place were some kind of prince. The whole thing made him want to punch something. With that thought, Aidan slammed his fist down on his desk, causing everything — papers, pens, laptop — to vibrate violently.

"So I'm guessing this is not the best time

for a visit from an old friend?"

Aidan's eyes popped up at the sound of the sultry and familiar old voice. Kate. "What are you doing here? I thought you were settled in the middle of a cornfield or something."

Kate looked great, though quite different from the woman he'd known out in the field. Gone were the snug, well-worn khakis and T-shirts she lived in; today she was a picture of polished elegance in a body-skimming black blazer, skirt, and heels that showed off her toned legs well. Her hair also was longer than he was used to; it now swung teasingly around her shoulders. Aidan came over to give her a hug and was surprised by the fact that he felt friendly but no sexual attraction to the woman he'd shared so much with in the past. He pulled back and looked at her. "So what are you doing in New York?"

"I'm here to talk with the suits about moving to Washington and taking the position as correspondent there. From what I hear, you're one of the suits now, and I have you to thank for it. So thank you. I know you put in a good word or three for me, and for that I'm grateful."

"You don't have to thank me for anything. You very much deserve it. Though I was surprised to see you wanted to go for the job. Is life at home not what you wanted?"

Kate shook her head. "No, it's great, though slower-paced than both I and Tim would like. If I get the job, he's happy to relocate with me and work there. His company has a location outside of DC, so it would work out fine."

Aidan smiled then, happy for Kate. It would seem that someone was finally getting a happily-ever-after from this, after all. He looked at the TV and saw the segment was over. When he turned back, Kate was staring at him hard.

"So do you care to share what or, better yet, who it is that has you so bent out of shape? I bet she makes a hell of a story, and you know how much I love your stories." Kate grinned, pulling him out of his mood. Aidan nudged her shoulder, then slung an arm easily over it as he led her to the doorway and out into the hall.

"Watch it, Harmon, I am one of those suits, and you don't have the job yet."

Kate's head fell back as she laughed at him. She hugged him, then gave him a kiss on the cheek as she ducked under his arm and out of his grasp. "Oh, please, Walker, now I know it's woman problems. You were always way too easy to read. Remind me to invite you over for our monthly poker night when Tim and I are settled in DC. And bring your girl because, knowing you, you'll find a way to fix things. You always do."

Eva stopped short as she made her way out of the ladies' room and ducked back into the conference room, where she and Kevin were meeting with Louise, Carter, and the rest of the crew, putting the finishing touches on the wedding preparations.

She'd be fine. This would all be fine. So what if Aidan wasn't at this meeting or the segments and had essentially cut himself off and out of her life. So what if she'd just seen him embracing, kissing, then happily laughing with a gorgeous woman with legs that went on forever, looking for all the world like he didn't even remember the name Eva Ward.

None of that mattered at all. She'd be fine because in a matter of days she'd have all she wanted. All she'd planned for and worked so hard for all this time. Soon she'd be Mrs. Kevin Rucker Esq., and she would have it all.

"Are you feeling okay, honey?" Kevin asked from the seat that Aidan had sat in just weeks before.

"I'm fine. Just a little tired," Eva said, taking the seat next to him. She looked over at Carter and put on her best smile, ignoring the questioning look in his eyes. "Let's continue. You were saying you'd like to be sure the sponsor's name is prominently displayed on the dais? It's tacky, but I can compromise and go with a named place card on the cake table. Deal?"

Eva gave Carter a look that left no room for argument, and with all that was going on, she had pushed the image of Aidan to the back of her mind. Now was not the time for hurt feelings or aching hearts. She had a wedding to map out.

CHAPTER 22

"You don't know how happy I am that you made it. I don't think I'd be able to go through with this without you by my side," Eva said to Cori in between taking huge gulps of air.

She felt woozy, but still she was determined to soldier on. They were in the studio's dressing rooms turned bridal changing and staging area, and it was currently seven thirty-four. The quicker this was over and done with, the better. The way Eva had it figured, she and Kevin and their splashy morning Midtown wedding were going on as a big lead into the nine o'clock hour. If all went as planned, by this time tomorrow she would officially be old news, and she could go on with her life of making news of the people who really wanted to be in front of the cameras and splashed all over the papers. Eva sucked in one more giant gulp of air, but the tight stays of her corset-style dress prevented her from taking it in fully. When she got up too fast, once again she felt dizzy.

Instantly noting her distress, Cori grabbed hold of Eva's shoulders and pushed her forward. The tightness of the dress strained against the pressure of her bending. "Okay, lady, no standing for you just yet. And of course I made it. Where else would I be but with my best friend when she's getting married? And after your last text, I knew you needed me here." Cori looked around and lowered her voice. "Though for the life of me, I still can't understand why you're going through with it. Get pissed at me if you want, but I have to say it: It's obvious that this is not what you want."

Eva's head shot up again, and she gave Cori a hard stare. Cori rolled her eyes and pushed her head back down. "Oh, save it, girl. I know you better than your own mama. You're not fooling me one bit with this 'old is new again' and 'I've found love' bullshit."

"Cori please, just let it go. No, it's not ideal and not the 'dream,' and of course this is not what I want, but I don't want to talk about that now. This is what it has to be to get things back on track. Besides, my mother will be back here in a second. The last thing

I need is her hearing you spout off, and then I'd have to deal with her today, on top of everything else."

Cori crossed her arms. "Everything else like what? The fact you're about to marry tall, dark, and spineless when you're really in love with tall, dark, and —"

Eva put up a hand, fighting to keep a hold on her quickly spiraling emotions. "Tall, dark, and doesn't care about me? That was a short-lived fantasy that needs to go into the file of forgotten memories. What good does it do for me to think about him now? It's not like he's here, suddenly declaring his love." Eva felt a lump that signaled threatening tears. Just freaking great. She blinked rapidly. "I swear, Cori, if you make me cry and I have to go through makeup torture again, I may never forgive you. He's not here, so this conversation is just a silly, waste-of-time exercise in self-flagellation. Now, can we drop it?" Eva didn't want to rehash things with Cori. It was painful enough being where she was and going through with this sham without Cori's interjections about the obvious.

These past three weeks had been her own personal torture — seeing Kevin again and going on a few staged dates for the cameras, all the while hoping, like out of some dream movie sequence, that Aidan would come for her and sweep her off her feet to ride off into the sunset. What the hell? She was an idiot for even dreaming it. Sunsets were overrated anyways.

For his part, Kevin wanted to pick things right back up. Bring his box of crap up from the lobby and straight back into her apartment. Pretend what they went through was just a blip, his on-air humiliation just a mistake, his time with the hostess just a momentary lapse.

But Eva knew it wasn't. She knew it by the way his eyes still wandered, and the times when they didn't, she even saw it in his over-attentiveness when they were out and he was supposedly courting her. Sure, he said all the right things and made all the right moves, but she knew nothing had changed. Or maybe everything had changed. Her eyes were finally opened, and she could see that Kevin was in this for all the wrong — or, hell, maybe it was all the right — reasons.

So she made up a story about him having to win her over before he could bring that damn box back up from the lobby and into her apartment again. But that wasn't the truth. She and Kevin were probably perfect for each other. They were two fakers, making their way in the big city, paying their dues in the most expensive possible way. The truth was she was keeping Kevin at arm's length and her nights free in the sad hope that Aidan would come to her. That he'd say he had changed his mind and she could say she had changed hers. That he'd say he wanted more and wanted to be with her. That he'd say he wanted not just her nights but her days too — forever, as she now knew she wanted his. But within a short time, Eva came to know it was nothing but a foolish dream, one that had her constantly blinking back her tears and swallowing down her true feelings.

She'd tried her best to let that dream go after the night she'd sung her song and gone into Kevin's arms. Aidan made his choice when he sent Kevin back to her, and she, like the dutiful talent she was, had followed through and finished the job. The camera caught it all, and the segment the following Monday was an instant hit. Social media had gone crazy, the majority of watchers clearly in the #TeamKevEva camp.

For his part, Aidan never returned to the set for any of her dates with Kevin, and Lou was now fully in charge and doing a great job of playing up the — couple, and if Eva played this right, her new life — the one she'd had planned from the very start — would begin in a few hours.

It was odd, though, because in some strange way she still always felt Aidan's presence over her shoulder. And a voice in her head kept asking her that question he had posed all those nights ago: "Why are you getting married?"

The question still gnawed at her, rubbing along her spine in the most uncomfortable way. Now when she closed her eyes and saw herself at the altar, it was never with Kevin or any of the men she had dated, but always with some faceless man. The longed-for image of Aidan remained just beyond him, out of her reach, the man she longed to be with, married or not; that somehow didn't seem to matter, as long as wherever she was, it was with him by her side.

But it was Cori who mimicked those words now, brought her back to reality, and summed up her true feelings so easily. "Okay, fine. Whatever you say. But just so you know, I've got your back, and we can blow this joint in a hot minute. Run away to what truly makes you happy."

"As if I'd let you run off with my talent." Both women turned toward the sound of Carter Bain's voice. Eva felt her eyes automatically roll, and she shook her head as

Cori stepped between her and Carter.

"A, she's not your property. And B, if I ran off anywhere, I doubt you or anyone else here would be able to stop me," Cori said, looking Carter in the eye.

Carter gave her a stare-down that Eva was sure worked well on his underlings, but she was pleased to experience her first smile of the day when he looked away, eyes cast down in defeat, as she'd anticipated. She'd not met a man yet who was a match for her best friend.

"You're right," Carter started. "Excuse me if I came off as impertinent." He put out a hand. "I'm Carter Bain, and you are?"

Cori put out her hand. "The best friend and general bullshit blocker. You, Mr. Bain, needed no introduction since you were already on my blocker radar." She then floored him with a smile that could cut glass.

Eva looked up between the two of them and let out a long sigh. The potential blowup was dangerous and there was no way she was getting into the middle of it. "Do you two want me to leave you to battle this out, or can you table the fight for later?"

Carter laughed nervously as he turned back Eva's way. "It's that sharp tongue of yours that's made you a star, Ms. Ward."

Eva raised a brow, noting that neither he

nor Cori gave her a real answer.

Aidan told himself he wasn't going to the wedding. That there was no real reason for him to be there. None at all, besides torturing himself, of course. Though not being there was torture enough. He should have listened to his gut and booked himself far away. Taken a trip somewhere. Madagascar, maybe? Just any place where he'd be safely away from the image of her, especially the image of her while she made sacred vows declaring herself the life partner, bound together, for real, and no joke in the eyes of the law, to some asshole. The same ass with whom — though Aidan knew she didn't really love him and maybe never really had — she still shared a past connection and who could make, or most probably already had made, his way back into her heart and her bed. Fuck! This couldn't have worked out any worse if it had been planned that way.

Over the past three weeks, Aidan had successfully extricated himself from her segment and thrilled his father in the process by delving into the larger-picture projects at the network. He'd even planted seeds about projects that were top on his list. On the surface, his plan was working out well. All he had to do was stay focused, and soon he'd have the best of both worlds. He'd have a seat at the table when it came to decision making at the network and the freedom to go on the road whenever the story needed him.

The road. It was supposedly just what he wanted, and now the thought of it made his mouth so dry it seemed filled with sawdust. He couldn't imagine being on the road without her by his side or here, waiting for him when he came back home. How ridiculous a thought was that? The man who thrived on having no attachments, the lone wolf, was now howling for a place — no, a person — to call home. It was ridiculous, and he should — no, he needed — to just push the thought aside, to block it out and be the man he was meant to be. Life was perfect, and it was high time he started acting like it. Aidan paused to study his reflection in the window. So what was he doing at the moment, pacing around his office like a caged lion, the television trained on the damned *Morning Show* and him hanging on every word spoken by that annoying Jim and the overly animated Diane?

He stopped mid-pace when it was announced that coming up was the montage of Eva and Kevin's journey. His stomach twisted at the use of the overused term, and he leaned back against the edge of his desk and watched as Eva's image came on the screen.

Journey. What the hell did they know about such a thing?

He didn't know why he was surprised at the lump that formed in his throat with that first glimpse of her image. Maybe he was going soft. That's what he got for hanging out so long stateside and getting comfortable in one place. But looking at her in the first stills of the too-sappy montage and seeing her in her little matching sweater set and those damned pearls brought it all back. First, that surprising kiss in the greenroom and the searing ball pain that came along shortly thereafter. Then the surprising pleasure that somehow took over his being. He never wanted to let go of that pleasure, but knew he must for both their sakes.

Shit. Who would have thought he'd be in even more pain today?

He wanted to turn away, perhaps prepare for this afternoon's meeting, but instead he rubbed his jaw and stayed rooted where he was, watching and feeling the twisting in his gut as the montage weaved a web, painting Eva and Kevin as a picture-perfect couple.

By the time the morning was over and done, they would again be the golden couple, at least for the time being. And she would be the standard of the modern working woman, no longer pitied but now looked up to; she'd have all she wanted. And wasn't that all that mattered?

The camera cut to a more recent image of the two of them on their last date. They were on the top of the Empire State Building, with violins playing, and Kevin asked Eva to marry him once again, pulling out the ring she'd stopped wearing eight weeks before. Aidan closed his eyes and ran his hands across his face before looking at the screen again. Eva nodded and smiled, and once again went into Kevin's arms. The camera edged in, doing a close-up on the ring. To the untrained eye, it all looked like a modern fairy tale. Only a person who knew Eva could see the pain behind that smile.

"Can I please have a moment alone with your friend?" Carter asked, this time coming at Cori with all the cordiality Eva knew she felt was her due. Still, she raised a brow and deferred to Eva, who let out a sigh and nodded, letting her friend know it was fine to leave her alone with the slick producer.

"It's okay. Why don't you go and please check on my mother. I'm sure she's out there driving the crew mad and can use a little reining in."

"So what is it?" Eva asked once Cori left the room. "Do you want me to cartwheel down the aisle, or would juggling make you happier?"

Carter shook his head. "Do I really come off as that evil? Should I twirl my dastardly mustache now and complete your picture of me?"

Eva let out a long sigh and leaned back. "No, you really don't. I'm sorry, I don't blame you. You're just doing your job. I understand that." She got up and went to the mirror to check her makeup and smooth her chignon. "Don't worry. I'll be ready to walk down the aisle, and things will go off without a hitch."

"What if I told you I don't want you to walk down the aisle?"

Eva whipped around too quickly and got a little woozy once again. She had to have heard him wrong. "Excuse me?"

"You heard me right. What if I don't want you to walk down the aisle?"

Eva waved a disbelieving hand in front of her face. "And what, I don't walk down the aisle, and you sue me for breach of contract?

Or what, you continue these farce dates and torture me forever? What's your angle now, Mr. Bain?"

"Neither, and no angle. You don't walk down the aisle, and you walk away and go on with your life. Free, not saddled to a man who doesn't care for you."

"What would you know about how Kevin feels about me? This conversation is over. Shouldn't you be out there giving orders to minions or something?"

"You're right, I don't know how Kevin feels about you, but I do know how Aidan feels. And he really cares for you. I've known him for years, and I've never seen him like this."

Eva closed her eyes against the words. When she opened them again, they were full of hatred for the man in front of her. "I think you need to go. I'm not having this conversation with you."

But Carter didn't move. Instead he flipped open a small tablet. "You have a good friend there who would go to bat for you, and Aidan has always been that kind of friend for me, whether I was being a jerk, which was most of the time, or not. But it's time I stood up for him. I've never seen him as twisted up about anyone as he is about you. With him, it was always the story first. Mission first. He didn't have to stay here or on your project. It was never about your story, but always about you."

Eva watched as he pressed PLAY and she came on the small screen live, loud, and in screaming bright color, having a full-on fit. Carter hit pause. "I wanted to use this. I was all ready to go. Aidan told me he'd have me fired if I did, and, worse, he'd never speak to me again. That was when I knew. Aidan's been my friend since our school days, and he never makes idle threats. He would have never said that if you didn't mean something to him. Even then."

He hit PLAY again, and there she was coming at him, straight for the camera and then past it and out of sight for their first kiss before the camera went out of focus and headed south. Carter laughed. "I will admit I got a kick out of that part. Though I don't know what happened when the camera fell, I have my suspicions." Eva shot Carter a look that he brushed off with a grin before hitting PLAY again. This time the footage was of Aidan, and he looked so beautiful — all tall, dark, sexy strength — as he helped move a piece of equipment, and then in another shot he looked great as he gave directions to some riggers.

Eva turned to Carter. "Why are you wasting my time with this?"

"Patience, please."

She let out a frustrated huff, though she continued to look. The images changed, and there she was, getting ready as he watched solemnly from his back corner in her apartment. She was climbing the rock wall as he stood poised ready to run forward to catch her. Then it was her on the screen at the opera, in her red dress, and him watching once again, this time through the monitor, but intent on her every move and even more so on every move of her date. She watched as his face went through every possible emotion from ambivalence to irritation, and from there to anger and then undeniable pain. Then there were the odd times when he was simply looking at her and his eyes would get all dark and full of passion and something she couldn't quite put her finger on — a soft, soulful look that Eva couldn't dare to hope was love. And she was there too. Right back with the same chill, the same thrill she only got from him. Her eyes began to water. Crap, her makeup.

"Come on, don't cry, please. Aidan would kick my ass if he knew I'd made you cry. Hell, he'd kick my ass if he knew I was here showing you this," Carter said, surprising her by handing over a handkerchief. "I didn't do this to make you cry. I only wanted to show you how much you mean to him."

Eva blew in the handkerchief and then looked up at Carter. "Well, I'm afraid you're totally overestimating things. He's a big boy and can speak for himself, and it speaks volumes that he's not here. No matter what you say, he left me, and then he practically threw Kevin back at me. He's not the hero you're trying to portray with your little video and cute, emotionally manipulative editing." She flipped the screen closed and looked up at the clock. "Now, if you'll excuse me, I'd like to go and get married and be done with this nightmare once and for all."

Eva was about to walk past him on that note, but Carter stopped her with a hand to her elbow. "Well, about that. It may not have been his idea to bring Kevin back on the show."

Eva's brows drew together as her heart begin to race. "Just how much of not his idea are we talking?"

Eva stood inside the makeshift, curtained-off tent and waited for her cue. She watched the scene outside the tent on the monitors and was once again overwhelmed by the spectacle of it all. She would be so relieved when this was all behind her and just a story of her distant past.

The normally bustling concrete tourist center had been turned into a square-block, floral-fantasy film set with about every flower imaginable decorating the space. It was almost too much to take in, and Eva felt a twinge of guilt seeping into her melancholy over the spectacle of it all. It was sad, really. This could be a fairy-tale dream for someone, but not for her. She supposed for her it could be too, if she were marrying her true love or even if she were marrying Kevin, the one she thought she knew months ago before the curtain had been lifted and her world had been turned inside out. But now she couldn't take in the tulle, the crystals, the flowers or the fantasy of it all. All she could see now was the artifice in the background, the little tech wizards behind it all, pulling the strings and making this spectacle happen.

Eva let out a calming breath and told herself once more that focus was what was called for here as she waited for her cue to come from the assistant PA, letting her know it was time to walk down the aisle. Don't think of the spectacle or the little wizard or the big wizard, Carter Bain, and what he had told her about Kevin and his part in bringing him back. She just had to play her part, and this would all be over soon. It was all timed out, and she had only thirty seconds to get down a rose-petaled aisle to Kevin, and they had three minutes and thirty seconds after that to say their vows before the next commercial break, or the show's live timeline would be off.

She took in a breath and inwardly shook off the conversation with Carter. There was no need to think of that now. Looking at the screen, she watched as the camera scanned the assembled guests and the wedding party. It reached Kevin and focused. She saw how he checked himself out in the monitor yet again and let out a sigh when the fool didn't even hide checking out the ass of a young PA. Part of her almost laughed, but instead she just shook her head. Prince Charming he was not. The camera panned, and Eva saw her mother sitting rigid in her chair on the edge of the front row as the guest of honor. She wore a weary smile, and for the first time, Eva could see her as she was. Her mother had given up so much trying to prove herself to be something she wasn't, all to cover for a man who didn't love her as she should have been loved. Suddenly the waste of it all hit

Eva like a kick to the gut, and instead of taking a step forward, getting in cue position, she took a step back. When she did, she hit something — or better yet, someone — solid. Eva stilled.

"Getting cold feet, princess?"

Aidan's voice rumbled over her like a slow wave, and Eva felt she would have fallen if she hadn't had his chest to lean on or her anger to hold her up. She turned around and looked him in the eye. "Absolutely not. I'm just waiting for my cue, and then I'm heading down the aisle. You better than anyone know how important timing is in this business." She lowered her voice. "Now will you move so you're not mistakenly in my shot?"

"What if I won't?"

Instantly the white-hot anger bubbled up. "Are you freaking kidding me right now?" Her voice went high, and Aidan grinned.

"There's that fire, kitten. I told you I always finish my jobs."

Eva shook her head. "I so do not have time for this. Not today, I don't."

Aidan leaned in closer to her ear, and his warm breath caressed her with each word. "If not today, then when? If not today, then I risk being too late, and I can't wait another moment to ask you to forgive me."

Eva could not believe her ears. Thirty seconds. Thirty freaking seconds when he had had weeks, and now he came to her with this? She turned away and looked back at the monitors. So many people were waiting to watch her marry the not quite man of her dreams, and here he came with this, now. She found it hard to breathe as she imagined all the eyes focused and waiting for her to walk down the aisle. She felt Aidan's expectant presence, a welcome but heavy being engulfing her. She closed her eyes briefly. This definitely was not as romantic as it was portrayed in the movies.

The PA peeked his head around and announced fifteen seconds until she was up. Eva opened her eyes and looked at Aidan. "I don't know why you're saying this," she said through clenched teeth and a churning stomach. "We had an arrangement but no attachment. You did nothing wrong. There is nothing to forgive."

She heard Aidan clear his throat before he spoke up again. "But there is, princess. You were right. I am a liar. I'm so sorry. I should have been honest with you from the beginning and told you I'm in love with you."

Eva sucked in a breath and closed her eyes again as the impact of his declaration hit her, cutting off her air and sending her world spinning.

Just then the partition curtains opened wide, and the PA announced her cue to go. Eva forced herself to focus, then looked back, and her eyes locked with Aidan's. His were dark and glassy and, for the first time, full of hope. She gave him a half smile and blinked back her threatening tears. "You know you're a real jerk, Walker. Like I said, timing is everything."

The lights were so bright they were almost blinding, and the music of the piano and the violin had a shrill, almost screeching quality to it. But Eva blocked it all out and focused on the task at hand. She counted her seconds. All she had to do was watch her time, and this would all be over soon. She saw them. All the smiling faces looking at her with admiration. She was doing what had to be done. She passed her mother and saw something like acceptance reflected in her eyes, but still, lingering below the surface, there was that hint of sadness.

Looking up at the end of the aisle, she got to Kevin, so tall, so perfect in his tuxedo; he would be a perfect match for her. Him and her, the two of them wearing well-worn masks of socially accepted love. They created a beautiful picture, or would if only Kevin were looking her way and not watching himself on the monitor off to the left. Eva smiled as she reached Kevin's side and whispered in his ear.

"You have got to be kidding me! But we're supposed to get married. Here and now," Kevin yelled, and the crowd gasped. "You can't stand me up at the altar. Do you know how many women would kill to marry me?"

"Yes, Kevin, I think I do. It's just I'm no longer one of them," Eva said with a grin as she shoved her bouquet into his empty arms. She turned, catching Cori's wide grin and started back down the aisle with a newfound energy. She passed her mother and saw the shock and then the surprising smile that gave her the strength to take off into a run the rest of the way and into Aidan's waiting arms. She hit him with the full force of her body, making him grunt.

"So it seems your balls are in jeopardy once again, Mr. Walker."

His grin spread wide, and her insides went soft. "I'm not worried about my balls at all as long as you have my heart." His brows came together then, and Eva looked at him, confused. "But will you make me one promise, princess?"

"What's that?"

Aidan wrapped an arm tight around her waist as he lifted his other hand to her face.

At first, he brushed his fingers across her bottom lip; then his hand went farther down to the pearls at her throat as he fingered them seductively. "When you finally let me take you out on a date, will you promise to keep your pearls on?"

Eva let out a laugh as she caught the spark in his eyes and let it charge her from the inside out. She felt renewed as the rest of the spectators seemed to fade away. The idea of the millions of viewers from around the country judging her every action vanished to dust and she was left with nothing in her mind's eye but she and Aidan as she leaned forward once again toward his irresistible lips. "For you, my love, always."

The employees of Thorndike Press hope you have enjoyed this Large Print book. All our Thorndike, Wheeler, and Kennebec Large Print titles are designed for easy reading, and all our books are made to last. Other Thorndike Press Large Print books are available at your library, through selected bookstores, or directly from us.

For information about titles, please call:
(800) 223-1244

or visit our Web site at:
http://gale.cengage.com/thorndike

To share your comments, please write:
Publisher
Thorndike Press
10 Water St., Suite 310
Waterville, ME 04901